WHEN THE BLUES COME CALLING

WHEN THE BLUES COME CALLING

A Lizzie Crane Mystery

Skye Alexander

To Rob Logan, who awakened me

Praise for When the Blues Come Calling

"*When the Blues Come Calling* is the newest, and in many ways the best (or at least my favorite so far) in the Lizzie Crane series. This time, jazz singer Lizzie and her combo, The Troubadours, are performing in their hometown of New York City, where they sing and play their music live on the radio and in some of New York's tonier nightclubs. I found myself torn between wanting to devour this book in one sitting and slowing myself down to savor at length a very well-written and enjoyable work of fiction."—Gregory Stout, author of the Shamus Award-winning Jackson Gamble series

"Lizzie is a likeable heroine, and her character is drawn with depth, particularly with respect to her musicianship and relations with her bandmates. Dialogue is tinged with a pleasing amount of period slang. An enjoyable historical mystery for fans of the flapper era."—Brodie Curtis, Historical Novel Society

"A delightful mix of mystery, romance, and the Roaring Twenties. In actress and singer Lizzie Crane, Alexander has created a refreshing heroine, whose charm and keen understanding of human nature make her an amateur sleuth to watch. Highly recommended."—Paula Munier, *USA Today* bestselling author of the Mercy Carr series

"The Golden Age of Mystery is alive and well in Skye Alexander's clever and charming Lizzie Crane novels. Agatha Christie fans: You've found your next great read."—Lori Robbins, author of the On Pointe and Master Class mystery series

"Alexander skillfully captures the milieu of the Roaring Twenties, Prohibition, motorcars, and the Jazz Age. Her characters are realistic, intriguing, and filled with adventure."—Susan Van Kirk, author of the Art Center Mysteries

"Skye Alexander…vividly recreates the Roarin' 20s through her depiction of the architecture, fashion, literature, and language. She's also created a smart and sassy heroine in Lizzie Crane with a supporting cast that's the 'bee's knees'."—Kevin Kleusner, author of *The Killer Sermon* and *The Killer Speech*

"Alexander brings the period to life with a twisting tale of murder and mayhem that will satisfy any fan of historical mystery."—Edith Maxwell, Agatha-winning author of the Quaker Midwife Mysteries

"Alexander's protagonist, Lizzie Crane, is a ball of fire. You'll love her talent, her courage, and her clothes."—Kate Flora, award-winning author of *A World of Deceit*

Chapter One

"Jazz came to America 300 years ago in chains."

—Paul Whiteman, "If Jazz Isn't Music, Why Isn't It?" The New York Times, June 1926

Huddled under umbrellas in the warm summer rain, the three musicians splashed through puddles as they ran to the unpretentious two-story brick building in a Brooklyn neighborhood not far from where the saxophonist Bert Halley grew up. Radio station KDAZ had been broadcasting from this location for almost two years, and every day, listeners throughout New York City tuned in to hear the new sensation called jazz.

This would be the trio's fourth time playing live on the radio. Still, Lizzie Crane, The Troubadours' vocalist, found it incredible that their music would soon flow from this building into homes and businesses all over the city. She'd never dreamed she'd one day hear her own voice on the airwaves, and felt proud, excited, and a little nervous knowing that she and her friends were on the cutting edge of this new marvel that brought news, sports, and live entertainment to the world. Now, thanks to modern technology, people who couldn't hear the group perform in nightclubs or at private parties could listen to them.

A pretty receptionist with finger-waved blond hair greeted Lizzie and her colleagues and asked them to sign the station's guest book. Then she led them down a hallway toward the studio at the center of the building. A young technician whose paper-white skin suggested he rarely ventured out into the sunshine raised his hand in greeting as they entered the windowless room. Lizzie waved back.

Just outside the technician's booth, their host, a tall, slim, well-dressed man with chocolate-colored skin who went by the name of Sweet William Bly, stood at a microphone that looked like a gyroscope perched on a pole. Sweet William announced the acts in his deep, resonant voice, offered commentary about the musicians who played at KDAZ, and did interviews with them. Sometimes he took telephone calls from listeners, depending on his mood. He pointed his index finger at The Troubadours in greeting and winked at Lizzie—something he wouldn't have dared to do except in this private space.

Sidney Somerset, the troupe's pianist and business manager, took his seat at the studio's Steinway and began "warming up the ivories," as he called it. Bert Halley, the youngest and newest member of the group, unsnapped his saxophone, trumpet, and clarinet cases. Lizzie paced around the room filled with gadgets and gizmos she couldn't come close to understanding, trying to settle her nerves. Even after seven years as a professional singer, she still got butterflies before she performed. Finally, she stepped up to the microphone and sang a few lines of Al Jolson's "April Showers" to test the acoustics, although she already knew the radio station's sound quality was superb.

The studio door swung open, and the station's manager, Victor Fosse, strode in. Bald, broad-shouldered, with close-set brown eyes and a prominent nose, his shirtsleeves rolled up to his elbows exposing muscular forearms, he looked more like a gangster than a music lover. Yet rumor had it he owned the most extensive record collection of anyone in New York City. Maybe in America.

He shook hands with each of the musicians. "Welcome back. Say, we had a terrific response to your last appearance. Phone rang off the hook for an hour after you finished playing."

"That's good news," Sidney said. "It's always nice to know folks are listening."

"Pretty soon you're gonna want me to pay you."

Sidney chuckled. "I won't refuse an offer, but we appreciate the publicity."

"One hand washes the other, eh?" Fosse said.

The technician, earphones covering his ears, spoke through a microphone in an overly loud voice. "We're live in three minutes. Everybody ready?"

Sid gave him a thumbs-up. Bert picked up his clarinet and blew the opening to "Rhapsody in Blue." Lizzie combed her fingers through her brunette bob.

"I'll leave you to it then." Fosse slapped Sidney on the shoulder. "I'm gonna be listening in my office. Make me proud."

For the next twenty minutes, the three Troubadours played a medley of popular jazz numbers, blues favorites, and show tunes. As always, Sidney exhibited his proficiency at the piano, and Bert shone. Lizzie, however, who loved singing for a live audience, felt enervated in this stark room furnished only with machines. *I'm a professional,* she reminded herself. *I should be able to perform anywhere, anytime.* Yet she couldn't help wondering about her invisible listeners. What did they think of The Troubadours? Did they enjoy what they heard? Phone calls to the radio station after the fact didn't provide the immediate gratification of cheers and whistles and hands clapping.

When she first complained about singing into a void, Sidney had teased, "You're just a glutton for praise and applause. You don't get to show off your pretty face and swell figure on the radio. This was your idea, remember."

She had to admit there was some truth in her friend's accusations. Six months ago, she'd suggested that doing live radio performances would give them greater notoriety. She also acknowledged the broadcasts had boosted The Troubadours' popularity. Their bookings had increased in the past two months, and so had their fees. Her business sense proved accurate, but she'd overestimated the glamour involved. There was nothing glamorous about this claustrophobic studio with its squadron of machines, drab gray walls, and stale air.

When they finished playing The Hot Five's "You Made Me Love You," Sweet William stepped up to the microphone. "Woo-eee! That's the unmistakable sound of New York's own Troubadours: Sidney Somerset on piano, Bert Halley on sax and clarinet, and the lovely Lizzie Crane doing a sensational vocal rendition of Louis Armstrong's hit song. Music lovers, you can hear them in person at The Oasis on Saturday night—and a little birdie just told me they've got something big on the horizon. Thanks for listening, folks. I'm Sweet William Bly, and we're here to dazzle you at KDAZ radio. Now don't go away 'cause we've got more tunes coming your way after a word from our sponsor."

He circled his hand in the air, signaling the technician to cut the live feed and go to a recorded advertisement.

Victor Fosse pushed through the studio's door. "Wow, just wow!" he said, extending his hand to Sidney.

"Thanks for giving us airtime, Vic. You're the bee's knees," Sidney said.

Fosse, his bald head gleaming in the studio's lights, punched Bert playfully on the arm. "And you, kid. What can I say except holy moly, you blow the bejesus out of those horns. If you were colored, Fletcher Henderson would try to get you to play with him."

Twenty-two-year-old Bert blushed profusely, hugging his saxophone to his chest like a child clutching a favorite toy. "Thank you, sir."

Fosse turned to Lizzie and bowed dramatically. "Everyone knows I'm a huge fan of Satchmo. But just between you and me, I prefer your version of 'You Made Me Love You' to his. You're a whole lot easier on the eyes, too."

"Not that anyone can see me from here." Lizzie tossed her head and laughed. "Thanks, Vic. It's been fun. Can you come to our show Saturday night?"

"I hope so, if the wife lets me out for a night on my own. She doesn't like jazz, prefers the opera." He rolled his eyes, pretending to be a hen-pecked husband.

Bert packed up his horns. Lizzie waved to Sweet William and the technician, then the trio made their way down the radio station's hallway and out into the rainy evening. Sidney opened the passenger door for Lizzie, and she slid into his Buick convertible.

"What's this about 'something big on the horizon'?" she asked.

"It's a surprise," he answered, smiling and rubbing his palms together. "I'll tell you all about it when we get to the Blue Lagoon. Dinner's on me."

Bert stowed his instrument cases in the back of the breezer, then folded his long legs into the space between the front and back seats. "I'm all ears," he said, chuckling at his own joke because his prodigious ears stuck out from the sides of his head like conch shells.

"Why does Sweet William know what's going on, and I don't?" Lizzie asked, a hint of pique in her voice.

Sidney turned the key in the ignition. "William knows everyone in Harlem and the Alley. Word spreads faster there than a hooker's legs."

She frowned at him, but Bert laughed.

"Don't get in a tizzy, Lizzie," Sidney said, patting her hand. "I would've told you earlier except I only heard about it this morning myself. I dare say William knew long before I did."

* * *

Sidney found a parking space a block from the Blue Lagoon–they'd only get half-soaked running through the rain to the restaurant. One of many such establishments in the city, it was known as a "blind tiger." People who sought access to the upscale speakeasy had to pretend they wanted to see an exotic animal in order to get through the door. The Lagoon catered to a moneyed clientele, serving distinctive food and some of the best entertainment in town. Victor Fosse first heard The Troubadours play here and was so impressed he invited them to perform on KDAZ.

They entered the Caribbean-inspired restaurant with its fake palm trees festooned with expensive strings of electric lights. Murals depicting white sand beaches at sunset graced the walls. One panel, Lizzie knew, slid aside to reveal a staircase that led to an underground room where customers could savor alcohol and other illicit delights. She spotted Rory Moynihan, the club's owner, standing near the long mahogany bar and talking to a bartender who mixed drinks that contained nothing stronger than ginger ale. But if diners chose to surreptitiously spike their beverages with a little something they brought along, or buy an exorbitantly priced bottle of the club's secret stash from the Bahamas, well, no one at the Lagoon would notice. She also knew that Rory paid the local vice cops handsomely to look the other way.

When he saw the three musicians, Rory waved them in with both hands. As always, he wore a tuxedo custom-made to fit his short, stocky frame that gave him the appearance of being almost square. His dyed black hair, slicked back with Brylcreem, shone like patent leather. A veneer of class laid over a core of raw, ruthless power. Although no one would guess it now, Lizzie knew his family hailed from New York's infamous Five Points, a slum riddled with disease, filth, and crime that once bore the dubious distinction of having the highest murder rate of any neighborhood in the world. How he rose from his lowly roots was best left unexamined.

On a Wednesday night, the club had yet to fill to capacity, but no tables near the stage remained available.

"I should've made a reservation," Sidney muttered as the maître d' showed them to a table off to one side, halfway between the entrance and the stage.

"It's okay. We can hear the music fine from here," Bert said.

"We just won't be seen," Lizzie grumbled. "I'd hoped to show off my new frock."

She stroked the glittering, golden dress made from dozens of strips of embroidered silk that swayed suggestively, opening and closing as she walked. She surveyed the restaurant, studying the outfits worn by the other female patrons, and decided none of their finery surpassed her own.

Sidney laughed. "You'll just have to get up and parade around a bit. Make a lot of trips to the ladies' room."

A waiter brought menus to their table and took their drink orders: three tonic waters with slices of lime. After he returned, set the icy glasses on the table, and answered questions about the dinner offerings, he left the musicians to decide what they'd like to eat.

Sidney slid a silver flask from his jacket pocket. "Being shunted off to the sidelines has its benefits," he said as he poured gin into their glasses.

Lizzie stirred her drink with a swizzle stick. "So, when do we learn about this mysterious big deal? Or are you going to keep us in suspense forever?"

"We're going to make a record. This morning I got a telephone call from a fella named Jim Jenkins at Jupiter Records. He heard us on KDAZ and wants to meet with us to discuss a contract." Sid raised his glass and grinned at Lizzie. "Bearcat, you were right when you suggested making a recording. This could be our ticket to fame and fortune."

She clinked her glass against Sid's and took a sip, but Bert held back. A look of disbelief and something close to panic swept across his face.

"Jim Jenkins?" he asked.

Sid nodded. "You know him?"

"He was my father's best friend. Before..."

Chapter Two

"Life without music would be a mistake."

—Friedrich Nietzsche, Twilight of the Idols

Bert paused, cleared his throat, then continued, "Before my father died."

Lizzie knew Bert's father had been killed in an automobile accident three years ago, and that only a couple months later, his mother had taken up with another man. They tossed nineteen-year-old Bert out of his home to fend for himself. He ended up playing for change on the city's streets until Lizzie heard him in Central Park last fall and invited him to join The Troubadours. But that was all she knew. Bert, tight-lipped and shy, rarely spoke of his past or what had come between him and his family. She couldn't help wondering, however, why Jim "JJ" Jenkins, who owned a recording company—a close friend of Bert's father, no less—hadn't recognized the young horn player's talent and taken Bert under his wing.

Sidney fit a cigarette into his engraved silver holder, took a drag, and blew out a lungful of smoke. "Is that why Jenkins wants to talk to us about a record deal? Funny, he didn't mention the connection."

Bert shrugged. "I don't know. Haven't seen him in a couple years."

Before Lizzie could inquire further, the waiter approached their table to take their dinner orders. Sidney ordered for all of them: halibut for Lizzie, shrimp for Bert, and a sirloin steak for himself. And another round of tonic water.

"Jenkins wants us to come to his office in Queens tomorrow morning at eleven," Sidney said, tapping ash from his cigarette. "Okay with you?"

"Ab-so-lute-ly. This is so exciting," Lizzie said, anticipation tingling in her veins. *Our very own record,* she thought. *People all over the country, maybe even as far away as Paris, will hear us play. It's a dream come true.*

"Bert?"

The lanky young man leaned back in his chair and cracked his knuckles. "Yeah, okay."

* * *

After the waiter served their dinners and they'd had time to savor the fare, Rory Moynihan came to their table to say hello.

"Welcome to the Blue Lagoon," he said. "Swell seeing you again. It's been, what, three months since you played here? Four? Gotta remedy that."

Sidney stood and shook the restaurant owner's hand. "It's good to be here, Rory. You remember my colleagues, Lizzie Crane and Bert Halley."

"Sure do," Rory answered.

Lizzie flashed him a pretty smile. Bert pushed himself up from the table and extended his hand.

"How's your meal?" Rory asked.

"Superb as always," Sidney said. "Tonight, we're celebrating making a record with Jim Jenkins's company, Jupiter Records. Maybe you've heard of it."

"Congratulations," Rory said. "Jupiter Records, you say? Jim Jenkins?"

"That's right."

"What a coincidence." Rory nodded toward two men seated at a table across the dining room. "See those two fellas? They're musicians too, up from Mississippi. They made a record for Jupiter. Want me to introduce you?"

"Yes, please do," Lizzie answered.

Rory crossed the dining room and spoke with the two men, whose clothing and demeanor instantly cast them as outsiders. No upscale Manhattanite would've sported a bushy beard like that of the bigger man—it reminded Lizzie of a woodchuck's pelt. And no one would have come to the fashionable Blue Lagoon dressed in a cheap, ill-fitting suit ten years out of date like the one the short, skinny chap wore.

As the two southerners approached their table, Sidney and Bert stood and shook hands with the men. Lizzie knew Sid, who always dressed as if he expected a photographer from *Theatre Magazine* to snap his picture, must find these rubes coarse, but he greeted them pleasantly and introduced Lizzie and Bert.

"I'm Charlie Tippett," the bearded man said, "an' this here's Hank Fowles. Pleased to meet y'all. Mind if we sit down?"

Although she was curious to learn more about their experience with Jupiter Records, Lizzie cringed when Tippett pulled up a chair and sat so close to her that his leg nearly touched hers. She scooted her own chair toward Bert, as far away from the bearded man as possible.

"I understand you gentlemen made a recording with Mr. Jim Jenkins of Jupiter Records," Sidney said.

Tippett replied, "Yessir, we did. An' I don't mind tellin' you it was a big mistake."

"Oh? In what way?"

"He cheated us," Tippett said. "Told us we'd make a pile of money, but we never saw a dime."

"Why do you think he cheated you? Is it possible your record didn't sell well, and you didn't earn any royalties?" Sidney cut a bite of his medium-rare steak and chewed it slowly, considering the man's accusation.

"That's what ol' JJ claimed, but it weren't true. He led us to believe we'd get paid every time our songs got played on the radio, as well as takin' in 10 percent of each record that got sold."

The thin, badly dressed man named Hank Fowles chimed in. "I had folks everywhere listenin' to the radio for our music. A lot of 'em heard it too. Not jest here in New York City, but in stations all over. Even as far off as Chicago. They wrote down when and where they heard it–I got a list with more'n a hundred dates and times on it."

"What are the names of your songs?" Lizzie asked. She doubted the story these yokels told, but if The Troubadours planned to consider a partnership with Jenkins, she needed to learn everything she could—the bad as well as the good.

Tippett named several songs. "Me an' Hank call ourselves the Delta Jazz Boys."

Surprised, Lizzie said, "I've heard of you. I've heard your songs too. KDAZ plays them, and so do other stations around here." Her appreciation of the two Mississippi musicians ratcheted up a notch. *They may lack class, but they've got talent.*

"JJ never did answer our long-distance telephone calls or letters, so we come up here to talk to him face-to-face," Fowles said.

"Have you met with him and rectified the problem?" Sidney asked.

"Nope. No, sir, he won't give us the time of day. Come all this way for nothin'." Tippett snorted and tugged at his beard. "Shoulda known I couldn't trust no Yankee." Too late, he realized he might have insulted his companions and added, "No offense intended to y'all."

"How did you meet Jenkins?" Lizzie asked.

"He had a scout that come down south lookin' to sign colored musicians to record contracts, seein' as how much folks everywhere liked Jelly Roll Morton an' King Oliver. Once that ol' boy started nosin' around, he found out there's a whole lotta white fellas in Dixie who can play a dandy tune too."

Fowles nodded. "We all been raised up on the blues an' jazz."

"So you signed with him?" Lizzie asked.

"Yes, ma'am, we did, and we were proud to do it," Tippett answered. "Now I'd run the other way as fast as I could if I saw ol' JJ comin' towards me with a paper and pen in hand."

"Have you sought legal remedies?" Sidney asked.

Again, Tippett snorted. "You think some country lawyer from Miss'ippi would stand a chance against the kind of city slicker Jenkins would hire? No sir. I signed that there contract, yes, I did, so I'm to blame. But I gotta say I barely understood a word of it."

Sidney longed to enhance his glass of tonic water with gin, but not in the presence of these strangers. Trying to wind up the conversation, he said, "Thank you, gentlemen, for sharing your experience with us. I hope you enjoy the rest of your time in New York and have a safe trip back to Mississippi."

The two southerners took the hint and stood. "A good evenin' to y'all," Tippett said. "Didn't mean to throw water on your fire with our tale of woe."

"I hope you can reconcile your differences and work out an equitable agreement with Mr. Jenkins," Sidney said.

Tippett shrugged. "We're not countin' on much, but at least we got to see the bright lights of the big city. I don't expect we'll ever come back this way again, so we been doin' it up right while we're here. Like eatin' at this here fancy restaurant. Went to a Broadway show too and heard a lot of good music. We've had us some fine times along with the disappointments, haven't we, Hank?"

"You only go around once," Fowles added.

"Don't give up," Lizzie urged them. She thought of her childhood living in a tenement in the Bronx, washing other people's laundry with her mother to make ends meet, dropping out of school at fifteen, and working in kitchens to help her parents feed her six younger siblings. She thought about Bert playing for change on the streets. "There's magic in music. You never know where its spell might take you."

* * *

"What do you make of all that?" Sidney asked after the Mississippi musicians had left the restaurant.

Lizzie sipped her drink, recently refreshed with a splash of gin from Sid's flask. She couldn't help noticing Bert hadn't said a word during the entire discussion. *Maybe he's angry that they spoke badly of his father's friend.*

"I think it's worth looking into further," she said. "Those fellas may be country bumpkins, and maybe they're way off-base, but they're good musicians. If Jenkins took advantage of them, well, we might want to

12

consider letting someone else make our record."

Sidney looked at Bert, who seemed more interested in his dinner than the conversation. "What do you think? You know Jenkins. Can we trust him?"

"When I was a kid, he was like an uncle to me. Now, I'm not sure."

Lizzie finished her dinner and crossed her knife and fork on the plate. "Let's go to Jupiter's studio tomorrow afternoon as planned and see what's what. We don't have to make a commitment yet. After we've assessed the operation and heard Jenkins out, we'll have a better idea what to do."

"Bert, what do you think?" Sidney asked.

"I think it's time for dessert."

Chapter Three

"Music is the tonal reflection of beauty."

—Duke Ellington

Lizzie had expected Jim Jenkins's office to be swanky. But Jupiter Records occupied a nondescript building on a side street in Queens, far from the city's music scene. No doorman greeted them, no red carpet showed the way to their destination. A directory hanging on the lobby wall indicated that Jupiter Records was housed on the third floor. She pulled her cloche hat tight over her bobbed hair and glanced around, searching for an elevator, but saw none.

"Guess we'll have to hoof it." Sidney started up a stairway bordered by pine wainscoting stained dark reddish-brown to imitate mahogany.

Lizzie, Bert, and Bert's seventeen-year-old sister Daisy followed. Bert's request to bring Daisy along today surprised Lizzie. He'd rarely mentioned his younger sister during the nine months he'd been a member of The Troubadours. This was the first time Lizzie had met the girl. But Bert insisted Daisy loved jazz and was a talented musician despite her youth.

"Takes after her big brother, does she?" Lizzie asked, studying his younger sister who resembled him with her tall, gangly frame and gapped teeth. Her unruly brown hair looked as if she'd cut it herself with sewing scissors.

"Plays piano, clarinet, and guitar," he said proudly. "Besides, I need somebody to help carry my instrument cases."

"Okay by me," Lizzie said, and Sid nodded in agreement.

Sidney pushed open a door with Jupiter's brass nameplate on it, and the musicians entered a small, simply furnished reception room. Framed photographs of the company's star acts decorated the pale green walls. Lizzie spotted several she recognized, both white and Negro performers.

A young woman looked up from her typewriter. "May I help you?"

"We're The Troubadours, here to see Mr. Jenkins," Sidney said, handing her his business card. "We have an eleven o'clock appointment."

"Oh, yes," she said. "He's expecting you. Let me tell him you've arrived."

A few minutes later, the woman returned, followed by a man in his mid-forties with a large, round head perched on a scrawny neck. He made Lizzie think of a lollipop. His salt-and-pepper hair was slicked back from a high forehead, and a pencil-thin moustache lined his upper lip.

"Welcome to Jupiter Records," he said, extending his hand to Sidney.

Sid shook it, then introduced Lizzie. "And of course, you know Bert Halley and his sister Daisy."

"I've known them since they were in diapers," Jenkins replied and flashed a big smile. "Good to have you kids here. Imagine us making a record together. Your dad would have been proud."

Lizzie noticed neither of the "kids" smiled back at Jenkins. Instead, Daisy cast her eyes down at the floor. Bert, who was several inches taller than the record producer, looked over the man's head. He opened and closed his hands at his sides, as if he didn't know what to do with them when he wasn't holding a musical instrument.

"Bert tells me you and his father, Tommy Halley, were friends," Lizzie said. "Is that why you wanted to work with us?"

"Let's say that's why I initially took an interest in you. But once I heard you play, I knew you had a great future ahead of you." Jenkins motioned for them to follow him down a narrow corridor that led to the studio. "C'mon, let me show you the inner workings of this business."

On the walls hung posters of Ma Rainey, Jelly Roll Morton, and Blind Lemon Jefferson.

"Did all these folks record with you?" Lizzie asked.

Jenkins shook his big head. "No, but I like their music."

The studio's drab gray walls and tan carpet gave no indication of the colorful musicians who'd recorded here. The stark, industrial ambiance was tinged with the odor of cigarette smoke and something acrid she couldn't identify.

Jenkins poured himself a mug of coffee from a percolator and asked, "Anybody want some java?"

"I do, black please," Lizzie said, but the others declined.

He filled a cup for her, then set his own on a wooden table scarred with cigarette burns while he led Lizzie and Sidney around the spacious room. A baffling array of devices and mechanical instruments lined the walls. More equipment, replete with dials, wires, gauges, and switches, perched on shelves and tables situated about the studio. Jenkins proudly described each one in detail. By the time he directed the musicians to sit at the table where Bert and Daisy waited, Lizzie's head was spinning.

"We're entering a brand-new era of record-making," Jenkins said, then took a swig of his coffee. "Up until a year ago, performers had to cluster around a huge flaring horn and play into it. The horn funneled the vibrations generated by their music to a stylus that manually cut grooves into a cylinder or a wax master disc. From that prototype, we made the records. The sound quality was poor. Drums and horns overpowered the other instruments and voices–it was hard to balance the mix. Surface noise caused a problem, too."

"Have you found a way to fix that now?" Lizzie asked. "I wouldn't want our record to give the wrong impression of us to our audience."

"You happen to be in luck, little lady," Jenkins said, enthusiasm lighting up his face like a full moon. "In just the past year, the industry has shifted over to modern electronic devices. Now all you have to do is use a microphone. We can capture, amplify, and balance everything electronically. That gives us a wider range of frequencies and better audio quality. Your music will be directed to an electrically powered synchronous turntable motor that runs at 3600 rpm with a 46:1 gear ratio that produces 78 rpm–that's revolutions per minute. An electronic signal is applied to a stylus that cuts precise grooves into a wax disc. When finished, that master disc will be sprayed with silver and serve as the prototype we'll use to cast your record in shellac."

Lizzie stared at him in bewilderment. "I haven't a clue what you're talking about."

"Don't worry your pretty head about it. That's my job," Jenkins said in a patronizing tone. "What do you say we give it a test run? See how you sound? You can get an idea of how the equipment operates. It's not as complicated as it seems."

"Nothing is," Daisy said, her voice as flat and matter-of-fact as the gray studio walls.

Lizzie frowned at the girl, wondering what she meant. Then she glanced at Bert, who turned away.

Sidney stubbed out the cigarette he'd been smoking and said, "Before we record anything, we need to discuss contractual issues."

"Such as?" Jenkins asked.

"Well, let's say, hypothetically, you died, or the company went belly up before The Troubadours signed a contract with Jupiter. Who'd own the rights to what we might record here today?"

The record producer laughed nervously. "I'd rather not think about such things. Don't want to jinx the project."

"Nevertheless, we need to iron out the details before we record any of our music," Sidney said. "You've already heard us perform, and you know how good we are. You wouldn't have invited us here otherwise."

"True," Jenkins admitted.

Lizzie wondered if Sid was contemplating what the Mississippi musicians told them last night at the Blue Lagoon, about Jenkins cheating them.

"Maybe we should have our lawyer meet with yours to hammer out an agreement before we proceed," she suggested, although The Troubadours didn't have an attorney and the only legal matters they'd been involved in previously were murder cases.

While Jenkins appeared to consider the prospect of getting lawyers involved, Daisy slipped away from the group and began wandering around the studio. She paused in front of the numerous gadgets and gizmos, one after another, occasionally reaching out to touch something that caught her fancy.

"Let's talk about how you plan to get our record out to the public," Sidney said. "Will radio stations here in The City and elsewhere play it?"

"Sure, they will. Most definitely," Jenkins said. "Are you members of ASCAP?"

"Yes," Lizzie said, before Sidney could admit they weren't.

It took her a moment to remember what the acronym stood for: American Society of Composers, Authors and Publishers. The three-year-old association required radio stations to pay a licensing fee if they wanted to play members' music on the air. That way, the musicians as well as those who used their music profited.

Jenkins ran a fingertip along the thin, dark line of his mustache. "Well, then, ASCAP will monitor your on-air presence. If you write your own music and hold the copyrights to your songs, you'll get paid whenever a station plays your record."

Lizzie sipped her coffee while she pondered the Mississippi musicians' claim that their songs had gotten a lot of airtime, but they hadn't received any payments. Maybe they signed over their copyrights to Jupiter Records, or some other legality prevented them from getting what they believed they were due. *I only understand a smidgeon of what Jenkins is talking about.* Without the backing of a watchdog organization like ASCAP, she realized, musicians had no power against unethical record companies or radio stations. *We have to join up post-haste if we're going to do this.* One of the many logistical steps The Troubadours needed to take if they planned to continue growing professionally. Already, she felt overwhelmed. Things were so much easier when they played in local nightclubs and accepted payment in cash at the end of the night.

"When do you envision our record coming out?" Sidney asked.

"I'm thinking September," Jenkins answered.

"What will people do if they want to buy our record?" Lizzie asked.

"Listeners will be able to buy it from record dealers like Sam Goody's, as well as in stores that sell musical instruments or furniture," Jenkins said.

"Why furniture stores?" Bert interjected, his first words since entering the studio.

"When someone purchases a phonograph cabinet, he's gonna want records to listen to on it, right? It's an easy sell," Jenkins pointed out. "Notice how furniture stores play music in the background? That's not to entertain their customers, it's to entice them to buy."

Bert nodded and looked past Jenkins's shoulder at his sister. Daisy was running her fingertips along a row of levers that protruded from a long black box, as if trying to ascertain their purposes. Jenkins turned around to follow Bert's gaze.

"Daisy, don't touch the equipment," the studio owner ordered sharply.

Chastened, the girl shoved her hands in the pockets of her skirt. She moved down the hallway, studying the photographs on the walls, leaving the adults to their discussion.

Sidney fitted another cigarette into his engraved silver holder and lit it. After taking a drag and exhaling the smoke, he asked, "How much will The Troubadours earn from each record sold?"

"Ten percent. That's the going rate," Jenkins answered.

"Who keeps track of our sales?" Lizzie asked.

"We do. Jupiter carefully accounts for all sales that come through this office and provides quarterly reports to musicians." Jenkins withdrew a handkerchief from his pocket and dabbed at his high forehead, which shone with a sheen of sweat even though the temperature in the studio was far from warm. "Listen, I've got a draft of the contract already drawn up. I'll get it for you. You can have your attorney examine everything, Miss Crane."

"I'm a novice at all this, Mr. Jenkins. I'm only trying to understand how things work in your business."

"Of course," Jenkins said. "And you should. It will be a partnership, after all. We need to be able to trust one another."

He excused himself and returned a few minutes later with a manila folder in hand. He placed it on the table in front of Sidney. "Take it home and read it over. Let your attorney have a look-see."

"Thanks. Does anyone else have questions?" Sidney asked his colleagues.

Bert shook his head, and Lizzie noticed he avoided eye contact with

Jenkins.

"Not at the moment, but may we get back to you if we think of something?" she asked.

"I hope you will," Jenkins said.

Sidney crushed his cigarette butt in a heavy glass ashtray and stood up. He held out his hand to the studio's owner. "Thank you for meeting with us, Mr. Jenkins. I think we've acquired some useful information. My associates and I just need a little time to discuss this project further."

"I understand, Mr. Somerset," Jenkins replied. "But don't take too long. You're riding a wave, and you don't want to miss the crest."

As the musicians started to leave the studio, Jenkins called out to them, "Say, if you're free this evening, how about coming to my birthday party? It's gonna be a doozy. Plenty of music, food, booze. The works." He pulled a calling card from his jacket pocket and jotted an Upper East Side address on the back. "Things probably won't get jumping 'til around ten, but show up whenever you want."

Sidney took the card. "Thanks, that sounds swell."

"Happy birthday," Lizzie said.

"See you tonight then," Jenkins said. "Think about playing a song or two—good advance publicity for your new record."

* * *

After dropping Bert and Daisy off in Brooklyn, Sidney and Lizzie drove back to Greenwich Village.

"Are you game for tonight-ski?" Sidney asked.

"All right-ski," Lizzie answered. "I agree with Jenkins, this could be a good opportunity for us."

"It's a swanky address. Maybe we'll get some jobs out of it."

"What do you think I should wear? Jenkins didn't say whether it's a formal affair."

"I'm going black tie," he said. "Remember, we're trying to make an impression. Get dolled up—think of it as advertising."

"You're right," she agreed. "I wish Melody could play with us on the record. She's been part of our group through all the ups and downs."

"Isn't she busy with her wedding arrangements? The big event's next Saturday."

Lizzie was still trying to adjust to Melody's absence. The blond flutist had joined The Troubadours right after graduating high school. In the two years since then, Melody had become more like a sister than a business colleague, and Lizzie missed her friendship as much as her music. Where would they find someone who not only had the talent but also the temperament to fill the gap she'd left behind?

"Yes, I know. She's agreed to continue performing with us occasionally, when we do private parties locally. But after she's married, her husband will probably put a stop to that. And once she's in a family way, well..."

"So, convince her to join us on the record, for the sake of posterity," Sidney said.

Lizzie nodded. "You're right. She'd want her children to be able to hear her perform in her early days."

Sidney lit a cigarette, inhaled deeply, then blew out a lungful of smoke. "Considering I'm not likely to have any children, this record will be my baby."

Mine too, Lizzie thought. She was twenty-six—practically an old maid— and although she'd had lovers, she'd never conceived. Nor did she feel called to the role of motherhood. As the eldest of seven children, she understood firsthand the hardships of raising a family and the limitations that would place on her career.

"What songs do you think we should record?" she asked. "Jenkins said we'll have one three-minute song on each side." *Assuming we can come to an agreement with him, that is.*

"What about 'Oh, Lady Be Good' or 'The Man I Love'?" Sidney suggested. "You're smashing on those."

"Hmm, what would you say to 'Big Butter and Egg Man'? It's one of Bert's favorites. Louis Armstrong made it popular, but we can give it our own special flavor. Of course, we'd have to get permission from whoever holds the rights," Lizzie pointed out.

Sidney drummed the breezer's steering wheel with his fingertips as if he were playing a keyboard. "What about the flip side?"

"You know what I'd really like to record?"

"What?"

"Our own songs. Ones you've written. We've never even performed any of your songs publicly. I'd rather play original pieces. We'll never get to the top just covering someone else's tunes."

He shook his head. "It's too soon. As you said, we've never even performed my songs publicly. Maybe nobody would like them."

"We won't know unless we try."

Sidney puffed on his cigarette, but didn't answer.

"What's the problem, Sid? Don't you think they're good enough?" When he didn't reply, she continued. "Okay, how about we test a few of them on a live audience? See what kind of response we get. Rory Moynihan wants us to play the Blue Lagoon again. That's the perfect venue to introduce your work."

"Are you saying I should set up a date to play my songs at the Blue Lagoon?"

She rapped him lightly on the top of his head. "Hello, is anybody home in there? Yes, that's exactly what I'm saying. Or maybe Eve and Ruth would let us perform at Eve's Hangout, if you'd feel less pressure there."

He turned off Cherry Lane and pulled up to the curb in front of the Village brownstone where Lizzie occupied a three-room apartment on the third floor. "Want me to see you inside?"

"Thanks, but it's barely two in the afternoon. I think I'm old enough to find my way home," she said in a teasing voice. "Think about what I said, Sid. Everybody knows what a talented pianist you are, but you're a darb songwriter too. Don't shove your stuff in the back of a closet and let it grow mold there."

Chapter Four

"[M]en and girls came and went like moths among the whisperings and the champagne and the stars."

—F. Scott Fitzgerald, The Great Gatsby

At half past ten, Sidney squeezed his Buick convertible into a narrow space on East 79th between Central Park and Park Avenue. He opened the passenger side door for Lizzie and offered his hand to help her out of the automobile.

"You look smashing, by the way," he said as she linked her arm through his.

"Thanks, so do you."

They made a handsome couple, she knew, both of them tall, slim, dark-haired, and elegant in their evening clothes. When they first met eight years ago, Lizzie had entertained fantasies about a romance with Sidney—until she realized he preferred men. Since then, they'd formed a bond that was closer and less complicated than most couples she knew.

They mounted the steps of a brownstone built about sixty years ago that had undergone a recent facelift, its original façade updated with limestone in keeping with the trend toward Beaux-Arts architecture. A doorman dressed in a black tailcoat, gray trousers, and a top hat greeted them. Sidney showed Jim Jenkins's calling card to the man, who nodded and opened the heavy oak door for them. Inside, a housemaid wearing a black dress with a white lace collar and white cuffs took Lizzie's fox stole and Sidney's top hat.

Music cascaded down the flight of stairs that led to the townhouse's second floor. At the top of the staircase, another maid directed them toward a ballroom where at least sixty people–all attired in the latest fashions—milled about, drinking and chatting. Lizzie was glad she'd worn her new rhinestone-spangled black silk evening dress with a V-neckline that showcased her cleavage.

"Looks like we've come to the right place," she said.

"And how," Sidney replied enthusiastically.

Along one wall stretched tables laden with an array of culinary delights: shrimp, scallop, and oyster appetizers; platters of sliced roast beef, lamb, and turkey; vegetable dishes and salads of all kinds; and fresh-baked breads, pies, and cakes. Servers stood ready to heap piles of food onto guests' plates. At the far end of the ballroom, three men—one at a piano, another on clarinet, and a third plucking an upright bass–played an instrumental version of "Sweet Georgia Brown."

Sidney took her elbow and drew her into the crowd. Waiters bearing trays with flutes of champagne maneuvered through the guests. He grabbed two glasses of bubbly and handed one to her.

"Cheers." Lizzie touched her glass to his, then sipped the sparkling wine. "Mmm, this is top shelf."

"In a place like this, I wouldn't expect anything less." Sidney's dark eyes scanned the room. "Which gent do you think is our host? I want to make sure to meet him while we're here. Those geezers he's got playing ought to be put out to pasture."

Lizzie laughed and shook a finger at him. "Don't be mean. You'll be a geezer one day, too."

"If that happens, promise you won't let me embarrass myself in public."

"Oh, look, Sid. There's Jim Jenkins."

He turned and followed her gaze. The record producer was talking to a man with a head of thick, graying hair whose athletic build made him seem younger than he probably was. Beside him stood a woman half his age with perfect features, finger-waved blond hair, and dollar signs in her eyes.

"Let's go make our acquaintance," he said.

Just as they started weaving their way through the clumps of guests, the musicians stopped playing. As they vacated their position at the ballroom's east end, two others took their place. A heavy-set man raised his trumpet and launched into a Dixieland jazz number. His cohort, a man in his middle years wearing an ascot instead of a bow tie, quickly joined in on his tenor sax.

Sidney stopped to listen. "Now that's more like it."

The duo followed up with a lively rendition of King Oliver's "Riverside Blues." Then they relinquished the limelight to yet another musician, a solo guitarist who never looked up from his instrument the entire time he played.

"I'm not familiar with that song, are you?" Lizzie asked.

"It's one of Blind Blake's, if I'm not mistaken," Sidney said.

"Who?"

"Kind of a mystery man. I'm surprised you haven't heard of him, Bearcat. Darb guitarist. Plays around Chicago now, but he's probably from Florida or Georgia."

"Is that why he doesn't look at the audience, because he's blind?"

"Silly, that's not Blake. Blake's colored."

"I know plenty of musicians in this city, but I don't recognize any of these guys," Lizzie said. "Do you suppose they're out-of-towners? All on the Jupiter Records label? Maybe we could talk to some of them, find out more about Jenkins."

Sidney shrugged. "Maybe, but let's first see about getting a chance to play tonight. Are you game-ski?"

"To fortune and fame-ski," she said, raising her glass.

He took her hand and led her across the ballroom's well-waxed walnut floor toward Jim Jenkins, who was still engaged in conversation with the athletic-looking man and his pretty companion. As they approached, Lizzie wondered what sport the man might play to acquire that tan. Tennis? Golf? Polo in the Hamptons?

"Happy birthday, Mr. Jenkins," Sidney called out.

Jenkins turned around and greeted them, his full-moon face breaking into a grin. "Well, hello there. Good of you to come." He slapped Sidney on the back as if they were old chums.

"Thanks for inviting us. Swell party," Lizzie said.

"Let me introduce you to our host. Malcolm MacGregor, please meet Lizzie Crane and Sidney Somerset with The Troubadours. I'm trying to convince them to sign with me."

"Welcome. I trust you're having a good time," MacGregor said, a hint of the Scottish Highlands in his voice. Almost as an afterthought, he introduced the blond woman at his side. "This is Nadine. You're making a record with this chap JJ, are you now? Be sure to negotiate a good fee—he's a right tightwad, he is."

"This, coming from a Scot?" Jenkins punched him playfully on the arm. "It's my birthday, Mac. Go easy on me for once."

"Might I have heard your music?" MacGregor asked Lizzie.

His eyes slid down to the V of her dress and lingered there until she wanted to put her hand under his chin to tilt his head back to its upright position. Accustomed to men's appraising looks, Lizzie had to admit she often used her charms to get what she wanted. It was an old game, one she'd mastered over the years. She just wished this fellow would show a tad more discretion. MacGregor's companion, pencil-thin and fashionably flat-chested, noticed too. She elbowed him.

"I need another drink, Mac," the blonde said, waving her empty glass.

"Ah, so you do, lass." He signaled to a waiter, who hurried over with a tray of champagne flutes. Turning his attention back to Lizzie, he asked, "Would you consider favoring my guests with a song or two this evening?"

"Ab-so-lute-ly."

"We'd be delighted," Sidney agreed.

MacGregor consulted his Rolex. "In fifteen minutes?"

"Perfect," Sid answered.

"How many musicians are performing here tonight, Mr. MacGregor?" Lizzie asked.

"Eighteen, plus you two. Quite a tribute to our man JJ, don't you agree?"

She turned to Jenkins. "Are they all with Jupiter Records?"

"Most of them. A few are, shall we say, auditioning tonight. Like that fat ol' gal."

He pointed at a woman shaped like an overstuffed armchair who'd stepped up to the microphone. She began to sing, a cappella, in a rich alto that flowed like maple syrup through the ballroom.

"She's good. Better sign her while you can," Lizzie said, and Jenkins nodded.

Before the singer finished, however, a man with a sunburned nose and wearing a daytime suit instead of a tux like most of the other male guests pushed through the crowd. He grabbed Jenkins's arm. JJ's glass crashed to the floor, splattering the birthday boy's trousers with bourbon.

"Leave my Marie alone, ya hear?" the man growled. "Just cuz she sang a song for you don't make her your property."

While a housemaid hurried over to clean up the whiskey and broken glass, Jenkins roughly peeled the man's fingers off his arm, bending them back and causing him to wince. An amused look crossed MacGregor's face. Several nearby couples turned to watch the scene unfold, hoping for a bit of excitement.

"I don't know anyone named Marie," Jenkins said. "Now go crawl back under your rock and leave me alone, while you still can."

The sunburned man stepped away, rubbing his hand. "You've not seen the last o' me," he called out as the crowd parted to let him pass.

Sidney nudged Lizzie. "I think it's time to excuse ourselves."

"Now you're on the trolley."

"We need to get ready for our set," Sid said to Jenkins and MacGregor. "Nice chatting with you."

"Thanks again for inviting us to your party," Lizzie added.

"I look forward to your performance," said MacGregor, and once again Lizzie felt him undressing her with his eyes.

Jenkins grinned. "Knock 'em dead, kids."

"He gives me the creeps," she told Sidney as they snagged two more glasses of champagne from a passing waiter's tray.

"Which one?"

"Both of them, actually."

"Maybe you should have worn something more modest, Bearcat," he teased her. "Men can't help leering. It's an occupational hazard for a tomato like you."

She took a sip of her champagne, then changed the subject. "What shall we play? I'm thinking 'Bye Bye Blackbird.' Sam Lanin's Dance Orchestra recorded it only a couple months ago—it's getting a lot of play time."

Sidney nodded. "Good choice. How about we follow up with 'Cake Walkin' Babies?'"

"Without Bert's horn, it's a little flat, but I guess we can pull it off." She thought a moment. "I'd rather sing 'Wild Women Don't Have the Blues' if that's okay with you."

He laughed. "Sending a message to Jenkins and MacGregor?"

"Something like that."

"You're on, Bearcat."

The alto finished her set and moved out of the spotlight, clearing the way for the two Troubadours. Sidney played a few scales to test the piano's action as Lizzie stepped up to the microphone and introduced the duo. For ten minutes, they held the audience in thrall. Once she caught Jim Jenkins's eye, and he gave her a thumbs-up.

They bowed to their cheering listeners as two men rolled an enormous birthday cake, perched on a wheeled platform, into the center of the ballroom. Dozens of sparklers flickered atop the gaudy confection decorated with yellow icing, blue swags, and red roses. Sidney slid onto the piano bench again and began playing "Happy Birthday." Soon, other musicians around the room joined in on saxophones, clarinets, trumpets, fiddles, guitars, and accordions.

As the last notes of the song rang through the ballroom, the top of the cardboard cake burst open. A lovely young woman wearing a short, nearly transparent dress popped out. She waved her arms in the air and did a full-body shimmy. Several players switched to a burlesque tune, while the cake woman did a bump-and-grind.

Lizzie laughed and nudged Sidney. "Look at Jenkins and MacGregor—

those old lechers' eyes are bugging out of their heads."

"You don't mind being upstaged?" he teased her.

"Not in the least."

Amid cheers and catcalls, MacGregor's kitchen maids pushed in another cake—this time a real one—on a stainless steel cart, along with stacks of dessert plates and silverware. Guests lined up to be served.

"Do you remember the story about a party given for the famous architect Stanford White at the end of the last century, where a scantily clad lady popped out of a cake just like this one?" Lizzie asked Sid.

"Can't say as I do."

"A chorus girl named Evelyn Nesbit supposedly bedded White that night and went on to have an affair with him. Later, she married railroad scion Harry Kendall Thaw, who never got over his jealousy of White and insisted the architect had ruined his wife. He shot and killed White on the rooftop theater of Madison Square Garden."

"Holy moly. Who knew a cardboard cake could lead to murder?" Sidney said, grasping her arm. "Maybe we should skedaddle while the getting's good."

Chapter Five

"He had two lives: one, open, seen and known by all who cared to know, full of relative truth and of relative falsehood, exactly like the lives of his friends and acquaintances; and another life running its course in secret."

—Anton Chekhov

The telephone jarred Lizzie out of a dream of walking along a white sand beach in Massachusetts, collecting seashells. After about a dozen insistent rings, she climbed out of bed, shuffled into the living room, and picked up the Bakelite receiver.

Suspecting Sidney might be on the other end of the line, she said, "I hope you have something cheery to tell me, because it's barely eight o'clock. I didn't get to sleep until nearly three."

"Sorry," he apologized, "but I've been awake all night thinking about this recording deal."

"So if you can't sleep, neither should I?" she asked irritably.

"I think we should present Jim Jenkins with a list of our requirements, ask him to draw up a potential contract, and then get input from a lawyer about how to proceed."

"We don't have a lawyer," she reminded him.

"We need to get one straight away, if we're going to do this deal."

Lizzie yawned. It was too early to discuss business. She needed a cup of coffee at least to clear her head. "I agree. Can we talk about this later?"

"I telephoned Jupiter Records before I called you," Sid continued. "JJ's secretary said he has an opening at half past eleven today. I can pick you up at quarter 'til."

"Do I have a choice?"

"I'd rather you came with me, but I'll go alone if I have to."

"Oh, all right," she said and hung up.

* * *

Jupiter Records' pretty young secretary was busy filing her fingernails when Lizzie and Sidney entered the reception room.

"Hello, Mr. Somerset, Miss Crane," she said, setting aside her emery board.

Sidney nodded. "Good morning. Is Mr. Jenkins ready for us?"

"Let me check." She pushed her chair away from her desk. "I haven't seen him since first thing this morning. He wasn't feeling well and asked me to hold his phone calls."

A few moments later, a scream sliced through the office. Lizzie and Sidney hurried down the hallway, following that scream, into the studio.

Jim Jenkins lay on his back in a pool of vomit, blank eyes staring at the ceiling. The secretary clapped her hands over her mouth, as if she feared she too might vomit. Sidney stepped toward Jenkins and knelt beside him, careful to avoid the smelly mess congealing on the carpet. He felt the man's wrist for a pulse.

"Telephone the police," he told the secretary.

* * *

A nervous-looking technician ushered a stocky policeman with a jutting chin marked by a gumdrop-like mole into the recording studio. As Sidney had done earlier, the officer knelt cautiously and felt for Jenkins's pulse. He found none. After telephoning a coroner, the policeman approached the secretary, who stood with her back against a wall as far away as she could get from the body while still remaining in the same room. She wept quietly and dabbed her eyes with an embroidered handkerchief.

"Miss, are you employed here?" he asked.

The young woman sniffed, then answered in a shaky voice, "Yes, I'm his secretary. I'm the one who found him…like this…and called the police."

The policeman turned to Sidney. "What about you?"

Although Lizzie knew her friend was rattled, Sid assumed his professional stage persona and answered calmly, "I'm Sidney Somerset, and this is my colleague, Elizabeth Crane. We're local musicians. We were scheduled to meet with Mr. Jenkins today to discuss a recording contract. Unfortunately, we found him like this when we arrived."

"I'm Detective Lawrence Perry with the New York Police Department. People just call me 'Law.' It has a nice ring to it, don't you think?"

His harsh, raspy voice, Lizzie thought, sounded like a saw gnawing through wood. "A detective?" she asked. "Don't detectives usually investigate murders?"

"Murders and other crimes, but it's a slow day. In nice weather like this, people have better things to do than kill one another. Now, what can you tell me about Mr. Jenkins and this situation?"

"Not a thing," Sidney answered. "We only met him yesterday."

Sid's fingers fidgeted at his sides, as they often did when he needed a cigarette. Lizzie hoped the big cop wouldn't notice and interpret the nicotine shakes as a suspicious sign. This was the fourth dead body she'd encountered in less than a year. Although inwardly she still recoiled in horror from the scene, she'd learned to hide her reactions from the police.

"It's quite a shock," Lizzie said, glad Bert wasn't here with them to see his family friend's lifeless form. "What do you think caused Mr. Jenkins's death?"

Perry shrugged. "That's not my call. A medical examiner will determine cause of death."

Lizzie considered the angry Mississippi musicians they'd met at the Blue Lagoon the night before last. What would they think when they heard of

Jenkins's demise? What would happen now to the men and women who'd contracted with Jupiter Records? She felt a wave of relief wash over her. Despite her initial excitement at making a record, she thanked her lucky stars The Troubadours had been spared the complications of such a deal—just in the nick of time.

Detective Perry pulled a small notebook and pencil from his pocket, then motioned them toward the studio's wooden table and chairs. "I need to ask you a few questions." When the distraught secretary hung back, he called out, "You too, miss."

Sidney held a chair for Lizzie, then sat beside her. The blond secretary took a seat on the other side of Sidney, still dabbing at her eyes where the mascara had run. As Sid fitted a cigarette into his engraved silver holder, Lizzie wished—not for the first time—that he'd dispense with the fancy holder in front of strangers, especially strangers who were capable of making life difficult. His sleek good looks, stylish clothing, and slightly effeminate mannerisms drew enough disparagement from people who disapproved of three-letter men. Detective Lawrence Perry, she suspected, fit into that category.

Perry sat at the head of the table and asked the secretary, "Now, Miss… what's your name?"

"Irene Warner," she answered in a voice so soft Lizzie could barely hear her.

He wrote it down in his notebook. "Did Mr. Jenkins have a family?"

"A wife."

"Has she been notified of his death?"

Irene shook her head. "I didn't want to be the one to tell her."

He passed Irene his notebook. "Give me her name and address. I'll have one of our men do it."

She jotted down the information and handed it back to him.

"How long have you worked here, Miss Warner?"

"Four years."

"Do you know anything about Mr. Jenkins's health that might have contributed to his death?"

Irene twisted her handkerchief nervously. "His birthday was yesterday, and some of his friends threw a big party for him last night. This morning, when he said he wasn't feeling well, I thought he might've been a tad hungover."

"Did you attend the party?" Perry asked.

"No, sir."

"What made you suspect Mr. Jenkins had been drinking?"

Irene looked up at the ceiling, perhaps wondering how much to reveal about her boss's behavior. After a few moments, she answered, "Well, he drank quite a bit."

"Can you give me the names of the friends who threw the party?"

"Um, I'm not sure."

"Not sure you know their names or not sure you're willing to give them to me?"

"I don't know them," the young woman said, but Lizzie felt certain she was lying.

Lizzie studied the secretary's face, trying to decide if Irene was reluctant to divulge information that might be incriminating to her employer's friends. The Volstead Act and the Eighteenth Amendment didn't prohibit drinking spirits—only making, selling, or transporting them. Nonetheless, the cops might make things difficult for the people at JJ's birthday party, considering the record producer had died in the wake of that party. Maybe Jenkins drank some bad booze with methanol or wood alcohol in it, but she couldn't imagine a rich man like Malcolm MacGregor serving rotgut.

Detective Perry jotted a few lines in his notebook, then turned his attention to Sidney. "How did you become acquainted with Mr. Jenkins?"

Sidney stubbed out his cigarette and slipped the silver holder back into his jacket pocket. "He heard us perform on KDAZ radio and proposed making a record with us."

"And when did you last see him?"

"Alive? Last night. At his birthday party. He invited us to perform there."

Detective Perry scribbled in his notebook, then looked at Lizzie. "Miss Crane, did you attend the birthday party too?"

"Yes, sir."

"Where was this party held?"

"At the home of Malcolm MacGregor, on the Upper East Side."

The policeman paused and tapped his pencil on the notebook. Lizzie wondered if the name meant something to Perry. Even though she'd never heard of MacGregor, she guessed he must be a big muckety-muck, with a ritzy townhouse like that and all those fancy guests.

"Who else was there?"

"Quite a lot of people. The only ones I spoke to, though, were Mr. MacGregor, Mr. Jenkins, and a few of the other musicians. Oh, and Mr. MacGregor's lady friend, but I can't remember her name."

She was glad Bert had declined the invitation to the party. It meant she didn't have to mention him or tell this big copper about the connection between the dead man and the saxophonist—at least not yet. Nor would she reveal that both Bert and his sister Daisy had met with Jenkins here at this studio yesterday, unless Law Perry asked. That would only invite more suspicion and unnecessary intrusion into their personal lives.

The door to the studio swung open, and two men wheeled a gurney into the room. Perry rose to greet them. "Thanks for coming so quickly. You can take him away."

Without squeamishness or fanfare, they lifted the body onto the gurney, then rolled their lifeless cargo out.

Turning back to his querents, Detective Perry said, "Thank you for your time." He handed each of them a card with his name and the telephone number of the police station on it. "Please give me your contact information in case I need to speak with you again, and don't hesitate to call me if you remember anything else."

Chapter Six

"Life is for the living.

Death is for the dead.

Let life be like music.

And death a note unsaid."

—Langston Hughes, The Collected Poems

"We have to let Bert know Jenkins is dead," Lizzie said as she got into Sidney's convertible.

Sid slid behind the wheel of the breezer and turned the key in the ignition. "How do you think he'll take it?"

"Haven't the foggiest. He's known Jenkins since he was a kid, said the fella was like an uncle to him." She pulled off her straw hat and held it in her lap, so the wind wouldn't blow it away. "This isn't going to be easy."

"Bert doesn't reveal much about himself," Sidney said as he eased into the midday traffic. "He didn't even tell us he knew the man until Wednesday. And we'd never met his sister Daisy until yesterday."

"Now we may finally meet Bert's mother, though I wish the circumstances were better," Lizzie added.

Sidney drove toward Brooklyn, his fingers tapping on the steering wheel as if he were playing the piano. "I've always wondered about the Halleys' family life. It couldn't have been good, considering Bert's mother tossed him out on the street to fend for himself after his father died. He's been living in a boarding house only a mile from his childhood home, yet he doesn't speak of his family unless you ask him a direct question."

"His father was a music teacher," Lizzie said. "Bert got his talent from his dad. Apparently, his sister did too. But that's all I know."

"And that Jim Jenkins, the deceased owner of Jupiter Records who sought us out to make a record with his company, was Tommy Halley's longtime friend." Sidney almost missed his turn and took a sharp right without signaling. The driver behind him blew his horn angrily. "I think we're going to find out a whole lot more about our pal Bert soon."

* * *

All families have their problems, Lizzie knew well enough. Her immigrant parents struggled constantly to provide for their seven children, and she had to drop out of school at fifteen to go to work to help put food on the table. Sidney's well-to-do family had rejected him because of his sexual preference for men. Practically everyone she knew had a painful story to tell. What was Bert's?

Sidney pulled over to the curb in front of the modest, three-story boardinghouse where Bert rented a room. Nine months ago, after finding him playing for change in Central Park, Lizzie had cajoled the owner into taking the saxophonist in, against the woman's better judgment.

"Musicians stay up all night, making a racket. They take drugs, drink. Bring in loose women," the boardinghouse's owner protested, shaking her head.

Lizzie wrote her telephone number on an envelope stuffed with cash that Sidney had given her to cover Bert's room and board for six months. She handed it to the landlady. "If he causes any problems, let me know."

No complaint ever came.

Sidney knocked on the door, waited a minute, then knocked again.

Another minute passed before the plump, gray-haired widow who owned the building cracked the door a few inches and peeked out. She frowned, then recognized Lizzie and opened the door wider.

Sidney handed the woman his calling card. "We've come to see Bert Halley. Is he in?"

"Ah, dear Bert. Yes, he's fixing the steps on the back porch," she said. "Come in, come in."

Despite her initial resistance to having a musician under her roof, the landlady had developed a doting affection for the shy, surprisingly quiet, and well-behaved young horn player who often helped out with handyman chores that her own sons eschewed.

"I'm afraid we have some bad news for him," Lizzie said.

"Lawdy be." The woman clasped a hand to her ample bosom. "Let me just go and fetch him. You can sit in the parlor if you like."

A few minutes later, Bert loped into the parlor with springy strides that made his long legs seem fashioned of rubber. Apparently, the boarding-house's owner hadn't revealed the nature of their visit, because a crooked smile spread across his face as he joined his colleagues and dropped down onto a worn mohair sofa.

After briefly greeting her friend, Lizzie said, "I hate to tell you this, Bert. We've just come from Jupiter Records. Jim Jenkins is dead. We found him there this morning." She waited for a reaction, but when Bert remained expressionless, she continued, "The police are looking into the cause of death now. I'm so sorry."

Bert cracked his knuckles one by one. "Does my mother know?"

"Not from us, though the police may have told her or she might've heard about it elsewhere." Lizzie glanced at Sidney. "Maybe we could all drive over there now and tell her together. Daisy too. Sometimes it's easier to have friends with you during times like this."

Bert nodded and pushed himself up from the sofa. "Okay, let's do it."

* * *

The mile-long drive to Bert's family's home took only a few minutes, but to Lizzie it seemed endless. She'd expected Bert to react with sadness, surprise, anger—anything other than nothing. True, the young man was shy and guarded, the rare performer who barely showed emotion and never purposely drew attention to himself. But surely this sudden news must have hit him hard. *Maybe he's in shock,* she thought.

When Sidney parked and shut off the breezer's engine, the three of them sat in awkward silence until Lizzie asked, "Would you prefer to tell your mother by yourself?"

Bert shook his head, but still didn't move from the backseat. "No, I'm glad you came with me."

Finally, Lizzie opened the Buick's passenger side door and stepped out into the sunny day that seemed too pretty for such bad news. Sidney followed. Bert slowly unfolded his long legs and climbed out onto the cracked sidewalk that edged the scruffy yard in front of the house where he'd grown up. As they approached the plain, two-story brick building, Lizzie slipped her arm around Bert's waist and gave him a quick hug.

Bert knocked on the front door, then tried the knob. Finding it unlocked, he pushed it open and called, "Mom? Daisy?"

Uncertain whether to enter or wait to be invited in, the three musicians stood at the doorway staring into a parlor with floral wallpaper, its curtains drawn shut. A multicolored rag rug lay on the floor. A green davenport with two matching chairs and an upright piano, its key lid closed, furnished the room.

"Mom?" Bert called again. His reluctance to enter gave Lizzie the impression he didn't visit here often.

"Bert?" a thin voice sounded from the upper floor. A reed-like woman appeared at the top of the stairs, her loose brown hair spilling down her back. Unlike her tall, long-limbed son and daughter, Gladys Halley was small and delicate, almost frail. "Bert, is that you?"

"Yes, Mom." He stepped into the narrow foyer and motioned for Lizzie and Sidney to follow him.

Bert's mother squinted at them. "Who are these people?"

"My colleagues," he answered. "My musician friends, Lizzie and Sidney. You've heard me talk about them."

"Oh, yes. I remember."

"Come downstairs, Mom. We have something to tell you."

Slowly, carefully clinging to the banister, Bert's mother descended the staircase. When she reached the bottom, Lizzie could see that the woman, with her high cheekbones and large blue eyes, had once been pretty. But although she couldn't have been more than mid-forties, she looked older. Faded. Tired. Resigned. The death of a spouse sometimes did that to people, Lizzie knew. And now the poor woman was about to learn that yet another person close to her had died.

Bert hooked his arm through his mother's to support her and guided her into the parlor. "Where's Daisy?"

"At a friend's house. She'll be home directly," Gladys said. "Why are you here?"

Gently, Bert seated his mother in one of the armchairs, then remained standing beside her. He looked at Sidney and mouthed, "Tell her."

"Mrs. Halley," the pianist began. "I regret to inform you that your friend Jim Jenkins has died."

Gladys Halley gasped. "What?"

"Lizzie and I found him this morning in his studio."

"Jim? Dead?"

"Yes, ma'am," Sidney said.

"Why? How?"

"The police are examining the body for cause of death," Lizzie explained.

Bert's mother turned to look up at him, her face a mixture of grief, fear, and confusion. She reached for his hand and clung to it. "Is it true?"

"I'm afraid so."

"Stay with me, son?"

"Of course, Mom."

* * *

Sidney drove Lizzie to her Greenwich Village apartment and came in for coffee.

"After all this, I don't feel much like eating lunch," she said as she handed him a cup of strong, dark Jamaican.

He shook his head and lit a cigarette. "Me either. Frankly, I'm still in a daze." He blew smoke rings at the ceiling, watching them drift until they broke apart and dissolved. "One thing's for sure. We're not going to be making a record with Jim Jenkins and company."

Lizzie slipped off her shoes and curled her feet underneath her on the sofa in her cozy living room. "New York has other recording companies. Ones with less stigma attached to them." She thought again about the Mississippi musicians' claim that Jenkins had cheated them. About the jealous man who'd crashed JJ's birthday party. And now Jupiter Records' owner had died unexpectedly. "I'm glad we didn't sign a contract with Jenkins."

"And how," he agreed. "I'm concerned about Bert, though."

Lizzie held her coffee cup with both hands and took a sip. "His mother seemed a bit strange. Frankly, she gave me the creeps."

"She reminded me of a balloon that's lost all its air. You think she's daft?"

"The idea crossed my mind," Lizzie said, then brought the subject back to business. "What's our next step?"

"I'll contact other recording studios and see what our options are before word gets around about Jenkins's death."

"My guess is word's already gotten around. I suspect Sweet William Bly has heard about it, and that means everyone in the music scene knows by now."

Sidney took a long drag on his cigarette, then blew out a cloud of smoke. "Maybe the publicity surrounding JJ's unexpected death will be a plus. It's sure to make the papers. You know what they say, even bad publicity is better than none at all."

"Maybe so, but I wish people would stop dying around us," Lizzie grumbled. "We've already been linked with three murders and one manslaughter in less than a year."

"We have no reason to think Jenkins died of anything other than natural causes."

"I hope you're right-ski."

"Hang tight-ski."

She finished her coffee and got up to refill her cup. "Want some more java?"

"Sure, thanks." After she poured him a fresh cup, he asked, "What's your read on our man Bert?"

"He's always been tight-lipped, but he's not hard-hearted. Wouldn't you think he'd show some emotion at the death of a close family friend?"

Sidney, who'd lost a dear friend only a few months ago, nodded. "I hope he'll be okay to play tomorrow night. We're booked for a show at the Oasis. I don't want to cancel at this late date."

"Leave Bert to me."

Chapter Seven

"Only he who is without anything is without enemies."

—Rafael Sabatini, Captain Blood Returns

After Sidney left, Lizzie telephoned Alan Peabody, the man who'd been the object of her fantasies for ten months and her lover for five. They'd met last summer at the home of a Massachusetts industrialist who hired The Troubadours to perform at his daughter's engagement party. Lizzie still couldn't quite believe the handsome, sophisticated, and wealthy Boston Brahmin—relative of the famous philanthropist George Peabody for whom the city of Peabody, Massachusetts, was named—actually cared about her. He could have any woman he wanted, yet he'd courted her all this time, a showgirl and high school dropout who'd grown up in poverty in the Bronx. She kept waiting to wake up one morning and find it was all a dream.

She didn't like to interrupt Alan at his office in Boston's financial district, where he invested enormous sums of money for prestigious clients. Lately, though, he spent many of his evenings with his mother, who was dying of heart disease, and Lizzie felt even more reluctant to bother him then. But she needed to tell him about Jim Jenkins's death before he heard about it elsewhere.

Alan's secretary answered the phone. "Mr. Peabody is with a client. May I take a message?"

"Would you please tell him I telephoned and ask him to call me when he has time?"

"Certainly, Miss Crane."

Lizzie hung up and gazed out the living room window of her apartment. Golden sunlight splashed the streets of Greenwich Village. People hurried here and there, going about their business on this salubrious day. It was too nice to stay indoors. She pulled on a pair of comfortable walking shoes, a sweater, and a straw hat with a red feather in its band. After applying a bit of lipstick, she grabbed her purse and hurried downstairs.

As usual, Sixth Avenue bustled with activity. The sun warmed her shoulders. Sounds and smells tantalized her senses. She hadn't felt like eating lunch earlier, after discovering the body of Jim Jenkins. Now her stomach growled. She stopped at a vendor's stand and bought a soft pretzel drizzled with mustard. Continuing her stroll, she peeked in the window of a bookstore and then an avant-garde boutique. She paused to listen to a street guitarist play flamenco music and dropped a few coins in his open case.

When she reached 28th Street, Lizzie turned into the block-long section known as Tin Pan Alley. On this pleasant day, the windows of the brownstones that lined the street were open to invite in the gentle breezes. The cacophony of dozens of tunes spilling from those windows all at the same time gave the Alley its name. It did, indeed, sound like a busy kitchen full of pans banging against each other.

Lizzie entered the shop of a trombonist who stopped performing several years ago because of lung problems. Born François du Bois to a mulatto mother and white father in the swamps north of New Orleans, he changed his name to Frank Woods and came to New York more than two decades ago with only a cardboard suitcase and a dented trombone to his name. His wavy brown hair, hazel eyes, and skin almost as light as Lizzie's own enabled him to pass when necessary. As the blues and then jazz captured the imagination of New Yorkers, he managed to eke out a living performing in second-rate nightclubs and brothels. Now he sold sheet music and records as well as gramophones and instruments, while keeping tabs on everyone and everything in the music world.

"Hello, Frankie," she called to him.

The man stopped dusting a phonograph and turned around to look at her. "Lizzie Crane," he said, a wide grin splitting his face. "Haven't seen you in a month of Sundays. What you been up to, lady?"

"Work mostly. We've been playing in Massachusetts." She held out her hand, and he shook it. "It's good to see you. How have you been?"

"I get by," he answered. He took a few puffs on a cigarette–the agent of the lung problems that had ended his musical career—and then carefully set the stylus of a gramophone on a record. The ragtime piano of fellow Louisiana musician Jelly Roll Morton filled the room. "What brings you here now?"

"I guess you heard Jim Jenkins died."

Woods nodded.

"I found his body," Lizzie said.

"Holy moly, hadn't heard that part."

"We were supposed to make a record with his company," she added. "Now it's gone bust."

"Sorry 'bout that. I would've liked to sell your songs here in my shop." He watched the record spin on the gramophone's turntable for a few moments before continuing. "The street has it ol' JJ didn't die of natural causes."

"Really? Spill."

He set his cigarette in a nearly full ashtray and held out his hand. "First, *mademoiselle*, may I have this dance?"

Lizzie joined him in a lively "Grizzly Bear," until he grew short of breath and had to sit down. She sat too, waiting until his breathing returned to as normal as it was ever likely to get.

"What really happened?" she prompted.

" 'Course I wasn't there, so this is all hearsay. But rumor says somebody poisoned the man."

"Think he might've drunk some bad booze?"

"Maybe. Plenty of panther piss around. Easy way to poison a fella."

"Who'd want to bump him off?" Lizzie thought again about the two disgruntled men from Mississippi. Were they angry enough to kill Jenkins? Had he cheated other musicians, too, who might have sought revenge? What about the irate man who accosted Jenkins at his birthday party?

Woods shrugged. "He stepped on some toes."

"Tell me more."

He ran a finger over his lips as if sealing them. "Best you don't know. And you didn't hear it from me."

The door to the shop opened, and a well-dressed white couple entered. Although the temperature outside was in the low sixties, the woman wore a mink stole. They paused for a moment and looked around, as if assessing the store. Woods got up to greet them.

Lizzie stood to leave. "Take care, Frankie."

"You too. Don't make yourself scarce around these parts."

She walked the length of the block, entering a shop here and there, greeting fellow musicians and music lovers. A few had heard about Jim Jenkins's death but offered nothing more than she already knew. Finally, she headed back toward her apartment.

On MacDougal Street, she stopped in at Eve's Hangout near Washington Square, a popular tearoom for bohemian types. Established last year by Swedish painter Ruth Norlander and her Polish partner Eve Adams, the nightspot had quickly become a favorite haunt of intellectuals, artists, and political activists. Emma Goldman and Anais Nin showed up from time to time. Lizzie always smiled when she read the sign at the entrance to what was recognized as a lesbian club: "Men are admitted but not welcome." However, both Ruth and Eve adored Sidney–he and Lizzie had performed here on several occasions. Lizzie also attended some of the poetry readings and discussions of women's rights that Eve organized.

It took a few moments for her eyes to adjust to the dimly lit semi-basement room after being outside in the bright sunshine. At half past two in the afternoon, only a handful of women sat together at tables in the tearoom, chatting and sipping their drinks. In one corner, a group of four played bridge. Lizzie took a seat and asked a young woman with white-blond hair and skin so pale it seemed almost translucent to bring her a cup of Assam.

Instead, a woman with dark, wavy hair and a plain face free of makeup carried the tea to Lizzie's table and sat down. Although people frequently described Eve Adams as "mannish," Lizzie had always thought of her as strong.

"Eve, it's so nice to see you."

"And you as well. It's been a while since you visited us here."

"I've been in Massachusetts lately. Singing for my supper, you know."

Eve nodded. "How is Sidney?"

"Sid's good. How's your book doing?" A few months ago, Eve published a book titled *Lesbian Love* that had attracted attention in the Village.

"People seem to like it—at least the ones who matter. I plan to read from it this evening. Are you free to join us? Others will be reading their work too, not only me."

At another time, Lizzie might have enjoyed listening to an eclectic bunch of women sharing their poetry, provocative essays, or radical political pieces. But she didn't feel up to it now. Jim Jenkins's death and the possibility that he might have met with foul play had cast a dark cloud over this otherwise pretty day.

"Not tonight," she said. "I'm feeling kind of grummy."

"What is the reason for this bad mood?"

Lizzie told her.

"Ah, yes, I heard you were going to make a record. It is unfortunate, but there are other record producers."

"Yes."

"Then you will find one even better. I'm sure of it. We'll sell your record here, and you will sing it for us, okay?" She patted Lizzie's hand, then stood. "Tell Sidney *cześć* for me."

* * *

When Lizzie unlocked the door to her apartment, the telephone was ringing. She hurried to answer it, happy to hear her lover's voice on the other end of the line.

"Sorry, I couldn't speak to you earlier today. To what do I owe the pleasure of a phone call from the most beautiful lady in New York?" Alan asked. "Let me amend that, the most beautiful lady in the world?"

Lizzie laughed at his hyperbole, but it delighted her nonetheless. "I apologize for disturbing you at work."

"You're not disturbing me," he assured her. "What's up? Are you all right?"

"Yes, but I've had a dreadful morning." She related the story as succinctly as possible, then added, "Somebody may have killed him."

"What makes you think that?"

She told him what Frankie Woods said. "It's just a rumor, but it seems Jenkins had enemies."

"Stay out of it, Lizzie. Find someone else to make your record. Leave the rest to the cops."

"I intend to."

She changed the subject and asked about his mother's health. Although Mrs. Peabody had lived longer than expected, she continued to decline with each passing day.

"Why don't you catch the next train to Boston?" he suggested. "You can be here by nine o'clock."

"That's a lovely idea, but you've got your work and your family to tend to. And we've got a performance tomorrow night." She paused for a moment before saying, with more confidence than she felt, "I'm okay. I just wanted to talk to you. I miss you. I'm looking forward to seeing you next weekend for Melody's wedding…" Her voice trailed off, leaving the unspoken hanging in the air between them: *if your mother doesn't die before then.*

Chapter Eight

"I frequently hear music in the very heart of noise."

—*George Gershwin*

At half past seven, The Troubadours arrived at The Oasis, a fashionable Greenwich Village nightspot that rivaled The Blue Lagoon. In an attempt to appear exotic and capitalize on the popularity of the motion picture *The Sheik of Araby* starring Rudolph Valentino, the restaurant had decorated its interior with colorful tapestries, mosaic tiles, and alcoves defined by arches where small groups of diners could enjoy a sense of intimacy. Dozens of lanterns with stained-glass set in metal latticework hung throughout the room. The Oasis even prided itself on its selection of Middle Eastern lamb dishes seasoned with cardamom, nutmeg, and turmeric. *All it lacks is a camel,* Lizzie thought.

A modest stage had been built into one of the alcoves, and the trio stepped onto it. Sidney began making friends with the piano, while Bert unsnapped his instrument cases. The evening's first wave of diners looked up from their meals in eager anticipation.

This was what Sid enjoyed most, working in nightclubs and restaurants where he could interact freely with the audience. Lizzie met him in such a place, a nice but unpretentious establishment called Marco's. He played piano, she waited tables. It was the first decent job she'd ever had. Soon they began performing together. But after Prohibition took effect on January 17,

1920, the restaurant's owner couldn't make a go of it and closed his doors forever. Lizzie and Sidney shifted gears and began entertaining at private parties, weddings, and other events around the city.

Then last summer, they landed their first big job, a week-long extravaganza of music and dramatic performances to celebrate the engagement of a wealthy Massachusetts industrialist's daughter to a Russian count. Soon, New England's rich and famous started hiring The Troubadours and paying them more than Lizzie could ever have imagined earning. But their success had a dark side too, that began with the murder of their previous saxophonist.

Lizzie approached Bert while he checked the mouthpieces of his horns. "How are you doing?" she asked in a low voice.

He nodded. "Okay, I guess, all things considered."

"Thanks for coming tonight despite Jenkins's death. I'm sure it's tough on you and your family."

Bert nodded again. "Mom's taking it pretty hard."

"And your sister?"

"She's not shedding any tears over him. After Dad died, Daisy and JJ had a falling out. She resented him hanging around, trying to fill a gap that couldn't be filled."

Lizzie wondered if Bert felt the same way, but when he didn't comment further, she asked, "What about JJ's wife?"

"I call her Auntie Edith. Nice lady. Treated Daisy and me like her own kids."

"How's she holding up?"

"I don't know. Gonna see her tomorrow." Bert ran a hand through his unruly brown hair, trying unsuccessfully to tame the cowlick. "They didn't get along very well, what with him out drinking and carousing so much—you know how guys in the music world can be." He blew a few notes on his sax, then said, "Maybe she's better off without him."

Sidney pushed away from the piano and stepped up to the microphone. Lizzie and Bert stopped talking.

"Good evening. ladies and gentlemen," Sid said. "We're The Troubadours, and we'll be playing all your favorite jazz numbers tonight, along with some blues songs and show tunes. I'm Sidney Somerset, and these are my illustrious colleagues. Bert Halley, the man of many horns."

A few people snickered at the double-entendre as the saxophonist blushed.

"And this is our lovely chanteuse, Lizzie Crane. The sirens of old have nothing on her, so you ladies better hold on to your fellas tonight, lest they get swept away."

Lizzie smiled and waved to her audience. She'd have to speak with Sid later about using that line. Although the men found it funny, their female companions usually didn't, and Lizzie had enough trouble dealing with women's jealousy as it was.

"Get up and dance if your feet start itching," Sidney continued. "And if you've got a special song you'd like to hear, we'll try to accommodate you."

For the next hour, the trio performed hits made popular by Louis Armstrong, Ben Bernie, Willy "The Lion" Smith, and King Oliver. They even played "The Sheik of Araby." The younger couples danced. The older ones tapped their feet and swayed in their chairs in time to the music.

One elderly woman joined them onstage for a lively rendition of "Oh, Lady Be Good." Her breath reeked of bourbon, but Lizzie had to admit the old girl still had a swell voice. Sidney urged her to curtsy to the audience. She did—and would have fallen if Sid hadn't caught her. Applause and even a few catcalls filled the room, and the woman blushed like a girl under her face paint.

"Folks, we're going to take a break now," Sidney said. "We'll be back soon with more music, so don't go away."

The three musicians retired to what The Oasis's owner euphemistically called a dressing room that was barely more than a closet with a mirror nailed to one wall. As Sidney pushed the door open, a heady aroma enticed them. Someone had left a pot of lamb stew with rice, pine nuts, and pomegranates on what passed for a dressing table, along with three plates, napkins, glasses, and silverware. A bottle of tonic water and another of gin sat in a bucket of ice.

"Dinner is served," Sidney said. "Anyone hungry?"

"Ab-so-lute-ly," Lizzie answered, grabbing a plate.

"Bert?"

"I'm always hungry."

"Don't they feed you at that boarding house?" Lizzie asked.

"Well, yeah, but…"

She tousled his hair and laughed. Like many young men, the lanky twenty-two-year-old seemed to have an insatiable appetite.

"Dig in," Sidney said, filling his plate. "It's one of the perks of performing at a restaurant."

Twenty minutes later, the musicians returned to the stage. Lizzie spotted KDAZ's manager Victor Fosse at a table near the front of the room—apparently, his wife had given him the night off. She smiled at him, and he pointed his finger at her in greeting.

Sidney spoke into the microphone. "Thanks for hanging around, ladies and gentlemen. Hope you're having fun tonight."

Applause rippled through the restaurant.

"Before we begin our next set, I'd like to welcome Victor Fosse, the power behind KDAZ radio and well-known music aficionado. Over the years, Vic has brought many of the best and brightest stars to our fair city, and we're indebted to him for keeping us all up to date on what's happening in the jazz world. Hey, he even lets us play on KDAZ once in a while."

Sid motioned for Fosse to stand, which he did, as the audience clapped enthusiastically. He nodded his bald head and grinned, soaking up the attention.

After Fosse seated himself again, Sidney continued, "For those of you who've just joined us, we're The Troubadours—Lizzie Crane, Bert Halley, and yours truly, Sidney Somerset. We're here to sing and dance and entertain you tonight, so kick back or kick up your heels, but whatever you do, have a good time."

Bert lifted his clarinet to his lips and launched into "Rhapsody in Blue," one of Lizzie's favorite songs, even though the instrumental piece didn't give her an opportunity to sing. Sidney joined him on the piano. Melody used to play violin when they performed this Gershwin hit, and Lizzie felt a twinge of sadness at the loss. Although Melody lived only an hour's train ride from

Manhattan, these days her fiancé, family, and wedding plans consumed all her time. Once she moved to Connecticut with her new husband, the visits would grow even fewer and farther between.

An hour later, the musicians took another break. After briefly greeting Fosse, Sidney headed back to the dressing room for a smoke and a drink, followed by Bert, who may have hoped to find dessert had materialized in their absence. Lizzie, however, accepted Fosse's invitation to join him at his table. She smoothed the skirt of her gold lamé dress and sat down.

"Great performance," Fosse said.

"Thanks. Glad you could come."

"What are you drinking?"

"Whatever you've got in your flask."

Fosse signaled a waiter and ordered two Coca-Colas. "I hope you like Jamaican rum," he said.

"It's one of my favorites, along with gin, scotch, bourbon, vodka, wine, champagne, cognac, and sherry. I'm particularly fond of grasshoppers."

"Well, we're not likely to get grasshoppers here tonight, but this rum has the voodoo gods' seal of approval." He held her glass underneath the table and splashed a generous amount of the golden liquid into it. "Trust me, you'll love it."

They toasted, drank, then Fosse set down his tumbler and leaned toward her, resting his elbows on the table. "You heard about Jim Jenkins, I presume?"

"Actually, Sidney and I found his body. We were supposed to make a record with his company. But when we arrived at Jupiter Records yesterday morning, Jenkins was dead, lying in a pool of vomit."

Fosse shook his head. "Sorry you had to see that. No lady should come upon a dead man like that."

"It's not my first time," Lizzie said, recalling the three other murder victims she'd discovered. "Any idea what happened to him?"

"Not a clue."

She decided to press further. After all, Fosse had his finger on the music scene's pulse. Maybe he knew more than he let on. "A friend of mine in the Alley hinted that Jenkins had enemies. Wednesday night, Sid, Bert, and I met two musicians from Mississippi who'd made a record with Jenkins. According to them, he cheated them out of their royalties. They seemed pretty angry about it."

Fosse stared into the dark recesses of his glass, contemplating the implications.

"What do you think, Vic?"

"In this business, you can't avoid making enemies. If you're lucky, they'll sue rather than kill you."

"That sounds like a line out of a ten-penny crime novel." Lizzie took a sip of her drink, savoring the seductively sweet beverage. "Music's not like the booze biz. We're not violent people. I can't imagine guitarists toting Chicago typewriters around in their instrument cases."

"Jenkins didn't die from a gunshot wound."

"What did he die from?"

He fingered his cufflink, turned it around a couple of times as if it were a dial on a radio. "I wouldn't know," he said, but she didn't believe him.

"I didn't see you at his birthday party Thursday night."

"You went?"

Lizzie nodded. "And quite the bash it was. I've never heard so many musicians in one place at the same time. Sid and I even played a couple songs."

"I wasn't invited," Fosse admitted.

"Oh? Why not? I thought you and Jenkins were pals. Two big shots in the New York music scene."

He shrugged. "We had a disagreement, I guess you could say."

"Spill," she said, hoping to glean more information from him.

Before he could reply, Sidney and Bert returned from their break and took their places onstage. *Drat,* she thought. *A few minutes more, and I might have learned something useful.* She finished the last of her rum and cola and stood up.

"Showtime. Thanks for the drink, Vic."

Chapter Nine

"Truth is so often disconcerting."

—Rafael Sabatini, Scaramouche

J ust as Lizzie sat down at the dropleaf table in her living room with a cup of coffee, a bagel with cream cheese and lox, and a crossword puzzle, the telephone rang. She got up and answered it, surprised to hear Detective Lawrence Perry's voice on the other end. Five days had passed since their unfortunate meeting at Jupiter Records. Five days during which she'd managed to push Jim Jenkins's death from center stage into the wings of her priorities. Alan would arrive in New York tomorrow night. Melody's wedding was only three days away. The last thing she wanted to bother with on this warm, windy, almost-summer day was the questionable demise of the record producer.

"Miss Crane, I'd like to speak with you today," Perry said, then added, "if it's convenient."

"What's this about, Detective?"

"Jim Jenkins. The medical examiner has determined the cause of his death."

"What's the verdict?" She crossed her fingers, hoping he'd died of something perfectly ordinary, a heart attack or a stroke perhaps. Nothing criminal or even suspicious.

"I'd rather discuss this with you in person."

"Why me?"

"I'm hoping you might provide some additional information."

"I've told you all I know," she said, wondering why the police might need additional information if the reason for the man's death had been determined. Detective Perry's request put her on the defensive, bringing back memories of other police interrogations into other untimely deaths.

"You met with Mr. Jenkins the day before his death," Perry continued. "You attended his birthday party that night, too. Not only were you one of the first people to find him dead, but you were also one of the last to see him alive."

"Me and at least fifty of his closest friends."

"I've tried to reach Mr. Somerset and Mr. Halley, without success. I'd like to speak with them too."

"Mr. Halley wasn't with us at the party or when we found Jenkins's body," she pointed out.

"Miss Crane, could you come by the police station to answer a few questions? Nothing formal, I'm merely trying to establish a timeline for Mr. Jenkins's last day or two on earth—and to make sure I haven't overlooked any details that might be relevant."

If Jim Jenkins died of natural causes, why do the cops want to look into the days leading up to his death? Lizzie wondered. If they need more details, wouldn't they be better off talking to his doctor? This whole conversation was giving her the heebie jeebies.

"Detective, I don't know anything. I'm sorry, but I can't help you."

"Forget the police station, I know it can be a bit intimidating," Perry said. "There's a little café not far from your apartment called The Place. I believe you're familiar with it?"

"Yes."

He knows where I live. He knows where I eat. What else does he know about me? A chill ran up Lizzie's spine. She realized Detective Perry wouldn't insist on talking to her if Jenkins had dropped dead from a heart attack or a stroke. There was more to this than he let on. More than she wanted to know.

"Please meet me there in an hour," he said. It sounded more like an order than an invitation.

She'd planned to do some last-minute shopping today for Melody's wedding, and she needed to clean her apartment in preparation for Alan's arrival. But she'd learned from past experience that getting on the wrong side of the police never turned out well. With any luck, she could avoid revealing the connection between Jenkins and Bert. Convince the cop that The Troubadours only had a brief—and quickly terminated—business association with the dead man.

"Okay," she agreed reluctantly and hung up the phone.

* * *

The Place was part café, part art gallery. Ornately framed paintings in the classical style covered most of the dark red walls. Eighteen tables in various sizes and shapes, accompanied by bentwood chairs, sat on an oak floor, stained dark with age. Benches with richly carved backs lined one wall. From a pressed tin ceiling hung frosted-glass globes that emitted enough light for diners to find their way to their tables, but barely enough to allow them to read the menu. Lizzie always suspected the restaurant's owners of discouraging newcomers in favor of regulars who already knew what they wanted to eat.

Detective "Law" Perry sat at a small round table near the back of the café on a delicate chair that seemed it might buckle under his weight. As she approached, the stocky policeman stood. In the overly warm room, his broad face glistened with sweat. Even though he didn't wear a uniform, he looked like a cop.

"Thank you for meeting with me, Miss Crane," he said in a voice as rough as sandpaper.

"Would you like something to eat or drink?"

"A cup of coffee, please. Black."

Perry raised his hand to signal a waiter, and Lizzie noticed the first joint on his right index finger was missing. *Does that interfere with his ability to pull the trigger of his pistol?* she wondered.

"Black coffee for the lady, and I'll have chai tea," he told a sullen young man who eyed the policeman warily.

"What's chai tea?" Lizzie asked. She didn't realize The Place served such a thing; it wasn't on the menu.

"Black tea mixed with cinnamon, cardamom, cloves, ginger, peppercorns, and milk. It's quite popular in India. I acquired a taste for it when I lived in Mumbai as a boy. My father was a colonel in the British Army."

"You don't have a British accent."

In an authentic Brooklyn accent, he said, "My mother's a native New Yorker."

While they waited for their drinks, Lizzie shifted her gaze to the painting of a bucolic landscape hanging above Perry's head in an attempt to keep from staring at the protuberant mole on his chin.

Her curiosity finally got the better of her. "You didn't drag me here on this beautiful morning to discuss tea. What's the story? Spill. How'd Jim Jenkins die?"

"From mercury bichloride poisoning."

"What's that?"

"$HgCl_2$. A highly toxic substance first written about by a medieval Persian physician named Muhammad ibn Zakariya al-Razi, who used it to cleanse wounds. Today it's often diluted in water and applied topically as a treatment for syphilis."

"Did Jenkins have syphilis?"

"According to the medical examiner's report, yes."

That the big cop would reveal details of a police investigation surprised Lizzie, but she felt certain it wasn't a careless indiscretion. Perhaps he'd decided an information swap was the best way to get her to open up. *Give and you shall receive.*

While the waiter served their drinks, she pondered Perry's revelation. *How sad,* she thought, her mind running through a list of famous people who'd suffered from the awful disease, including Vincent van Gogh, Christopher Columbus, Friedrich Nietzsche, Henri Toulouse-Lautrec, and Charles Baudelaire. Did Bert know Jenkins had syphilis? Did JJ's wife?

"I don't understand how this caused his death," she said. "People with syphilis usually drag on for ages, gradually getting more and more debilitated until they finally check out. Jenkins seemed fine when I saw him last week."

Perry sipped his chai tea before answering. "It appears he ingested the mercury bichloride."

"So?"

"When ingested, it causes internal bleeding. It doesn't take much to kill someone; a couple grams can do in a grown man." He took another sip of his tea, then continued. "Are you aware of the scandal involving David Curtis Stephenson, Grand Dragon of the Indiana Ku Klux Klan? It was in all the papers last year."

"It sounds familiar, but I don't recall the details."

"Stephenson beat, raped, and inflicted other injuries on a woman he'd been seeing named Madge Oberholtzer. Ashamed and afraid of him, she bought mercury bichloride tablets at a local chemist's and swallowed them, intending to commit suicide. When Stephenson found her, she was in bad shape but still alive. He didn't take her to a hospital or seek medical treatment, which might have saved her life. After she died, Stephenson was sentenced to prison for second-degree murder."

Lizzie contemplated what Perry said. "Are you suggesting Jenkins committed suicide by eating mercury bichloride?"

"Whether he committed suicide has yet to be determined," Perry answered. "I was hoping you might be able to shed some light on that."

"Me? I only met the man twice and talked to him for a few minutes about business. That's the extent of it."

But even as she spoke, she sensed there was more to this story. A story that might lead Law Perry to Bert and his family once the cop learned that Bert's father and Jenkins were longtime friends.

"Mercury bichloride can kill in a matter of hours or days, depending on the strength of the dose and the person's constitution," Detective Perry continued. "That's why I'm talking to people who had contact with Jenkins shortly before his death. To see if they observed anything that might aid our investigation."

Sipping her coffee, Lizzie read between the lines of what the policeman said. *Perry thinks somebody may have bumped off Jenkins. And maybe that person was me.*

"Well, you've got your work cut out for you, Detective. Jenkins crossed paths with a great many people in the music world. You'll be questioning possible suspects from now 'til Christmas."

Perry raised an eyebrow. "Suspects, Miss Crane? Do you have reason to think Jenkins met with foul play? Surely, I didn't suggest such a thing."

"Not in so many words, but you're beating around that bush."

Perry signaled the waiter to refill her coffee cup. "Did anything unusual happen at the party?"

Lizzie expected him to pull out his notebook and pencil and start taking notes, but he simply listened, committing her answers to memory. "Only that so many musicians showed up to wish him happy birthday—and not just local musicians either."

"What's your connection with Malcolm MacGregor? I understand he hosted the party."

"None. Never met him before the party. Seems like he's rolling in dough. What's his story?"

"He has businesses in South Africa. Gold and diamonds," Perry answered before bringing the conversation back to his primary concern. "Do you know of anyone who might have wished Jenkins ill?"

Lizzie thought about the Mississippi musicians who claimed Jenkins cheated them. She considered the jealous man who confronted JJ at the party. She recalled what the music store owner Frankie Woods told her last week: "He stepped on some toes."

"I don't, Detective. But word on the street has it Jenkins made some enemies."

"Miss Crane, if you hear anything else 'on the street' I must insist you report it to the police."

Before the waiter returned with his coffeepot, Lizzie stood up and pushed in her chair, eager to get away. "This is sounding more and more sinister with each passing minute. Detective, I really have to be off now. I have a busy afternoon ahead of me."

Perry handed her his card, although she still had the one he gave her on Friday. "Thank you for your time, Miss Crane. Please contact me if you have any information that might be of help."

Chapter Ten

"He felt now that he was not simply close to her, but that he did not know where he ended and she began."

— *Leo Tolstoy, Anna Karenina*

Lizzie's tiny apartment had only two closets, plainly inadequate for her extensive collection of daytime, evening, and performance outfits. The rest she hung in a massive, old-fashioned wardrobe that took up a good portion of her bedroom. Flinging open its doors, she began pulling out one frock after another. She held each one up to her hourglass figure, assessed her appearance in the wardrobe's mirror, then tossed the dress aside on her bed. Melody had chosen Lizzie's maid-of-honor gown, a mid-calf French blue silk number with a high neck and elbow-length sleeves, more modest than most of Lizzie's garments. But she still had to decide what to wear at the formal Friday night rehearsal dinner and during her performance with The Troubadours at the wedding reception.

And what about tonight? She planned to meet Alan's train at Penn Station in a few hours, then dine with him at the Blue Lagoon. Thursday nights at the Lagoon weren't as fancy as weekends, but still, she wanted to impress her lover. Besides, as an entertainer, she had an image to uphold. Finally, she chose a short peach-colored frock made of delicate layers of silk that resembled feathers to wear tonight. *One down, two more to go,* she thought. Next, she set aside a floor-length pink gown emblazoned with rhinestones and seed pearls—elegant but not terribly revealing—for tomorrow night's rehearsal dinner. And a more risqué turquoise dress with a plunging neckline and zigzag hemline that barely skimmed her knees for the reception. She hoped Melody's family would approve, or at least not be shocked.

"Who knew getting dressed could be such an ordeal?" she asked the jade figurine of the Chinese goddess Quan Yin, who occupied a place of honor on Lizzie's vanity. As always, the goddess stared back at her with a serene expression that suggested she cared little about the petty problems human beings brought on themselves.

After returning the cast-aside frocks to the wardrobe, Lizzie carefully folded the chosen ones in tissue paper and packed them in a leather suitcase, along with daytime garments, underwear, and a nightgown. She wanted to have everything ready before Alan arrived. Once he was here, she'd have little time to think about anything but him.

* * *

Slowly, the electric locomotive pulled into Penn Station, and the train opened its doors to discharge its passengers. Lizzie scanned the men descending from it until she noticed Alan's fiery red hair amid the drab clusters of people waiting to meet the arrivals. As he put on his fedora, she waved, but he didn't see her. Hiking up her skirt, she ran toward him. When he spotted her, he set down his suitcases and opened his arms to gather her in. He picked her up and spun her around and around, until she felt dizzy not only from the swirling motion but from his closeness.

Alan kissed her cheeks, her forehead, and finally her lips. "It's good to see you, Lizzie."

"It's good to see you too," she replied as a familiar tingling thrummed through her body. "How was your trip?"

"Uneventful, fortunately. It gave me time to finish up some last-minute business and put my everyday affairs behind me." He squeezed her hand, then signaled a porter to wheel his luggage to a waiting taxicab. "I don't want anything to interfere with this weekend."

Lizzie gave the cabdriver the address of her apartment, and the man hurled the automobile into the late afternoon traffic like a warrior charging into battle. A horn blared, and their driver jerked his car aside to let the other motorist whiz past.

"What's our plan?" Alan asked.

"I made reservations for dinner at the Blue Lagoon–I hope that's okay. It's a nice place. We've played there a few times."

"Good choice," he said. "How's Rory Moynihan doing?"

Surprised that he knew the restaurant's owner, she answered, "Okay, as of yesterday."

After a mile and a half, the cabbie pulled over to the curb. While Alan collected his luggage and paid the driver, Lizzie bought a bunch of apple blossoms from a girl selling flowers on the street corner. She recalled what the elderly antique dealer from whom she'd purchased her Quan Yin statue told her, that in Victorian times, people conveyed messages with flowers; each had a special meaning. According to myth, apples were the favorite fruit of Aphrodite, the Greek goddess of love. The blossoms meant "I prefer you above all others."

They rode the creaky old elevator that reminded Lizzie of an oversized birdcage to her building's third floor. She unlocked the door to her apartment and, while Alan deposited his suitcases in her bedroom, she filled a vase with water and plunked the flowers in it. When he joined her in the galley kitchen, he'd removed his jacket and tie and unfastened the top two buttons of his shirt.

"Would you like a drink?" she asked.

"Later. Right now, I seek to quench a different thirst."

Laughing at his declaration, which Lizzie thought sounded like a line from a sappy movie, she slid into his embrace. An hour later, they still lay on the linen sheets she'd put on her bed this morning, which now smelled of their lovemaking.

"I think we should make this a ritual," Alan said. "Do it every hour, on the hour."

"Is that even possible?" Although she wasn't totally ignorant of the body's capabilities, she'd never attempted–or even contemplated—such a feat.

"I doubt it. But it's a nice idea, don't you agree?"

Lizzie considered what Honoré de Balzac wrote about routine being a monster that devours everything. "I'm afraid you'd soon grow tired of the routine. Perhaps periods of separation make our time together sweeter."

"Maybe so, but we've been separated for twenty-eight days. That's twenty-seven more than I need to sweeten this weekend." He ran a finger along her collarbone. "What time's our dinner reservation?"

"Seven-thirty."

He glanced at the clock on her bedside table. "It's quarter to six now. Shall we ring in the hour?"

* * *

Fake palm trees strung with electric lights welcomed them to the Blue Lagoon. As the restaurant's dapper maître d' led them into the dining room with its murals of white sand beaches and turquoise sea, Lizzie thought *how much more interesting it would be if he wore a loincloth and a lei instead of a tuxedo.*

"Would you like to sit near the stage?" the man asked.

Alan pointed to a table tucked into the shadows along one wall, about halfway between the stage and the restaurant's entrance. "I think we'd rather have something a bit more private."

"Of course, sir." He led them to a table draped with a crisp white tablecloth and held a chair for Lizzie. "Your waiter will be with you in a moment."

Before the waiter arrived, however, Rory Moynihan spotted them and came over to their table. Alan stood and shook hands with the restaurant owner, who was nearly a head shorter, but probably equaled him in weight.

"Well, this is a surprise," Rory said, motioning for Alan to sit. He glanced at Lizzie, then Alan, then back at Lizzie again. "How do the two of you know each other?"

"We met at a party in Massachusetts last summer," she answered. "Alan's visiting for the weekend. Remember Melody, the blond flutist in our band?

We're going to her wedding on Saturday."

"Sure, sure. Give her my best wishes, okay?"

"I will."

"What's the best thing on the menu tonight?" Alan asked.

Rory grinned, revealing a gold molar. "Everything. Hey, I don't mind tooting my own horn. Besides, it's the truth. But you won't go wrong with the lamb chops."

"Lizzie?"

She nodded. "Sounds swell."

"I'm sending out some Oysters Rockefeller for starters, too," Rory said. "Gotta eat 'em while they're in season, right?"

"Thanks, Rory," Alan said.

"Bon appétit," the restaurateur said with a New York accent that would have made a Frenchman wince.

When their waiter appeared a few minutes later, Alan waved away the menus. "Mr. Moynihan has already decided what we'll be eating tonight. Would you please bring us two club sodas while we wait?"

"Certainly, sir."

After the waiter departed, Lizzie asked, "How do you know Rory? Do you come here often when you're in town on business?"

"Sometimes."

"Don't be so mysterious. Spill."

"He helped me out in a tight situation a few years ago. Three men tried to rob me on the street right outside this restaurant. Well, let's just say Rory's pretty good with his fists. And a Colt."

It took Lizzie a moment to realize he meant a pistol, not a horse.

"Later, I made some investments for him that turned out to be profitable," Alan continued.

The waiter set two glasses of club soda on their table and promised to return shortly with their oysters. *If I'd had the good sense to buy a garter flask, I'd be prepared to spike our drinks with a splash of spirits,* Lizzie regretted, making a mental note to rectify that detail soon.

"And you've been pals ever since?" she asked.

He chuckled. "I guess you could say that."

"Alan Peabody, you never cease to surprise me."

Chapter Eleven

"Dancing is poetry with arms and legs."

—Charles Baudelaire

Sidney picked them up at noon the next day, even though the trip to the town of Madison, New Jersey, should only take a couple hours at most, and they weren't expected until five.

"I want to be certain we've got plenty of time to get settled in at the hotel. Besides, we need to check out the restaurant and make sure everything's copacetic," he explained, as Lizzie and Alan settled themselves in the backseat of the Buick. "And I'm guessing you and Melody will have a lot to talk about, Bearcat."

"Right you are," Lizzie said.

She was glad her friend had found happiness, but Lizzie couldn't help feeling sad too. After two years of working and traveling together–not to mention the frightful ordeals they'd endured—Melody's wedding tomorrow would officially end their professional relationship. Would their friendship continue once she moved to Connecticut with her new husband and her role in life shifted to that of wife and mother?

After taking the ferry across the Hudson River, they motored west into New Jersey. Bert, riding shotgun, stared out the window and said little. Although never the chatty type, he'd been more withdrawn than usual since Jim Jenkins's death. Lizzie longed to talk to him about the loss, to offer some sort of solace, but the time never seemed right, and she hadn't a clue how to begin. Now that the police had released JJ's body, the man's widow—a woman Bert affectionately called Auntie Edith–had arranged to hold the funeral on Monday afternoon, the day after they returned to New York.

Poor Bert, Lizzie thought. She recalled her brief meeting with his mother, who seemed as fragile as gardenia petals that bruised if you touched them. Was he trying to prop her up during this difficult time? And what about his younger sister Daisy? Most likely, Bert was shouldering the burden for all of them.

Lizzie tousled her young friend's unruly brown hair, startling him out of his reverie. "A penny for your thoughts."

He turned around in his seat to look at her. "I guess…well, I hope Melody will be happy with Douglas…you know, in Connecticut and all." He paused a moment, then continued. "She was always so nice to me. We got to be good friends, especially when she was teaching me to play the flute. I don't have many friends. Don't get me wrong, Lizzie. You're my friend too, I know that." He turned away to stare out the breezer's passenger side window again. "I miss her."

Lizzie patted him on the shoulder. "I know."

But she sensed he wasn't talking only about Melody. She suspected he missed Jim Jenkins, too, the man who'd been, as he'd put it, "like an uncle" to him for so many years.

At half past two, they rolled into Melody's hometown, a pretty community that had avoided the industrialization of some of the other northern New Jersey cities, with middle-class houses on well-cared-for lots and a few grand estates built by titans of industry who wanted to escape from The City on weekends. Melody told Lizzie people called Madison the "Rose City" because its greenhouses supplied New York's florists with flowers, particularly roses.

They drove past Main Street's shops, the library, the YMCA, the high school, and the railway station. They located the Episcopal church where the wedding service would take place and the restaurant where the reception would be held. Finally, Sidney pulled into the parking area behind their inn, a three-story clapboard building with a mansard roof and arched windows.

After a porter deposited their luggage in their rooms, Lizzie said, "Sid, let's check out the church and the restaurant, okay-ski?"

"Whatever you say-ski," he answered.

"We need to make sure we've got all our bases covered. Don't want anything to mar Melody's big day." She looked at Alan. "Want to come with us?"

"If you don't mind, I'd rather stay here and make a few telephone calls. Unless you need me, that is."

"I'm sure we can handle it. If you talk to your mother, please give her my regards."

"I will."

"How about you, Bert?"

"Sure, I'll come. I don't have anything else to do 'til tonight."

Lizzie gave Alan a quick kiss. "We won't be gone long."

The three musicians motored back to the church, a pretty gray stone structure with a peaked roof pointing toward heaven and a bell tower that reminded Lizzie of a fortress lookout. Inside, polished wooden pews lined both sides of a central aisle that led to the chancel, where a rose window let in a rainbow of light. The church, Melody had told her, was well known for its choir and its interest in presenting liturgical music to the community.

Tomorrow, a dozen members of the choir–people Melody had sung with since she was a girl–would usher in the bride and groom to be joined in marriage. But before the couple took their vows, Lizzie would sing "Ave Maria" alone, a cappella. She looked around for microphones. Finding none, she stepped up to the chancel and sang the opening refrain of Franz Schubert's beautiful hundred-year-old song. As she'd expected, the sanctuary had excellent acoustics.

Bert clapped his hands and whistled as if he were at a ballpark instead of in a church.

"Sounds good to me."

"What do you think, Bearcat?" Sidney asked.

"I think it will do-ski."

"Me too-ski."

Lizzie smoothed the skirt of her linen traveling dress, imagining how she'd look in her blue maid-of-honor dress, standing here tomorrow afternoon at the front of the church before Melody's friends and family. Although long ago she separated herself from the Catholic Church in which she'd been raised and hadn't attended Sunday services in nearly a decade, she still hoped God, Goddess, the Creator, or whatever benevolent being presided over the universe would bless Melody and her husband Douglas.

"Let's see what we're in for with the reception," she said to Sidney.

They drove to the restaurant Melody had chosen for her reception dinner, housed in what once had been a handsome private residence in the Queen Anne style. Turrets with pointed roofs stood at either end of the building. A porch with a decorative white railing ran along the front. The owners lived on the upper two floors and had converted the first floor to a restaurant.

A man who seemed harried and fretful, with frown lines between his eyebrows, pursed lips, and a smudge of what looked like chocolate on his cheek, met them in the foyer with a curt, "We're closed."

"We're the musicians who'll be playing here tomorrow night," Sidney said. "Would you please show us where we'll be performing?"

The man pulled himself together, but didn't smile or offer any sort of greeting. "This way."

He led them down a hallway wallpapered with pink roses on a green background to a spacious room that Lizzie supposed had originally been three smaller rooms, the walls that once divided them now removed. At the far end, she saw a long table with twelve chairs lined up along one side. A baby grand piano occupied a corner at the other end. Eighteen round tables, each of which could accommodate six guests, filled the space.

"There's no room for dancing," Lizzie pointed out.

"Excuse me," Sidney said to the taciturn man who had yet to introduce himself or state his role here. "We need to clear an area near the piano where people can dance. Will you please have your staff rearrange the tables?"

"On whose orders?"

Jeepers creepers, Lizzie thought. *Where did Melody dig up this old grouch?*

"Mine," she said.

"And who are you?"

"Elizabeth Crane, the maid of honor at the Fitzgerald-Pitt wedding tomorrow. May I know your name?"

Grudgingly, he said, "Terrance Bolton."

"And what is your position here?"

"I'm the restaurant manager."

"Well, Mr. Bolton. I hope we can settle this ourselves, without involving the owners. The bride's father is a noted architect in New York, and her groom is a partner in Hartford's biggest insurance company. The bride is a native of your lovely city." She paused a moment to let that information sink in before softening her tone. "Now I'm sure you want to help make this a happy and memorable event for everyone. You and the staff here should be honored to share in the realization of a young woman's dreams and to celebrate the sacred bond of holy matrimony."

Lizzie glanced at Sidney and saw him roll his eyes. A smile played at the corners of Bert's lips, the first she'd seen all day.

"The Fitzgerald family could have selected any number of venues to mark the wedding of their only daughter. They chose yours," she continued. "Therefore, you have an obligation to uphold their trust in your establishment and to do your part to enhance the joy of this newly wedded couple on this special occasion."

She looked at Sidney again and rubbed her fingers together. He reached into his jacket pocket, pulled out his wallet, and withdrew a bill, which he handed to Bolton.

"Now, please call a couple members of your staff in here, so we can attend to this matter post haste."

"Yes, ma'am." Bolton tucked the bill in his pocket and exited through a door that Lizzie guessed led to the kitchen.

Sidney laughed and lit a cigarette. "Ball-breaker. Good thing you and I are on the same side."

"That supercilious prig isn't going to put a damper on Melody's big day," Lizzie said, struggling to keep her temper under control. "I'm of a mind to complain to the owners."

A few minutes later, Bolton returned with two young men in tow. "Direct them," he said to Lizzie.

Melody had told her that seventy-two people, plus the wedding party, would attend the reception. That meant they could get rid of six tables.

With a wave of her hand, she told the men, "Please take these away."

"What are we supposed to do with them?" one man asked.

She wanted to suggest shoving them in a place where the sun didn't shine, but said politely instead, "That's up to you. Just remove them from this space until midnight tomorrow."

While the reconfiguration took place, Sidney tested the piano and found it to be in good shape. Bert ambled about restlessly. Lizzie thought he seemed distracted, bored, wrapped up in a world of his own where no one else could follow.

To give him something to do, she asked, "Bert, would you mind helping these fellas? We'll finish up faster that way."

"Oh, sure," he agreed and picked up two chairs.

When the men had cleared an area suitable for dancing, she joined Sidney at the piano and sang a few lines of Gershwin's "Oh, Lady Be Good."

"Okay by you-ski?" he asked.

"It'll have to do-ski. The acoustics aren't usually good in old houses like this, but we can't do anything about that."

"Fortunately, the piano's fine."

"That's a plus. What time is it?"

"Three-thirty."

"Holy moly. We're due at the church at five to rehearse tomorrow's ceremony. I haven't even telephoned Melody yet to let her know we've arrived." She ran her fingers through her dark hair. "I want to take a bath and wash off the road dust."

They climbed into Sidney's breezer—Lizzie in the front passenger seat, Bert in the back—and drove to their inn. Sid parked in the paved area behind the building.

"Meet you back here in an hour," he said.

Chapter Twelve

"Happiness is a work of art. Handle with care."

—Edith Wharton

Melody and her entourage were standing at the front of the church when Lizzie entered, on Alan's arm, with Sidney and Bert following behind. The two women hadn't seen each other in three months, and Lizzie couldn't help noticing how radiant her friend looked, like a rosebud that had opened into full bloom. The blond flutist excused herself from the small cluster of relatives gathered around her and hurried to greet the musicians who'd been her second family for the past two years.

"I'm so happy to see you," Melody said, giving Lizzie a heartfelt hug. "Your gown is spectacular! Thank you for coming." She hugged Sidney and Bert in turn, then, after a moment's contemplation, hugged Alan too.

"All the Visigoths in Europe couldn't keep us away," Lizzie said.

Melody frowned. "Aren't the Visigoths gone by now?"

Sidney laughed and patted the top of her head. "Ages ago. Now introduce us to everyone. Lizzie and I have met Douglas and your parents, but Bert and Alan haven't. And we don't know the rest of your clan."

Melody motioned them toward the front of the church, where a dozen people awaited them. She went through the formal introductions, which involved a lot of smiling and handshaking, before her father clasped Lizzie's hand in both of his. His eyes sparkled with joy.

"If it hadn't been for you, none of this would've happened," he said.

"What do you mean?" Lizzie asked.

"That night, you convinced me to let Melody perform with your group, you told me she had great talent, and encouraged me to let her express it. You asked how I'd feel, as an architect, if I couldn't see the buildings I designed materialize—not because they weren't good enough, but because someone decided it wasn't the proper thing to do. I don't know what my daughter will do with her music now, but because she had an opportunity to perform, she met Douglas. A happy coincidence, don't you think?"

Lizzie couldn't decide if she was happier that Melody had met Douglas and proceeded along a path that pleased her parents, or that the young musician had been given a chance to perform. But before she could consider it further, the minister interrupted them.

"Welcome, everyone. Thank you for joining Melody Fitzgerald and Douglas Pitt in celebrating their marriage. Tomorrow afternoon, in the presence of God, family, and friends, these two young people will formally commit to one another in holy matrimony." The minister, a short, plump man in his middle years, paused to wipe sweat from his brow and cheeks, even though it was far from hot in the sanctuary. "Naturally, we want the ceremony to go smoothly, so let's take our places and run through the steps to make certain we've got it down pat."

The wedding party trooped obediently back to the church's entrance and queued up. Douglas and his father, who would serve as his best man, remained standing with the minister. Sidney, Bert, and Alan, who weren't part of the procession, sat in one of the pews to watch. As the organist played Pachelbel's "Canon," the ushers—Douglas's brothers—seated their mother and Melody's parents. Two flower girls skipped down the aisle, pretending to scatter rose petals. Next came Melody's cousins in the role of bridesmaids, then Lizzie as the maid of honor. Finally, Melody walked down the aisle, escorted by her father, and was handed off to her future husband. Lizzie stood next to her friend with the cousin-bridesmaids beside her, as the age-old ritual played out.

The betrothed couple held hands as the minister said a few words—not those tie-binding ones he'd speak tomorrow at the actual ceremony, however—and signaled Douglas's eight-year-old nephew to pretend to present Melody's wedding ring. The child burst into laughter, earning him a quick rap on the head from his grandfather. After acting out the exchange of vows with her husband-to-be, Melody strolled back down the aisle. Then the entire group, except Lizzie, traipsed into the church's narthex to go through the exercise again.

Despite her friend's obvious happiness, Lizzie saw the event as one man transferring property to another, almost as if he were handing over the deed to a house. Of course, Melody's parents weren't forcing her into this marriage—quite the opposite. She was enthralled not only by her groom but by the whole experience. A little girl's fantasy fulfilled.

"When am I supposed to sing?" Lizzie asked the minister.

"Excuse me?"

"I'm supposed to sing 'Ave Maria' before the procession begins."

"Hmm, well, I guess you should sing early on." He consulted his program, squinting as if he had trouble reading the small print. "Ah, yes, here you are. The 'Ave Maria.' After finishing, you can make your way along the side aisle over there and get in position."

Lizzie hurried down that aisle to join the rest of the group. To her, the whole affair seemed more like a parade than a sacred ritual. *If I ever get married, I'm going to have a celebration full of passion and joy and playfulness, not this tired old routine. Maybe something wildly pagan in an oak grove, with lots of flowers and music and dancing. Fertility rites on the forest floor would be good too.*

As they lined up for a second take, Melody singled Lizzie out. "I need to talk to you before we go to dinner."

* * *

The restaurant Douglas Pitt had chosen for the rehearsal dinner was smaller and more intimate than the one where tomorrow's wedding reception would be held. Pink tablecloths covered the tables. A vase of roses graced each, along with a candle in a glass container.

Before Lizzie could take her seat, Melody grabbed her friend's hand and pulled her toward the ladies' room. After peeking under the stall doors to make sure they were alone, Melody leaned against the sink and said, "Tell me the truth. What can I expect tomorrow night?"

"Haven't the foggiest."

"But you and Alan have been lovers for months, and he's not your first."

"Yes, but my experiences won't be like yours. The fundamentals will be the same, what goes where, and all that. Everything else is up for grabs."

"Will it hurt?"

"Probably, but not for long."

"Will I like it?"

"Maybe. Don't get discouraged if you don't right away, though. Women have been taught all kinds of negative stuff and nonsense about sex. It can take a while to overcome that conditioning. A lot depends on your partner, too. How he treats you and how you feel about each other."

"Douglas and I love each other. And he's always kind to me."

"I know, and I'm happy for you. That bodes well for your relations together."

"What should I do to please him?"

"I'm sure whatever you do will please him. He doesn't expect you to be a courtesan. Just relax. Let him guide you." Lizzie smiled at her innocent friend. "At least your relatives won't display your bloody sheets in the morning to prove your virginity."

A look of horror crossed Melody's face. "They wouldn't!"

Lizzie laughed. "Poor little bunny, certainly not. That custom went out of fashion centuries ago."

Melody studied her reflection in the mirror over the sink, combing her fingers through her golden hair. "Does Alan give you pleasure?"

Her friend's directness caught Lizzie off guard. Although she liked to consider herself modern and unflappable, she paused for an awkward moment before answering, "Very much."

The door to the restroom opened, and one of Melody's cousin-bridesmaids burst in. "Oh, there you are. Everybody's wondering what happened to you."

"Just having a little chat, girl-to-girl," Lizzie answered.

"Last-minute jitters?" the cousin asked.

Melody shrugged. "I guess."

"We haven't seen each other in months," Lizzie said. "We're just catching up. We'll be there momentarily."

"All right, but don't take long, Melody. The waiters are serving dinner, and the fathers want to make a toast."

A ginger ale toast, Lizzie knew. Even though New Jersey, like New York, scoffed at the Volstead Act, the Fitzgeralds and the Pitts were teetotalers. Tomorrow's reception would also be dry. *Surely Sid will have a little something tucked in his pocket,* she thought. *I really must buy a garter flask as soon as we get back to The City.*

The men stood as Lizzie approached the table, where a plate with a perfectly prepared crab cake on a bed of fresh greens sat at her place. Alan held a chair for her.

"Sorry to keep you waiting," she said.

"Everything okay?" Sid asked, taking his seat again.

"Fine. Melody just had some questions about what to do tomorrow night."

Alan raised an eyebrow, the golden flecks in his dark eyes sparkling. "What did you tell her?"

"I suggested several of the easier positions from the *Kama Sutra.* She's a beginner, you know."

Alan laughed. Bert blushed.

"You didn't!" Sidney said.

"No, of course not. But did you know the *Kama Sutra* advocates sexual freedom for women and nonjudgmental attitudes toward homosexuality? Two thousand years ago, those Hindus were way ahead of us."

Lizzie took a bite of her crab cake as Alan leaned toward her and whispered in her ear, "Perhaps you'll show me one of your favorite positions tonight?"

Before she could give her imagination free rein, however, Douglas's father tapped his knife on his water glass and stood.

"Welcome, everyone. Words can't express how happy my wife and I are that tomorrow, our son Douglas will formally bring Melody Fitzgerald into the Pitt family. Frankly, we were beginning to think Doug was a confirmed bachelor. By the time I was his age, he and his brothers were in high school."

A few of the guests chuckled. Sidney whispered to Lizzie, "They probably feared he was a homosexual."

"Now we realize he was simply waiting for the right woman," the elder Pitt continued. "And it was worth the wait, don't you think?"

Several guests clapped their hands. One of Douglas's brothers called out, "Hear, hear."

Pitt rambled on for a while, recounting stories of Douglas's youth that his relatives undoubtedly knew already, and the rest of them didn't care about. Lizzie turned her attention to her crab cake. It seemed odd to her that the Pitts hadn't asked The Troubadours to play music tonight—or hired other performers—considering their son was marrying a professional musician. Even if they didn't like jazz, they might have chosen a string quartet or a classical guitarist to perform. She couldn't help wondering if this was a subtle way of showing Melody they expected her to give up her career and devote herself entirely to her husband.

When the garrulous elder Pitt finally finished with a toast to the bride and groom and sat down, Melody's father stood. "Dear friends and family," he began. "I want to thank all of you for being here tonight to celebrate our beloved daughter Melody's transition from *kore* to wife."

"What's 'kore' mean?" Bert asked.

"It's Greek for maiden," Lizzie answered.

"Since her birth, Melody's mother and I have wanted nothing more than our only daughter's happiness. Tomorrow, we'll hand over that responsibility to a man we believe will give Melody the love and care she deserves, a man for whom we have the greatest respect. Tonight, we wholeheartedly welcome Douglas Pitt into our family."

Applause rippled through the dining room as Douglas stood. He pulled a piece of paper from his pocket, cleared his throat, and began reading Shakespeare's eighteenth sonnet. The paper trembled in his hand. He muffed two of the fourteen lines. Lizzie thought this successful businessman, who'd spoken before leaders of industry and state, who managed huge sums of money and governed policies that affected countless people throughout the nation, seemed more nervous than his young bride. Melody, though, looked up at him with adoration.

Next, it was Melody's turn. The flutist played Debussy's romantic song "Clair de lune" without missing a note. At the end, she bowed to her small audience of family and friends, a signal to the waiters to begin serving the main course. She snapped her flute into its case and made her way to The Troubadours' table. Sidney pulled out a chair for her to join them.

"That was lovely," Lizzie said. "You amaze me, Mel. You're so cool when you perform. I've been doing this ever so much longer than you, yet I still get butterflies before I go on stage. I don't know how you manage it."

"Music calms me."

"Like the savage beast?" Sidney teased.

Lizzie rolled her eyes. *There's nothing savage about Melody. She's as sweet and tame as vanilla custard.*

"I forgot to say earlier how sorry I am that your record deal didn't work out," Melody said. "Such a sad situation, that man dying and all. What will you do now?"

Lizzie realized her friend probably didn't know about the connection between Jim Jenkins and Bert. Didn't know that JJ's death was more than a professional loss. Or that it might not have been an accident.

"I've contacted several other recording outfits," Sidney said. "It will all work out."

"Would you consider making the record with us?" Lizzie asked her. "Even though you won't be playing with us much in the future, you were an important part of who we are today."

"Douglas and I will be traveling in Europe for a while, so I don't think that's possible."

"Well, maybe by the time you get back, we'll be so popular we'll have to make another one," Lizzie said. "Give it some thought."

"I will."

The waiters approached their table and set plates with Cornish game hens, wild rice, and asparagus with hollandaise sauce in front of them. Melody took the opportunity to excuse herself and moved on to talk with her cousins.

Bert, whose appetite never seemed to get sated, dug in enthusiastically. But after eating only a few bites, he jumped up suddenly and dashed to the men's room. When he hadn't returned after nearly ten minutes, Lizzie started to worry.

"Sid, would you go check on Bert and see if he's okay?" she asked.

Several more minutes passed before the two musicians came back. They sat down at the table again, but Bert ignored his dinner. His skin was pallid, his eyes dull.

Lizzie laid her hand on his arm. "Bert, what's wrong? Are you sick?"

He nodded. "A bit."

"Do you think it's something you ate?"

"I don't know, maybe."

"But we've all eaten the same things, and the rest of us are okay," Alan pointed out.

Visions of Jim Jenkins's body lying in a pool of vomit flashed in Lizzie's mind. She recalled her meeting the day before yesterday with Detective "Law" Perry at The Place, where he'd told her Jenkins died from ingesting mercury bichloride. A frightful idea slithered through her mind like a venomous serpent, an idea with no substance whatsoever, yet it made her shudder. If someone murdered Jim Jenkins, might that someone also try to eliminate the people who were close to JJ? People who knew something the killer didn't want known?

Chapter Thirteen

When Lizzie rolled out of bed at quarter past eight, Alan was already up, showered, dressed, and reading the *New York Times*, a cup of coffee in his hand. A financial advisor for numerous wealthy clients, he usually went to his Boston office a couple hours before the stock exchange opened to prepare for whatever opportunities or challenges the day might bring. Unlike Lizzie, who rarely saw the sun rise unless she hadn't yet been to bed.

He greeted her with a hug. "Good morning, Sunshine."

Rain splattered the arched windows of their room in the handsome old New Jersey inn.

"We could use some sunshine," she said. "I hope this crummy weather doesn't dampen Melody's wedding ceremony. You don't think it's a bad omen, do you?"

"I doubt it. Just an inconvenience," he answered. "Do you feel like having breakfast? There's a nice dining room downstairs that overlooks a rose garden."

"Ab-so-lute-ly."

He handed her a section of the newspaper and pointed to an article with the headline: *Man-Haters' Tearoom Raided.* "Are you familiar with this place? It's near your apartment."

Lizzie scanned the article, aghast. "Eve's Hangout, busted? That can't be. They don't serve booze there."

But as she continued reading, she realized the bust had nothing to do with alcohol. According to the article, New York's vice squad had organized the raid on the establishment. An undercover policewoman named Margaret Leonard seized a book of short stories titled *Lesbian Love* written by one of the nightclub's owners, Eva Zloczower, under her pen name Evelyn Adams.

"This is dreadful," Lizzie said. Angrily, she paced back and forth across the room, slamming her heels into the soft carpet. "The cops are just harassing her because she's a lesbian. Why do they care? Don't they have murderers and arsonists and bank robbers to catch?"

"I'm sorry to be the bearer of bad news, Lizzie. This should be a happy day, not one marred by inclement weather and intolerance."

She passed the newspaper back to Alan and headed for the bathroom. "Give me fifteen minutes to freshen up and get dressed, then let's go down to breakfast. Maybe I'll feel better after I've eaten."

* * *

Despite the rain, the wedding ceremony came off without a hitch. Bert had recovered from his bout with indigestion. The bride looked radiant in her white gown, embellished with seed pearls, silk ribbons, and antique lace. Guests filled most of the pews in Madison's pretty Episcopal church. The organist played well, and Lizzie sang exquisitely. The ring bearer didn't drop the ring. The flower girls didn't dissolve into fits of giggles. As the minister pronounced Douglas and Melody man and wife, the groom grinned broadly, and Lizzie felt confident he'd take good care of her friend. She crossed her fingers and prayed, *May all her fairy princess dreams come true.*

* * *

Usually, Sidney wore a tuxedo with tails when they performed. But this afternoon—not wanting to outdress the bridegroom—he'd donned a beautifully cut black suit and a black bow tie, as had Alan and Bert. The less formal attire did nothing to assuage Bert's awkwardness, however. He still looked like a little boy in his Sunday best, starched, spit-shined, and afraid to move. Lizzie pinned rose boutonnieres on the three men's lapels, then excused herself to go to the restaurant's ladies' room, where she changed out of her maid-of-honor gown into a fringed flapper dress that bared more skin than some folks might consider appropriate.

One of Melody's unmarried bridesmaids and a Fitzgerald cousin had been seated at the table with Lizzie and her friends. Lizzie greeted them both, wondering why they wore such sullen expressions on this festive occasion, and sat down beside Alan. Already she felt sorry for him, thinking he might feel obliged to amuse the two women while The Troubadours performed.

Leaning toward him, she whispered, "Don't think you have to entertain these ladies or anyone else this evening. Just because I've agreed to sing for Melody doesn't mean you shouldn't come and go as you please."

He laughed and squeezed her hand. "I can't count the number of dinners I've spent in the company of people I'd rather have avoided. But regardless of how dull the rest of this event may be, I'll have the pleasure of hearing you sing."

"It's only for an hour or so."

"Perhaps you'll take a break during that hour and dance with me."

"Ab-so-lute-ly," she promised. "And would you please dance a time or two with Melody? Douglas has two left feet."

"I'd be delighted."

* * *

After they'd finished a meal of spring lamb with mint jelly, new potatoes with parsley and cream sauce, green beans almandine, and Parker House rolls, the musicians excused themselves to perform. They wound their way through the tables full of guests toward the end of the room where the baby grand piano sat, shining like a black pearl. Halfway there, Lizzie heard a woman's voice utter a name she hadn't expected to hear tonight. Jim Jenkins.

The speaker, a bottle blonde who might have been in her early forties, wearing too much face paint and too much perfume, addressed her companions in a too-loud voice. "Serves him right. He was fooling around with another woman."

Lizzie paused, knelt, and pretended to adjust the strap of her shoe, hoping to hear more of the conversation.

"How do you know that?" asked another woman who wore a yellow hat adorned with a peacock feather.

"I have connections in the music world," the blonde said.

By now, word of the death of Jupiter Records' owner had made its way to the New Jersey suburbs, where many people who worked in The City lived. The newspapers had carried some of the story. The rest traveled on the faster train of gossip.

"That's rather unkind, don't you think?" a third woman asked. "The poor man died an awful death."

"If my husband was cheating on me, you can be sure I'd make him pay," the blonde said.

"You're not suggesting his wife killed him, are you?" asked the woman with the yellow hat.

Sidney played the beginning of a song Lizzie knew he'd written, signaling his colleagues to take their places. She stood, wishing she could eavesdrop longer on the three ladies' conversation. Who was this loud woman who claimed to have inside information about Jim Jenkins's affairs? Did she really know something about the record producer's alleged infidelities? Lizzie didn't recognize her as a fellow musician, but perhaps she worked in marketing or one of a dozen other areas of the music business. Maybe she had musical aspirations of her own. Lizzie tried to recall if she'd seen the woman at JJ's birthday party the night before he died, but drew a blank.

As she took her place beside her colleagues, Sidney pushed away from the piano and stood to address their audience. "Ladies and gentlemen, I'm Sidney Somerset of The Troubadours from New York City, and these are my colleagues Lizzie Crane and Bert Halley. As many of you know, Melody played with us for two years before choosing another path in life. She's a splendid musician, a dear friend, and we miss her. Tonight, we're here to celebrate her marriage to Douglas Pitt. We wish them all the best in the future and know that you, their friends and relatives, do too.

"We open tonight's entertainment with a song from George and Ira Gershwin, chosen by the new Mrs. Pitt to express her feelings for her husband: 'The Man I Love.' Please welcome our honored couple as they dance for the first time as man and wife."

Applause rippled through the ballroom as Douglas took Melody in his arms. The groom seemed even more awkward dancing than he had been reading Shakespeare's sonnet at last night's rehearsal dinner. But Melody gracefully led him, careful to keep her toes away from his shoes. *I hope he's got more panache in the bedroom than on the dance floor,* Lizzie thought.

Next, Melody danced with her father and Douglas with his mother. The Troubadours played Al Jolson's hopeful song "April Showers," a comment on the disappointing rainy weather as well as the ups and downs that inevitably came with married life. For the next half-hour, the trio performed a variety of jazz numbers, show tunes, and other popular pieces that brought many of the guests to their feet. Melody danced with both of Douglas's brothers and his father, who demonstrated more skill than the groom. She also danced twice with Alan. Then the flutist played a song with her former colleagues.

When they finished the song, Lizzie asked her friends, "Say, would you play 'Rhapsody in Blue' next? It's my favorite, and I want to dance with Alan."

* * *

At the end of their hour-long stint, The Troubadours took a break. Lizzie found Bert sitting on the restaurant's porch, staring out at the rain. She slid into an Adirondack chair beside him. "Are you okay?"

"Not really," he answered.

"Do you feel sick again?"

"No."

She leaned closer and noticed he was crying. Tears dribbled down his cheeks like a leak in a water pipe. Quiet, self-contained Bert rarely showed emotion. Perhaps the loss of his family friend had finally taken its toll. Maybe being surrounded by happy people having fun while he grieved was too much for the young man.

Bert pulled a handkerchief from his pocket and wiped his eyes. "I'm sorry, Lizzie. I just—"

"No apologies," she said, laying her hand on his arm. "This whole thing has got to be hard on you. I can't even imagine what you're going through. I know you miss Jenkins. But you've performed like a trouper. I'm proud of you, Bert, and I know Melody is glad you agreed to play at her wedding despite your own sadness."

For a few minutes, they sat in silence while Bert collected himself. At the far end of the porch, a couple leaned together, taking advantage of the band's break to enjoy a bit of romance. A few young men came outside to smoke and chat–Lizzie noticed they also passed a flask around.

"Not just JJ," Bert said finally. "It's my dad, too. It's all of a piece."

"I know. Each loss reminds us of all the others who have gone before and the many more that await us." Lizzie patted his hand. No one she loved had died, though, so she really couldn't understand what Bert felt.

Bert jiggled his long legs as he often did when he was nervous. "JJ and my father were together the night Dad died. They played at a local club that night as they often did."

His revelation surprised Lizzie. She longed to know more about what happened the night Tommy Halley died, but didn't want to pressure Bert. Instead, she said, "I knew your father was a musician, but I didn't realize Jenkins was."

"Yep, a pretty good one too. Played trumpet. That's how they relaxed and had fun. Got away from it all. Like me. Nothing makes me happier than playing music."

"I know what you mean."

"Well, they'd had a bit to drink—probably a lot to drink. My dad and JJ liked their booze."

After she met Bert playing his deceased father's saxophone in Central Park, Lizzie went to the library and read an old newspaper article about Tommy Halley, who died after stumbling into the path of a taxicab. The police report said he'd been drunk at the time, but she couldn't recall any mention of Jim Jenkins being at the scene.

"What would you do if a person hurt someone you loved?" Bert asked.

"I guess it would depend on the circumstances."

"There you are," Sidney interrupted them. "I wondered where you went. The bride and groom are ready to cut the cake."

Lizzie waved him away. "Give us a moment, please. We'll be there shortly."

"Okay," he said, retreating back into the bright lights and jovial atmosphere inside the restaurant.

Lizzie squeezed Bert's hand. "I'm so sorry. Do you want to play a few more songs tonight? You don't have to, you know. Melody will understand. We all will. Sid and I can handle it."

"I want to," he insisted. "Music's the only thing holding me together now."

Chapter Fourteen

"No friendship is an accident."

—*O. Henry*

Lizzie made an omelet with Gouda cheese, fresh chives, and smoked ham for breakfast and shared it with Alan at the dropleaf table in her Greenwich Village apartment. Outside, the morning sun had begun drying up the puddles from yesterday's rain. People dressed in their Sunday clothes hurried to church services. Boys wearing caps and knickers hawked newspapers. Young girls sold bouquets of flowers to passersby.

"If only the weather had been this nice yesterday," she lamented.

Late last night, while they drove home after Melody's wedding reception, the rain that had pelted them all day finally dissipated. The dark clouds parted, letting the moon and stars shine their light on the city that never slept.

"Nevertheless, I think the wedding went pretty well," Alan said. "Melody looked happy. So did Douglas."

"Yes, they seem to be good for each other, even though he's twice her age."

Alan took a sip of his coffee, then set the cup in its saucer and laid his hand over hers. "Have you ever considered living someplace other than New York?"

The question took her by surprise. "I've lived here my whole life. I can't imagine anything else."

"I know. But it's a big world. Aren't you curious to see it?"

"I'd like to see Paris," she answered, cutting a bite of omelet with her fork.

"Well, then, we'll go. What do you say? Rome and Florence, too, if you like. St. Peter's, El Duomo, the Uffizi Gallery."

"And maybe London?"

"Of course, London. And Barcelona–you'll love Antoni Gaudí's Sagrada Familia Cathedral."

"Athens?"

"No European tour would be complete without a visit to the Acropolis."

"The Swiss Alps?" she asked.

Immediately, she regretted it, remembering that six years ago his fiancée had died in a skiing accident at St. Moritz. His smile disappeared, and he turned to stare out the window at the street traffic below.

"Oh, Alan, I'm so sorry. How clumsy of me. I didn't mean to dredge up sad memories."

He shook his head. "It was a long time ago."

They finished the rest of their breakfast in silence; the moment of joyful anticipation swept away like a boat in a riptide. *How can you be so insensitive, Lizzie Crane?* she chastised herself.

Alan glanced at his Patek Philippe watch. "I should go. My train leaves at ten o'clock."

"When will I see you again?" she asked.

He took her hand and kissed each fingertip in turn. "Soon, I hope."

* * *

She'd intended to go with Alan to meet his train to Boston, but he insisted it wasn't necessary. "I'd rather kiss you goodbye here, in the privacy of your apartment, than with a crowd of people around us," he told her.

They took the elevator downstairs together. She watched him climb into a taxi that would drive him to Penn Station, to a train that would take him two hundred miles away.

Maybe he wants to put more than physical distance between us, she thought.

Maybe this weekend, entwined as it was with love and death, joy and sorrow, had opened old wounds in him—as it had in Bert. *Is it possible for love to shine without the shadow of loss always hovering over it?*

* * *

Lizzie knew Eve's Hangout wasn't open on Sunday, but she decided to walk to the tearoom anyway. Maybe she'd run into Eve or her partner, Swedish painter Ruth Norlander, who might tell her more about Friday night's raid. With the salubrious sunshine warming her, she strolled down Bleecker Street, then turned north and headed toward Washington Square. She passed women pushing baby carriages and old men sitting on their front stoops smoking cigarettes. Little girls played hopscotch or jacks on the sidewalks. Boys kicked cans in the street.

The popular tearoom occupied the bottom floor of an unpretentious townhouse at 129 MacDougal Street. Lizzie peeked through one of the windows, hoping to spot someone inside, but saw nobody. She knocked on the door, waited a minute, then knocked again. When no one answered, she walked to the proprietor's nearby apartment and found Eve outside, pruning the petunias in her window boxes.

"I'd say 'good morning' except it's not," Lizzie said.

Eve turned to face Lizzie, dropped a handful of withered blossoms in a bucket, and smiled slowly. She tilted her head back and stretched out her arms as if to embrace the sunshine.

"Nonsense, this is a fine morning."

"I read about the raid. What happened?"

"Do you wish to talk out here on this fine morning? Or shall we go inside and I'll make you a cup of tea?"

"Tea sounds good," Lizzie said.

In her kitchen, Eve Adams, born Chawa Zloczower in Poland to a Jewish family, brewed Indian tea for the daughter of Irish Catholic immigrants. She carried a tray with an English teapot, two porcelain cups, and a Spanish silver cream pitcher and sugar bowl to the living room, where she set it on a

Moroccan table.

When both women had filled their cups with the fragrant Assam, Eve said, "A woman named Margaret Leonard came to the tearoom several times. She seemed awkward, like she had never been to such a place before. I thought maybe she was still uncertain of herself and what she wanted." Eve paused to sip her tea before continuing. "I tried to make her feel comfortable. Safe. That she was among friends. Free to talk with the others. In time, I asked her if she wanted to go to the theater."

"How did she respond?" Lizzie asked.

"She was very eager. And so we went. After, I invited her to my home for tea—just as I am doing now with you—and she accepted."

"What went wrong?"

Eve shook her head. "Well, she was with the police, I found out. Undercover. What is it they call those deceptive women, the Flapper Squad? Anyway, she meant from the very start to trap me in some sort of crime. She said a neighbor complained, but not about noise or drinking alcohol. I am supposed to be a bad influence on young girls. That angry writer for the *Quill*, Bobby Edwards, I think he had a hand in it."

"What about your book?" Lizzie asked. "I heard it was confiscated."

"Yes," Eve said, sadly nodding her head. "Margaret needed evidence, not only the rumors. My book for her is proof that I am a danger to society."

"What happens now? Will they close the Hangout?"

Eve shrugged. "Who knows what's going on these days and where it will lead?"

"But the Hangout is one of the Village's most popular nightspots," Lizzie said. "You have so many friends who care about you."

"Ha. Do you mean Henry Miller, whose wife has taken up with a woman? Or Emma Goldman, an anarchist and Russian Jew, who insists women should be allowed to control their own bodies? No, I doubt my friends can be of help in this situation."

"What about the First Amendment? It guarantees freedom of speech."

"To say what is approved, yes. To say what threatens the status quo, no." Eve sipped her tea and stared at Lizzie, her dark eyes bright with indignation and fear. "These are confusing times, are they not?"

* * *

After leaving Eve to tend her flowers, Lizzie walked the mile and a half to Tin Pan Alley. On this sunny, seventy-degree day, the walk should have been a pleasant exercise, except she was too angry to enjoy it. Maybe the music, the activity, the cacophony of the Alley would distract her from what she considered blatant discrimination.

She turned onto West 28th Street, between Fifth and Sixth Avenues, and headed for Frankie Woods's music store. Even though it was Sunday, some of the shops along the Alley propped their doors open to welcome customers. Upstairs, the windows of music studios had been flung open, too, letting a jangling mix of instruments and voices spill out into the street below.

The music shook Lizzie out of her bad mood. When she came upon two adolescent boys tap-dancing on the sidewalk, she joined them. She tossed a few coins in a guitar player's open case. Then she climbed the half-flight of steps that led up to Frankie's store. The former trombone player had his back to her and was busy dusting phonographs when she entered.

"François du Bois," she called out his birth name. "*Bonjour.*"

The tall, slim Louisiana-born man turned around and grinned at her. "*Bienvenue, ma belle. Ça va?*"

"*Pas mal,*" she answered. "*Et vous?*"

He shrugged. "*Comme çi, comme ça.*"

"Okay, that's the extent of my French. We'll have to talk English now. Unless we want to order a drink–that I can do in a half-dozen languages."

Frankie held out his hand. "What you been up to these days, lady? Last I heard, you were chasing the ghost of Jim Jenkins."

"I guess I still am. Haven't gotten any closer to the truth of it all, though. Maybe that's why I'm here."

"C'mon in and set a spell, as folks down south say." He pulled up a chair for her, then sat himself and lit a Chesterfield. "What do you think you want to know?"

"Hmm, that's a funny way of putting it," Lizzie said.

He took a long drag on his cigarette and blew out a plume of smoke. "Sometimes when we get what we think we want, we discover too late it's not what we expected. Could even make things worse."

She wished he'd stop being enigmatic and just spill. "The last time we talked, you suggested someone might have poisoned Jenkins. That he'd made some enemies. You never said who."

"And I'm not gonna say now."

Lizzie switched to a different line of questioning. "I went to a wedding in New Jersey this past weekend. A lady there said Jenkins was having an affair. She suggested his wife might have killed him in revenge."

He flicked ashes into an ashtray on his desk. "Why do you want to mess around in all this anyway? You've heard the expression 'let sleeping dogs lie', haven't you?"

"Yes, and 'curiosity killed the cat' too. But Jim Jenkins was more than a business contact for me. He was like a second father to Bert Halley, you know, the saxophonist in our group. Bert's hurting, and I want to help him if I can."

He nodded. "The blues done come calling, have they?"

A well-dressed young man entered the shop and started flipping through the racks of sheet music for sale. Frankie stood up, crushed his cigarette butt in the ashtray, and held out his hand to Lizzie.

"My advice is stay out of it."

That's what Alan said, too, she reminded herself.

"I have to try to earn a living now," he said, politely dismissing her. "It's always good to see you, Lizzie. Stop by again."

"*Au revoir*, François." She waved goodbye as she left the music shop, no wiser than when she came in.

Chapter Fifteen

"Greenwich Village...the village of low rents and high arts."

—O. Henry

After leaving Frankie Woods's music shop, Lizzie stopped at her favorite thrift store. Run by a Methodist church, it was open for only a few hours each week after Sunday services. Sometimes she found quality, barely worn clothing there that she could never have afforded otherwise, handed down by wealthy, well-intentioned women.

She remembered the peddlers who rolled carts of secondhand goods through the streets of the poor Bronx neighborhood where she'd lived as a girl. Often, her mother took young Lizzie along when she went to buy the family's clothing and household goods from those carts. Among the Irish, Italian, and Polish immigrants who inhabited the Bronx, a stigma clung to what the Jewish vendors sold. Rumors claimed tuberculosis, scabies, and trench fever contaminated the very fibers of the garments and bedding. But the Crane family couldn't afford anything else, so Lizzie's mother soaked whatever she brought home in boiling water to remove any contagion.

In recent years, church-associated shops like this one had sprung up and conferred a sense of legitimacy to what had heretofore been considered a tawdry business. Donors could feel good about giving to worthy charities. Buyers could claim their purchases supported Christian outreach programs, instead of being only a way to save money.

Lizzie went directly to a rack of evening dresses, knowing that New York's society ladies wouldn't be caught dead wearing the same outfit twice. After flipping past a couple dozen items, she found a lovely turquoise silk gown that looked like it would fit her and plucked it from the hanger. She took it to the cashier, perhaps a church member doing volunteer work, who folded Lizzie's dress and slipped it into a brown paper bag.

"Enjoy your pretty frock," the woman said.

Lizzie handed her two quarters. "Thanks, I will."

Near-perfect days like this one didn't grace the city often, and Lizzie longed to make the best of it. She wished she could meet with a girlfriend, drink tea or a Coca-Cola together at a sidewalk café, walk in the park, and chat about superficial things. But she no longer had any girlfriends. The girls she'd grown up with had married long ago and devoted themselves to raising children. Women she met these days found Lizzie's beauty and unconventional lifestyle as an entertainer threatening. Even in the music world, where rules and roles blurred, competitiveness and envy made friendships difficult. And now that Melody, her colleague and companion for the past two years, had married, their relationship would surely fade as the flutist's focus shifted from music to her new home, husband, and family.

She popped into the Cherry Lane Theatre, where a rehearsal was underway, and took a seat a few rows back from the stage. Edna St. Vincent Millay had participated in renovating the three-story brick building a couple years ago. Before that, it housed a brewery and a tobacco warehouse; the aromas of its past tenants still permeated the space.

For about twenty minutes, Lizzie watched the actors practice an avant-garde play by a writer she'd never heard of. The playhouse was known for presenting experimental theater, and she attended performances there regularly. This one, however, failed to capture her attention. At the end of Act One, she quietly made her way outside again to the narrow, sun-splashed street.

She wandered around the Village aimlessly for a while, peeking in the windows of shops closed on Sunday. Mentally, she replayed scenes from her weekend with Alan. She'd decided not to bathe this morning, reluctant to wash his scent from her skin. *When will I see him again?* she wondered. Although they'd been lovers for five months and he lavished attention on her during their time together, she had no idea what he did to entertain himself when they were apart. A handsome, rich man from a prestigious family could find plenty of women to amuse him in her absence, and Lizzie worried that one day she'd wake up from her Cinderella dream to discover it was only that: a dream.

At a table outside one of her favorite coffeehouses, she spotted Sidney, sitting alone, reading a newspaper and sipping what she suspected was his signature café au lait with a sprinkle of cinnamon. She quickened her step, glad she'd fortuitously run into her friend. When she was still twenty feet away, he looked up as if sensing her presence and smiled.

He stood and pulled out a chair for her. "Bearcat, what a nice surprise."

"Top of the afternoon," she replied. "I tried to telephone you earlier but got no response."

"Have you had lunch?"

"No, and I'm ab-so-lute-ly famished."

He handed her his menu. "I was just about to order."

"What are you having?"

"Beef tongue on rye."

"Make that two. With dill pickles and potato chips."

A young waiter sporting a thin mustache took their order and brought Lizzie a cup of coffee.

Sidney fit a cigarette into his engraved silver holder. "I assume Prince Charming has gone back to Boston."

"He left this morning."

"Pray tell, what have you been doing in his absence?" he asked, a hint of sarcasm in his voice.

"Don't be a pill, Sid."

Sidney lit his cigarette, took a drag, then blew out a series of smoke rings. "Sorry, I can't help being jealous. Melody's just married the man of her dreams. You've got a hot sugar daddy, and I'm all alone with no romantic prospects in sight."

"That can change in an instant. Don't give up hope," Lizzie said. "Speaking of love, I talked to Eve this morning about the raid on the teahouse. She said an undercover female cop busted her because of her book *Lesbian Love.* What's going to happen now?"

Sidney shrugged. "Who knows? People like us don't have many friends in high places, at least not many who'll go to bat for us."

"The teahouse was a safe zone, a place of refuge for all women, not only lesbians. We could talk freely there about art, literature, and politics." Lizzie sipped her coffee pensively. *What if Eve goes to jail?*

The waiter brought their sandwiches, and they stopped talking briefly to eat. After a few bites, Lizzie steered the conversation toward a less emotional topic: business.

"Any jobs on the horizon? Other than Melody's wedding, we haven't played anywhere in nearly two weeks. I'm worried my pipes will dry up."

"Working on it," he answered. "Got a few parties in my sights. A twenty-fifth wedding anniversary celebration for a newspaper exec. Could net us some swell publicity. Xavier, the owner of the Queen of Diamonds, has expressed interest in us, too–that's one of your favorite posh speakeasies, as I recall."

"Definitely get us in there."

Sid snapped his fingers. "How about I set up an appointment with Xavier, and you come with me, dressed like the Queen of Diamonds? Red gown, tiara, the whole nine yards. He'll positively swoon."

Lizzie laughed. Although Sidney handled their bookings and finances, while she focused mainly on the production side of the business, the idea appealed to her. "I'm game. I've already got the red gown. Coco Chanel, no less," she said, referring to the extravagantly expensive strapless evening dress she'd worn a few months ago when she and Alan attended the dramatic performance of F. Scott Fitzgerald's *The Great Gatsby.*

The waiter stopped by to refill Lizzie's coffee cup and asked if they wanted anything else.

"Cheesecake," Lizzie said. When Sidney paused, considering his waistline, she prompted him. "Oh, c'mon, Sid. It's healthy. A couple thousand years ago, Olympic athletes ate cheesecake because they believed it gave them extra energy."

"I'm not exactly an athlete," he admitted, and Lizzie knew he'd probably never swung a tennis racquet or golf club in his life. "But, hey, bring it on."

While they waited for their dessert, Lizzie raised a subject she'd been pondering since Melody's wedding. "What would you think of inviting Bert's sister, Daisy, to audition for us?"

She could sense her friend's skepticism in the long pause that followed her question. They'd only met Daisy once, at the recording studio the day before Jim Jenkins's death. Bert had barely mentioned his sister before that. The secrecy surrounding the Halley family seemed curious, and the mother was certainly odd. But Lizzie had been willing to ignore all that because The Troubadours needed Bert—and because she genuinely liked the shy saxophonist. Now that the family's longtime friend had died unexpectedly, the curtains that concealed those secrets might soon be yanked open.

"She's only a girl," Sidney pointed out.

"Seventeen. Bert says Daisy's very talented."

"We're doing fine, just the three of us. Why do you want to bring in someone else who might be more trouble than she's worth?"

She'd asked herself the same thing. "I don't know."

But she did know. She knew what it was like to be a talented girl with big dreams. Lizzie had sought fame and fortune since she was Daisy's age, and she'd chased that dream ever since. She knew how hard it was to make it in the music world, especially for a young woman without money or connections. Although she'd only met Daisy Halley briefly, she could identify with her.

As the waiter set two slices of cheesecake on the table, Sidney said, "Well, I guess it can't hurt to hear what the girl's got."

Chapter Sixteen

"Life's but a walking shadow, a poor player,

That struts and frets his hour upon the stage,

And then is heard no more."

—William Shakespeare, MacBeth

Bert, his sister Daisy, and their mother Gladys Halley were already seated in the first pew with Edith Jenkins and her two sons when Lizzie and Sidney entered the church. Near the chancel rested a mahogany coffin with polished brass fittings, white lilies lying on the top. A bespectacled man wearing a choir robe sat at the organ playing somber tunes in what Lizzie considered a perfunctory manner, devoid of feeling, as people filed in to pay their respects.

Lizzie scanned the sanctuary and spotted a number of people she knew from the music world, including KDAZ radio's manager Victor Fosse. Malcolm MacGregor, who'd hosted the birthday party for the record producer on his last night on earth, was noticeably absent. Oddly enough, though, the angry man who accosted Jenkins at the party and ordered JJ to stay away from his lady friend had come to the funeral with a woman Lizzie guessed might be her.

At the rear of the church stood Detective "Law" Perry, wearing a black suit. In the mystery novels Lizzie read, the perpetrator usually showed up at the victim's funeral, and she wondered if Perry hoped to discover his quarry among the attendees.

She and Sidney slid into a pew near the back of the sanctuary. While Sid looked over the program, Lizzie continued searching for familiar faces in the crowd. She spotted the brassy blonde she'd overheard at Melody's reception, who claimed Jim Jenkins had a paramour, seated on the aisle about a third of the way back from the chancel.

"Such a sad business, his death," a woman in the pew in front of Lizzie said. "And so sudden."

The woman beside her, who wore a wide-brimmed black hat that partly obscured Lizzie's view, said, "I heard he died of mercury bichloride poisoning."

"Good heavens, that can't be. Isn't that a treatment for, um—"

"Syphilis," the woman with the big hat said. When her companion gasped, she quickly backpedaled. "Of course, it's used for other things too."

Lizzie glanced at Sidney, who raised an eyebrow as the first woman continued, "Poor Edith. We must give her our support in her time of need."

"Edith Jenkins is an upstanding Christian. Unlike...well, I shouldn't speak ill of the dead."

But before the two women could continue their conversation, the minister stepped up to the podium and began the service. Forty minutes later, Bert, Edith Jenkins's two sons, and three other men hoisted JJ's casket and carried it down the aisle outside to the waiting hearse.

A light rain splattered the windshield of Sidney's Buick as they followed the procession of automobiles to the cemetery. Lizzie longed to offer Bert some comfort, but she hadn't even managed to catch his eye. She wondered how he and his family were holding up. Seeing him crying last night at Melody's reception sparked her protective feelings for the young man, and she wished she could think of a way to help him during this painful time.

The church lady's insinuation that Jim Jenkins wasn't an "upstanding Christian" didn't surprise Lizzie. It would have surprised her more if she'd discovered he was a deacon in his church or taught Sunday school to the faithful's children. The musicians she knew could hardly be considered choirboys–even those who grew up singing in church choirs, as she had. They liked their booze and their drugs, their all-night parties, their floozies and their backdoor men. And Sunday morning came too early after a late night of carousing.

Last week, Detective Perry told her that JJ had syphilis and died from mercury bichloride poisoning. Apparently, word had leaked to members of the Jenkins' church. Did his wife know? Was the woman Bert called "Auntie Edith" also infected? The possibility gave more weight to the theory the loud blond woman had floated: Edith Jenkins had poisoned her cheating husband.

Jeepers creepers, I can't tell that to Bert, Lizzie thought. Then another idea crept out of the shadows, into the forefront of her mind. *Does Bert already know?*

* * *

Thirty or so mourners found their way from the cemetery to the home of Edith and the late Jim Jenkins. A half-dozen women—members of the Jenkins' church, Lizzie presumed—set platters of sliced turkey and ham, bowls of vegetables and salads, and trays of fresh-baked breads on the dining room table. Pies and cakes graced a sideboard.

As Lizzie plopped a spoonful of Waldorf salad onto her plate next to a slice of ham, she felt the prickly sensation of being watched. She looked up to see Edith Jenkins staring at her. She'd expected Auntie Edith to be a dowdy, gray-haired matron with thick ankles and a thick waist. The attractive, stylishly dressed woman in her middle years who'd been like an aunt to Bert surprised her.

Lizzie approached JJ's widow and smiled in a way she hoped expressed compassion. "Mrs. Jenkins?'

"Yes?"

"I'm Elizabeth Crane, Bert's colleague in The Troubadours. I wish to offer my condolences. I only met your husband briefly—as you may know, my musician friends and I planned to make a record with him. He impressed me with his knowledge of the recording business."

She didn't mention the birthday party at Malcolm MacGregor's townhouse or that she'd found Jenkins's body in his studio soon after his death.

"Thank you," Edith Jenkins said.

"Bert speaks highly of you and Mr. Jenkins. You were, well, a second family to him, I take it."

"Yes, our families were close."

Mrs. Jenkins didn't exude her husband's enthusiasm or friendly manner, and Lizzie couldn't picture her baking cookies or reading bedtime stories to Bert and his sister Daisy. Nor could she imagine the record producer's wife attending a bash like the birthday party MacGregor threw for JJ the night before he died.

Suddenly, a thought popped into Lizzie's head. "Bert told me both his father and Mr. Jenkins were musicians, and they played together sometimes. Did your husband happen to record any of their sessions?"

Mrs. Jenkins frowned and shook her head. "I don't think they ever made a recording together. They only performed in local pubs for fun. Mostly when they'd had a bit too much to drink."

"That's what Bert told me, too. He idealized them, you know. They were his inspiration, the reason he chose to pursue a career as a musician." Lizzie paused a moment, wondering if she dared broach the next topic. But she might never have this opportunity again, and so she pushed on. "I understand your husband and Bert's father played together at a neighborhood club the night Tommy Halley died."

The woman's eyes narrowed, then darted away from Lizzie's gaze and focused on the dining table laden with funeral food. "Excuse me, Miss Crane, but I need to check on things in the kitchen. Thank you for coming today."

Maybe Mrs. Jenkins couldn't bear to discuss the death of a close family friend right now while she mourned her deceased husband, Lizzie decided. Maybe the only way the widow could get through this ordeal was by keeping a stiff upper lip. Still, questions swirled in Lizzie's mind, and she made a mental note to learn more about the friendship between the two men.

She spotted Bert heading toward the dining table and hurried to catch up with him. The bounce had disappeared from her young colleague's long-legged stride, and he looked like he was sleepwalking. As he filled his plate, she called out to him.

He turned and forced a lopsided smile. "Hi, Lizzie."

She gave him a quick side-hug, careful not to bump his full plate. "I'm glad to see you're still able to eat."

"Gotta keep up my strength."

"What can I do to help?"

"Nothing, but thanks for asking."

Nudging him like a border collie herding a sheep, Lizzie gently steered Bert away from the other guests, into an alcove off the kitchen. She motioned for him to sit at an oak table beside a window that looked out on a small, neat yard. Seating herself across from him, she asked, "How are your mom and sister holding up?"

Bert shrugged. "Daisy's okay. Mom's kinda punch-drunk. She never got over Dad's death and now this…"

"Your mom's lucky to have you."

Bert forked some potato salad into his mouth.

"I hope you know I'm here for you," she continued. "Sid is, too. We care about you."

He nodded. "Thanks. You've always been a friend to me, Lizzie."

"I met your Aunt Edith a little while ago. I've got to say, she isn't what I expected. She's quite stylish and good-looking for an older woman."

Bert cut into a slice of roast turkey. "And cool as a cucumber."

His assessment took Lizzie by surprise. Always, he'd spoken favorably of his "aunt," but he'd never actually described her in definitive terms.

"JJ would never have succeeded without her. She was the driving force in their marriage and his business, too."

"He seemed to know a lot about making records," she said, recalling the tour of his studio that Jenkins gave her the day before his death.

"Oh, he was smart, for sure. But he liked going to parties, drinking with his pals, and hanging out with celebrities more than he liked working. Auntie

Edith kept him on track."

"The music world can be pretty seductive."

"And how," Bert agreed.

Lizzie wished she could ask him if Jim Jenkins also fancied women other than his wife, but she decided this wasn't the time or place to pose that question. Instead, she asked, "What do you think will happen to his business now?"

He shook his head. "No idea."

After Bert cleaned his plate, he and Lizzie joined his mother and sister. Gladys Halley, dressed in a plain black frock devoid of jewelry and a simple black hat with a veil, appeared even more pale and fragile than Lizzie remembered. Daisy's black garb, however, made the girl look older than her seventeen years and, like a judge's robe, gave her an aura of authority.

"Mrs. Halley, I'm Lizzie Crane. I wish to express my condolences for your loss."

"Thank you," she said, her dull eyes clearing as she recognized Lizzie. "You're Bert's friend, the one who came to our house to tell us Jim was dead, aren't you?"

"That's right."

"Well, thank you for coming today," Gladys said.

"Is there anything I can do for you, Mrs. Halley?"

An awkward smile that seemed more like a grimace crossed the woman's face. In an icy voice, she said, "Can you bring Jim back to life? No, I didn't think so. Well, then, I guess there's nothing you can do for me, Miss Crane."

Gladys Halley turned away abruptly and reached for her daughter's arm. Without a word, Daisy grasped her mother's hand and led her to a chair near the kitchen.

Confused, Lizzie looked up at her colleague. "Bert, did I say something wrong?"

He shook his head. "Mom's angry right now, but she doesn't know how to just be angry. She's used to being nice...what's the word, compliant?"

"Anger is a pretty common reaction when someone dies suddenly and leaves us alone," Lizzie said.

"She's mad at my old man as well. After he died, she hoped JJ would rescue us. But now he's gone too. They both abandoned her." Bert cracked his knuckles one by one. "Who's gonna help Mom now?"

Lizzie gave him a hug, then excused herself to get a glass of punch. As she dipped the ladle into a cut-glass bowl filled with pink liquid, she spotted the bleached blonde from Melody's reception dinner standing at the dessert table. The woman was nearly as tall as Lizzie and about twenty pounds overweight, but she carried it well. Her black-and-white polka dot frock seemed a bit gay for a funeral, Lizzie thought, and her black straw hat with its faille brim and oversized velvet rose couldn't help but attract attention. The woman slid a slice of chocolate cake onto her plate as Lizzie stepped beside her.

"Hello, didn't I see you at Melody Fitzgerald's wedding?" Lizzie asked.

The blond woman turned and instantly recognized Lizzie. "Hey, you're her singer friend."

"Lizzie Crane. How do you know Melody?"

"From church. I played the organ there for a while until they hired a professional. I grew up in Madison, but I live in Astoria now and work at the Steinway piano factory. In advertising. I'm Kitty Taylor." The woman balanced her plate on her left hand and held out the right one.

Lizzie shook it. "Pleased to meet you. And you knew Jim Jenkins, too?"

"Oh, yeah. We go back at least a dozen years. Used to bang out a few tunes together now and again. Just for fun, mostly at hole-in-the-wall joints and get-togethers with friends. Nothing upscale like what you do." Kitty paused to take a bite of cake. "By the way, you sang swell Saturday night."

"Thanks," Lizzie said, her mind sprinting ahead. If Kitty Taylor played music with Jenkins, maybe she'd also played with Bert's father. "Did you know his friend Tommy Halley? He was a musician too."

"We played a few tunes together. Nice guy, kinda quiet. Not like JJ and me, we could get raucous after a few drinks." She laughed loud enough that several people nearby turned to stare at her.

"Tommy died a couple years ago. He got hit by a car."

Kitty nodded slowly. "Yeah, I remember that. Drunk, wasn't he?"

"So they say. And now JJ's dead too." Lizzie leaned closer to Kitty and lowered her voice, as if sharing a secret. "I heard he died from mercury bichloride poisoning."

The blonde fingered the velvet rose on her hat. "Well now, isn't that interesting? So, the old lecher had syphilis. I heard he was fooling around."

"But as I understand it, he swallowed the drug. A person wouldn't ingest mercury bichloride to treat syphilis; he'd apply it topically," Lizzie continued. "Taken orally, it can kill you."

"Meaning either he committed suicide, or somebody dosed him?"

Lizzie shrugged. "Maybe he took it by accident, mistaking it for another drug."

"Hard to confuse it with another drug. Those pills are shaped like little blue coffins to warn people they're dangerous." She paused for a moment before adding, "Frankly, I can't imagine JJ committing suicide—he liked himself too much. I'm going with option number two."

"If that's the case, who'd want to bump him off?"

"My money's on the wife. Especially if he not only cheated on her but gave her the pox as well."

Lizzie recalled what she overheard Kitty say at Melody's reception, "If my husband was cheating on me, you can be sure I'd make him pay." She thought about Bert's description of Edith Jenkins, "Cool as a cucumber." Was she capable of murder?

Kitty wiped a dab of chocolate frosting from her bright red lips. "Unless he infected someone else, too, and she decided to get revenge."

"Who was Jenkins fooling around with?"

"I don't know. Never heard a name, only a rumor that he was double-dipping. What's your interest in it anyway?"

"Our saxophonist Bert, Tommy Halley's son, was close to Jenkins and his wife. He's pretty broken up over JJ's death."

"Well, you won't be doing the kid any favors by telling him what I just told you."

"You're right," Lizzie agreed. "I'd just like to know the whole story."

"If somebody bumped off JJ, that somebody's gonna do all he or she can to keep the story quiet. Might even try to rub you out of the picture if you get too nosy." Kitty set down her cake plate and stepped away from Lizzie. "That's all I have to say on the matter, and you'd be wise to zip your lips too."

Chapter Seventeen

"The nature of business is swindling."

—August Bebel

Rain pelted the windows of Lizzie's Greenwich Village apartment. Outside, people who didn't have the luxury of holing up indoors today, as she did, scurried through the downpour, delivering goods to shops and restaurants, collecting garbage, and hailing taxis to take them to their jobs in Manhattan's business district. A newsboy huddled under an umbrella with an armful of papers, hawking his damp product to people too rushed to stop and buy. A peddler selling vegetables from a horse-drawn cart lumbered down streets running with rainwater, but no one braved the inclement weather to purchase his wares.

Lizzie turned away from the window and poured herself a second cup of coffee. So much had happened in such a short period of time–Jim Jenkins's death, Melody's wedding, the raid on Eve's Hangout. Each event marked an ending, and she was still having trouble processing it all.

Her relationship with Alan Peabody perplexed her, too. Two days ago, he took the train back to Boston, yet except for a telephone call to let her know he arrived home safely, she'd heard nothing from him. She gazed at the sun-splashed Edward Hopper painting he gave her three months ago, hanging above her sofa. *Why does life have to be so confusing?* she rued as she sat at the dropleaf table near the window to sip her coffee and work a crossword puzzle.

She penciled in a few easy answers and passed over several words that stumped her. When she came to "Trick," the clue for a seven-letter word beginning with D, she wrote d-e-c-e-i-v-e. She paused, wondering if it had any relevance to her present situation.

"Now I'm starting to think like Cora," she said aloud.

Her tarot-reader friend saw meaning in all sorts of coincidences. Even though Lizzie didn't understand how signs and symbols–in tarot cards and in everyday life—could offer insights, Cora Delaney did. Furthermore, she'd done several card readings for Lizzie in the past few months that turned out to be amazingly accurate at foretelling the future.

Lizzie shook her head and moved to the next crossword clue. By the time she finished her coffee, she'd filled in about half the blank spaces. She carried her empty cup to her tiny galley kitchen, washed it, and set it in the drying rack. Then she switched on the radio and tuned it to KDAZ. Sweet William Bly's voice filled the room, rich and smooth and cheery as he introduced a quartet of musicians from Philadelphia. She listened to a few blues songs she rather liked, but on such a dreary day, their melancholy lyrics made her feel grumpy. Searching for something more upbeat, she turned to another station.

She curled up on the sofa in her living room and leafed through the latest edition of *Theatre Magazine.* But she couldn't stop thinking about her conversation with Kitty Taylor yesterday after Jim Jenkins's funeral. Somebody must know the name of his mystery woman—secrets didn't stay secret for long in this town. She made a mental note to ask Sweet William.

Next, her thoughts drifted back to the two Mississippi musicians she met at the Blue Lagoon two nights before Jenkins died. The words of her record store owner friend Frankie Woods came to mind, too: JJ "stepped on some toes."

Lizzie laid the magazine aside and picked up the telephone's handset. She dialed Sidney's number and waited while it rang three times. After the fourth ring, her friend answered.

"Good morning, Sidney Somerset here," he said.

"It's a miserable morning, Sid, in case you haven't noticed."

"I guess that depends on what you're doing, or want to do."

"What are you doing?"

"I was working on my opera, but now that you've interrupted me, what's on your mind, Bearcat?"

"Do you still have that contract Jim Jenkins gave you to review when we were planning to make a record with him? Before he died?"

"Yes."

"Have you read it?"

"No. I filed it away after his death," Sidney said. "It didn't seem relevant anymore. I don't even know why I kept it."

"I'd like to take a look at it."

"Why?"

"Just curious to see what's in these things. I've never signed a contract or read one, either for that matter. If we get an offer from another recording company, I'd like to have something to compare it to. I don't want to go into a deal totally naive."

After a long pause, Sidney asked, "When?"

"When it's convenient for you. Sorry, I disturbed your creative process."

"Well, since you have, you may as well come over. The Muse has decided to take a lunch break."

"Give me half an hour to dress and catch a cab."

* * *

In the bad weather, it took longer than she'd expected to snag a taxi, and the driver seemed annoyed that his fare only wanted a ride across the Village. On a more salubrious day, Lizzie could've walked to Sidney's apartment in less time. She tipped the cabbie more than she should have, considering his surly manner, then dashed through the rain into the building on the north side of Washington Square, where Sidney lived in an apartment on the top floor. She knocked twice, and after a few moments, he opened the door.

"I can't offer much in the way of lunch, just some cold chicken," Sidney apologized. "I can make deviled eggs and stuffed celery. Will that do? I don't feel like going out in this deluge."

Lizzie shrugged out of her rubber raincoat and hung it on a coat tree near the front door.

"Whatever you have is fine. I didn't expect you to make lunch for me."

"Coffee?"

"Yes, please."

While Sidney brewed the coffee and prepared their meal, Lizzie flipped through his collection of records. She found one of Louis Armstrong's Hot Five that featured the Louisiana trombonist Kid Ory and put it on the gramophone. Although she'd never heard Kid play in person, she liked listening to the man people said was the first Negro musician to perform live on American radio. Standing at the window overlooking Washington Square, she let his music carry her away. She was still swaying to the rhythm of New Orleans jazz when Sid said, "Lunch is served."

She joined him at a cherrywood table that could seat eight, although she'd never known her longtime friend to host a dinner party. The Troubadours sometimes ate take-out Chinese here after practicing, and on occasion, Sid invited a couple friends to his home to share a meal. But usually, whether for business or pleasure, he met with people at local restaurants. Lizzie generally did the same, mostly because her tiny apartment couldn't accommodate more than a few people, and her culinary skills were minimal. Sidney's apartment, however, was spacious and stylishly appointed, with high ceilings, tall windows, and paintings by up-and-coming artists hanging on the walls. A baby grand piano occupied pride of place at one end of the living room.

"Thanks, Sid," Lizzie said as she cut into a slice of cold chicken breast.

Sidney ate a few bites of his lunch and sipped his coffee, watching her eat. After a couple minutes, he asked, "So what's the sudden interest in contracts?"

"As I said earlier, I want to familiarize myself with how such things are done. You'll find us another company to make our record, won't you?"

"Working on it," he answered. "Sure, there's not something more to this?"

"Like what?" Lizzie crunched a stalk of celery stuffed with cream cheese, pimentos, and chives.

"You're not sticking your pretty nose into the investigation of Jim Jenkins's death, are you?"

"I only want to learn as much as I can, to protect us from getting swindled."

Sidney let out an exasperated sigh. "Lizzie, every time you involve yourself in a problem like this, it ends up a disaster. You've almost gotten killed a couple times because you poked around where you shouldn't. Haven't you learned your lesson by now?"

"I'm only interested in the business aspects of making a record," Lizzie lied. She hadn't told him about her meeting at The Place with Detective Perry or her conversation with Kitty Taylor. "It's well known that people in the music industry don't always play fair. We need to stay sharp. Oh, and by the way, have you looked into joining ASCAP yet?"

"No, but I will this week," he promised, then consumed a deviled egg in two bites.

"Remember those two Mississippi musicians we met at the Blue Lagoon who said Jenkins cheated them?"

"How could I forget the Dixie duo?"

Lizzie ignored his sarcasm. "I don't know if their accusations have any merit. I just don't want to leave ourselves open to con artists."

"Nor do I."

"Which is why we should familiarize ourselves with contracts and the legal side of this business."

After they finished eating, Sidney cleared away their plates and refilled their coffee cups. He dug around in his files until he found the contract Jim Jenkins had offered The Troubadours on behalf of Jupiter Records shortly before his death. He passed it to Lizzie, but she pushed the papers back.

"Would you please read it aloud, so we can assess it together?"

Sidney read the stilted, legal wording that described the entities involved and their powers, as well as the responsibilities of both parties in producing, promoting, and distributing the work. The contract stipulated the timeframe during which the record would be completed and made available for sale. It stated how much and when royalties would be paid to the performers. It forbade the musicians from entering into agreements that Jupiter considered competitive or that might undercut sales.

"'Should The Troubadours fail to fulfill any part of this agreement, engage in any behavior that might compromise the interests of Jupiter Records, or in the event of one or more of the musicians' deaths, all rights will revert to Jupiter Records. Any monies due will also be retained by Jupiter Records.'"

"Wow. That's a pretty sweeping claim, JJ staked," Lizzie said. "What might be considered failure to fulfill the agreement? What sort of behavior might compromise the interests of Jupiter Records? Leaves a lot open to interpretation, wouldn't you say?"

"And how," Sidney said as he fit a cigarette into his silver holder. "Good thing we didn't sign on with him."

Frowning, she twisted an earring as if trying to get a better signal from a radio antenna. Did the contract signed by the men from Mississippi contain this clause? And if so, had Jenkins withheld payments due to some real or fabricated charge against them? She thought about all the naive, idealistic musicians who longed to share their songs with the world. Who lacked the knowledge or legal expertise to understand what Jupiter Records proposed. How many had entered into agreements such as this one that gave Jenkins rights to their music and earnings in perpetuity?

Lizzie stood up and began pacing back and forth across the room, as she often did when she needed to think something through. "He could've trumped up any reason to avoid paying us. Once he got the rights to our music, he could do whatever he liked with it and reap all the profits."

"That's how it looks to me, too, Bearcat."

"And if one of us died, he'd be the beneficiary."

She crossed to a Palladian window, where she watched pedestrians huddled under umbrellas hurry across Washington Square. Had Jenkins swindled musicians, including the two Mississippi men who called themselves the Delta Jazz Boys? Or the man who'd confronted JJ at his birthday party and accused him of improprieties toward a female singer named Marie? Were there others? Had one of them taken revenge on Jim Jenkins?

Then another thought sneaked in through a side door of her mind and switched on a light. Victor Fosse, KDAZ's manager, hadn't been invited to JJ's birthday party at the posh Upper East Side home of Malcolm MacGregor. What caused the bad blood between Fosse and Jenkins, who'd been colleagues for years?

Sidney offered more coffee, but Lizzie refused. "I should be on my way and let you go back to your opera. Thanks for lunch. Sorry, I interrupted you."

He waved off her apology. "You're right. We do need to get up to speed on the contractual issues if we're going to make a record."

"I think we should hire a lawyer too," she suggested.

"Agreed. I'll look into it."

Lizzie hugged him quickly, then pulled on her rain slicker. "Things were easier when we just sang for our supper in nightclubs."

"And how. I'm starting to miss those good old days."

Chapter Eighteen

"What we play is life."

—Louis Armstrong

Daisy Halley set down her guitar and clarinet cases on the polished wood floor of Sidney's apartment. Her older brother Bert stood beside her, holding his own instrument cases. The girl scanned the spacious living room that housed a Steinway piano, sophisticated Biedermeier furniture, and plenty of good art. Golden sunlight beamed through tall windows that overlooked Washington Square.

Sidney crossed the room to welcome the tall, gawky seventeen-year-old. "Thanks for coming. Bert says good things about you."

Daisy nodded shyly, then looked at her brother.

"It's all true," Bert said. "Daisy's got real talent. She just hasn't had a chance to show it off yet."

Lizzie emerged from Sidney's kitchen, where she'd set the coffee percolator to brew. "That's why we invited you here today, Daisy," she said. "Now that Melody's married and moving to Connecticut, we've thought about adding another female entertainer to the group. Sid and I are eager to hear you play."

"Thank you, ma'am," Daisy said. The girl shifted her weight from one foot to the other, just as her brother did when he felt nervous.

"Please don't call me ma'am, it makes me feel old. My name's Lizzie."

"Okay."

"Do you have a favorite song you'd like to play?" Sidney asked.

"How 'bout 'Riverside Blues'?" Bert suggested, and his sister nodded.

With Bert on saxophone and Daisy on clarinet, the two young musicians belted out a lively rendition of King Oliver's popular Dixieland jazz tune. When they finished, Lizzie and Sidney clapped enthusiastically, and both siblings blushed.

"That was swell," Lizzie said. "Bert was right about you, Daisy."

"Thank you, ma'am, uh, Lizzie."

Lizzie got up to pour herself a cup of coffee. "Anybody else want a java jolt?"

"I do," Sidney said.

Bert and Daisy shook their heads.

"Want to play another song?" Sidney asked.

"Sure," Bert answered. "Let's try 'Sweet Georgia Brown.' Daisy does a darb job with her guitar on that one. I'll play clarinet."

Again, the duo gave an impressive performance. Having played together for so many years, they knew exactly what to expect from one another. Like her brother, Daisy overcame her shyness, and her plain face lit up when she lost herself in the music. *She'll never be pretty, but with a little makeup and a decent haircut, she'll look pleasing enough,* Lizzie thought as she sipped her coffee.

After a couple more songs, Lizzie asked Daisy, "Can you sing?"

"Not very well."

"Never mind, we've already got the best vocalist in the Big Apple," Sidney said. He glanced at his watch. "Thanks again for coming today, Daisy. Bert, I'll be in touch soon."

"Okay," Bert said as he nestled his clarinet and saxophone into their cases.

"Now off with you both," Lizzie said. "Sid and I have things to discuss."

After the Halleys left, she asked, "What do you think about having her practice with us? See how she fits in? You've got to admit she's good."

"Yeah, but she's seventeen. We can't risk taking her to any of the speakeasies. Most of the private parties we play at are out too. Booze, bad company." He shook his head. "No out-of-state stints or overnight jobs either."

"Hmm, good point," Lizzie said, remembering how she'd spent months convincing Melody's parents to allow her to join The Troubadours when she was the same age as Daisy. But Melody didn't start traveling with the group until two years later. Lizzie finished her coffee and set the cup down on a bird's-eye maple end table. "Maybe Bert qualifies as a chaperone."

Sidney shook his head. "No can do, Bearcat. I don't fancy getting charged with corrupting a minor. And you don't need to play wet nurse to a girl with a dead father and a loopy mother."

"You're right." *Daisy Halley would be more trouble than she's worth.* "What I'd really like is to add another horn. Bert's swell, but wouldn't it be the bee's knees if he played sax and we had another fella on trumpet? Like Coleman Hawkins and Louis Armstrong?" Lizzie asked, recalling nights when she'd heard Fletcher Henderson's orchestra perform at the famous Roseland Ballroom.

Roseland was unparalleled with its gaudy Art Deco ballroom, dance marathons, and taxi dancers. Where Negro and white musicians and music lovers of all persuasions mingled, putting aside their differences temporarily to share their love of jazz. Where racial barriers were broken, artistic borders were broadened, and history was made every night.

"Next, you'll want a drummer."

"And a bass player," she said, imagining herself singing to a thousand dancers, accompanied by a half-dozen musicians.

"We're not ready for that." He lit a cigarette and puffed on it pensively. "Are you hoping to play Roseland?"

"Ab-so-lute-ly. We have to think big, Sid. Unless we believe in ourselves, no one else will."

The telephone rang, and he excused himself to answer it. After a brief conversation, he hung up and grinned at Lizzie. "Your big dreams may be about to come true. That was Malcolm MacGregor."

"The guy who threw the birthday party for Jenkins?"

"The same. He wants us to play at a shindig on his yacht next weekend."

"How exciting! I've never been on a yacht."

"Me either," Sidney said. "I'm going to meet with him tomorrow to negotiate the deal."

"Charge him a bundle. A man who owns a yacht should be able to shell out a lot of clams."

* * *

Lizzie walked back to her apartment, fantasizing about performing on Malcolm MacGregor's yacht. Would they sail out into the open ocean or motor sedately down the Hudson? She envisioned herself entertaining a party of celebrities and industry tycoons–the city's biggest and brightest stars—captivating them with her sultry voice, pretty face, and sensuous figure. For a moment, she even let her imagination conjure up visions of Hollywood.

Jim Jenkins's birthday bash had brought a stroke of good luck for The Troubadours, even though it marked the end of the line for the owner of Jupiter Records. Not for the first time, Lizzie wondered about the association between MacGregor and Jenkins. Obviously, they shared an interest in music. But that didn't explain why someone with MacGregor's wealth and status, a member of New York's elite who had investments in South African gold and diamond mines, would socialize with a mere record producer from Queens.

That question raised another. Had a guest at JJ's party played a role in his death? According to Detective Perry, a person who ingested a significant amount of mercury bichloride would likely die within a day or so, maybe sooner. If someone wanted to kill Jenkins, he or she had a perfect opportunity to poison the birthday boy while blending unnoticed into the crowd of revelers. Anyone present that night could have slipped him the drug. *Assuming someone murdered Jenkins*, Lizzie reminded herself.

Kitty Taylor seemed convinced that Edith Jenkins had killed her unfaithful husband, but Lizzie wasn't so sure. True, the spouse was often the prime suspect. However, Frankie Woods's words echoed in a corner of Lizzie's mind: Jim Jenkins "stepped on some toes." Were those toes dancing at Malcolm MacGregor's Upper East Side townhouse the night before JJ died? If so, what motive did their owner have for wanting the record producer dead?

Chapter Nineteen

"The sudden disappointment of a hope leaves a scar which the ultimate fulfillment of that hope never entirely removes."

—Thomas Hardy

Thursday afternoon, Lizzie took the El to Brooklyn, where KDAZ Radio broadcasted from a nondescript brick building on a quiet side street. After saying hello to the receptionist and signing the guest register, she made her way down a long hallway to the studio. A red light shone above the door, signaling the station was live. For several minutes, she waited outside until the light snapped off, before entering the "inner sanctum" as manager Victor Fosse called it.

In a soundproof booth with a thick plate-glass window, a serious young man named Reggie fed records to a phonograph. On the other side of the studio, a tall, thin, dark-skinned man wearing a tan linen suit disassembled a microphone and carefully laid out its components on a wooden table. His black hair had been straightened, parted on the side, and slicked into place with pomade so that it glistened like patent leather in the studio's bright lights. In addition to hosting live shows and scouting promising new talent, Sweet William Bly kept KDAZ's equipment in good order.

When he saw Lizzie, he grinned and waved her in. "Hey, Miz Lizzie. You just missed Victor. He's gone to lunch."

"Actually, I came to see you, William," Lizzie said.

"Woo-ee, what's William done to get a visit from the hottest white lady singer in the Big Apple?" he asked, his voice as slow and rich as molasses.

Lizzie laughed. "Nothing yet, but I hope you can do something for me."

"Try me."

"Have you eaten lunch?"

He shook his head. "Not yet, I'll get something when Victor comes back."

"Let's order take-out from the deli around the corner. My treat."

"You making the big bucks these days, lady?"

"About to. We're playing on an honest-to-goodness yacht next weekend for a filthy rich guy named Malcolm MacGregor. I hear he's got money in South African gold and diamond mines."

William fingered his blue silk tie. "Hmm, would that be the same fella who threw a party for Jim Jenkins a couple weeks ago?"

"Bingo. That's one of the things I want to talk to you about," Lizzie said. "But let's eat first. I'm famished."

Fifteen minutes later, they sat down to thick ham-and-Swiss sandwiches on rye with dill pickles and potato chips. The sounds of Jabbo Smith's lively trumpet filled the studio. Although the Georgia-born musician had recently moved to New York, Lizzie hadn't heard him play in person yet, and she made a mental note to rectify that oversight as soon as possible.

Between bites of his sandwich, Sweet William said, "I hear Jenkins be eating dirt these days. Weren't you supposed to make a record with him?"

"That's gone bust, now that he's dead." Lizzie waved her hand dismissively. "What do you know about the birthday celebration MacGregor hosted for him?"

"Not much. I didn't get invited to no rich white man's party."

"Neither did Victor. I find that odd, considering he and Jenkins were friends and colleagues in the music scene for years."

William bit into a dill pickle and chewed thoughtfully for a few moments before answering. "Guess you could say they had them a falling out."

"Victor and Jenkins? What happened?"

Again, he took his time answering. He glanced around the studio as if checking to make sure no one else could hear him, although the only other person in sight was the young man spinning discs in his soundproof booth.

Lowering his voice almost to a whisper, William said, "It's like this. Victor wanted Jenkins to pay KDAZ for playing Jupiter's records. The way he sees it, we're doing record companies a service, promoting their musicians, giving them airtime. How else are folks gonna know about them? Vic calls it advertising and thinks we ought to get compensated for that."

Lizzie reached for a potato chip. "Go on."

"Victor charges a lot of other companies, too—and KDAZ isn't the only station that does. It's not against the law."

"But I gather Jenkins didn't like it."

"No, siree. They got into a big argument. Victor swore he'd never air another one of Jupiter's records unless Jenkins agreed to pay. Jenkins said 'over my dead body.' Those were his exact words."

"And now JJ's doing the graveyard shimmy," Lizzie said.

William nodded and took a big bite of his sandwich. A thin line of mustard dripped from the corner of his mouth. Lizzie tucked the revelation away in a cubbyhole in her mind and waited until he'd swallowed before raising her next question.

"There's this other bit of gossip making the rounds, too. Did you know Jenkins was cheating on his wife?"

William leaned back in his chair and laughed. "Well, who don't break free from the ball and chain if he gets the chance?"

"Was he seeing any woman in particular?"

"You mean a serious sweetie, not just a piece of goodnight candy?" He shook his head slowly. "Can't say as I ever heard a name."

"Here's the kicker. Jenkins had syphilis. He died from mercury bichloride poisoning."

"Yeah, that's the story on the street. Sure do up the ante."

"Looks to me like there's enough cause for somebody to bump off our man," Lizzie continued. "I can't help wondering if his wife found out about his mistress and bought Jenkins a ticket to the Pearly Gates. Or maybe he gave the pox to his side dish, and she got revenge."

She studied William for a reaction as he mulled over the possibilities, but his face remained expressionless. Perhaps he'd already gone down this road and knew where it ended. Given his reputation for having his finger on the pulse of New York's music scene–the down and dirty as well as the bright and beautiful–Lizzie suspected he knew more than he was telling.

"Think you can find out who JJ's lady friend was and let me know?" she asked.

"I'll give it a shot." He crumpled the brown paper bag in which their sandwiches had been wrapped and tossed it in a wastebasket. "I'm not gonna ask why you're poking around in this mess."

"Thanks. And William, let's keep this between us, okay?"

As Lizzie stood to leave, Victor Fosse burst through the door into the studio.

"Lizzie Crane, why didn't you let me know you were coming?" he asked, a surprised look on his face. He held out both meaty hands to grasp hers. "Tell me you're here to sing a song for our listeners."

Although she hadn't planned on it, she couldn't resist the opportunity to promote herself and The Troubadours. "Ab-so-lute-ly."

"Where are your pals?" Fosse asked, tossing his jacket and straw boater hat on a chair.

"Sorry, I'm on my own today. I was in the neighborhood visiting a friend and decided to stop by on a whim." She flashed him a pretty smile. "I hope that's okay?"

"It's swell. You plan to sing a cappella?"

"Unless you want to accompany me."

"The only thing I can play is a gramophone," Fosse said, then remembered something and snapped his fingers. "Hey, wait a minute. I think we've got a ukulele around here someplace. As I recall, you play the uke, right?"

Lizzie laughed. "I strum it sometimes. I'm not sure that qualifies as 'playing.'"

"Right-o, then." Fosse turned to William and pointed at the microphone that lay in pieces on the table. "I trust you've got another mic that works."

William touched two fingers to his brow in a mock salute. "Comin' right up, boss."

"Good. I'll go locate that uke and let Reggie know there's a change in the program. Now, Lizzie, what do you plan to sing?"

She hadn't played the ukulele in months, but she felt reasonably confident she could manage a simple tune. Nothing like her feisty, fellow New York musician May Singhi Breen, the "Ukulele Lady" who'd brought credibility to the underrated instrument and even had her own radio show. But on the spur of the moment, it would have to do.

"How about Breen's 'Waitin' Around'?" she suggested.

Fosse gave her a thumbs-up. While he went in search of the promised uke, William set up a round condenser microphone mounted on a pole. As he adjusted it to a height that was comfortable for Lizzie, she struggled to calm the butterflies that, even after all these years, still fluttered in her stomach before she performed.

"Here you go," Fosse said, handing her the ukulele. "It's probably out of tune. Been hanging around the storeroom a while."

Lizzie took it from him, blew off a layer of dust, plucked the strings, and handed it back. "Sorry Victor, I'm afraid there's no music left in this instrument. How about I just sing 'The Man I Love'?" She'd sung the Gershwin hit a thousand times, and she knew she could do it justice even without accompaniment.

"Sure, sure. Whatever you think."

Fosse glanced at William, who nodded, cleared his throat, and stepped up to the microphone. "Hello, music fans. Hope you're enjoying a salubrious June 17th in the Big Apple. I'm Sweet William Bly at KDAZ Radio, here to dazzle you with the hottest, the coolest, the all-time best jazz, blues, and more. Right now, we've got a surprise treat for you–Miss Lizzie Crane of New York's own Troubadours is right here in our studio, and she's agreed to favor us with an impromptu song. She's been a guest on KDAZ before, and I know many of you have heard her and her band play around town. So turn up your radios, sit back, and enjoy the dulcet voice of one of the city's most beautiful and talented soloists, Miss Lizzie Crane, singing one of my all-time favorite Gershwin tunes, 'The Man I Love.'"

Lizzie launched into the melody, calling up a vision of Alan Peabody and imagining she was singing to her lover. Although she would have welcomed Sidney's piano backing her up, without accompaniment, her words conveyed a message of longing even more poignant in its simplicity. After two additional songs, she said goodbye to Fosse and Sweet William and waved to Reggie.

"Come back any time," Fosse said, opening the door into the station's lobby for her. "Always a pleasure to have you here."

"Thanks, Victor. Next time I'll bring Sid and Bert with me, so you'll get more bang for your buck. Not that any bucks have ever passed between us."

Lizzie eyed him, curious to see if he caught her insinuation that KDAZ's manager pushed pay-to-play. But Fosse's small, close-set brown eyes and thick lips revealed nothing.

"See ya around," he said as Lizzie exited the station.

Daisy Halley stood outside on the sidewalk, holding her clarinet case. The stiff breeze tousled her chopped brown hair and whipped her calico skirt around her long legs.

"Hi, Daisy," Lizzie called out, surprised to see Bert's sister. "What a coincidence, meeting you here."

"Not really. I just live a few blocks away," the girl reminded her. "When I heard you on the radio, I rushed right over. I thought maybe you'd let me play with you, but the lady at the front desk told me I couldn't go inside."

"Well, you can't just barge into the studio unannounced and expect them to put you on the air."

"If you let me know next time, I can come with you."

A gust of wind lifted Lizzie's hat, and she quickly grabbed it to keep it from blowing away. "Listen, Daisy. I'm sorry, but you can't play with us. At least not yet."

Daisy's jaw dropped in disappointment. "Why not? You said I was good."

"You *are* good. But you're still in school."

"I can drop out of school. I hate it anyway."

"You've only got one more year," Lizzie said, wishing she could've finished high school instead of having to quit after tenth grade to go to work. "It's important that you graduate—you'll have many more opportunities if you do. Yes, you're talented, but it's tough to make a living in the music world. You'd be smart to get an education, so you have something to fall back on."

Lizzie started walking toward the subway stop. Daisy followed her, unwilling to give up.

"School's out for the summer. And when it starts back, I could play on weekends," the girl suggested. "Most of your jobs are on weekends, right?"

"You're only seventeen. A lot of the places we perform won't even let you in."

"I'm not a child," Daisy insisted. As if trying to shock Lizzie, she added, "I'm old enough to sleep with a man if I want to."

"I'm not going to discuss *that* subject with you," Lizzie said, growing tired of the conversation. "Keep practicing, Daisy. Maybe when you're older, we can talk about this again."

"You pretended to be my friend, but you lied!" Daisy stamped her foot, then turned and ran away down the sidewalk, her clarinet case banging against her thigh.

Chapter Twenty

"Those who can make you believe absurdities can make you commit atrocities."

—Voltaire

"No!" Lizzie cried, setting her cup down so hard coffee sloshed over the rim onto the morning newspaper. According to the brief article,

'Last night, police arrested Eve Adams, also known as Eva Zloczower, proprietor of Eve Adams' Teahouse located at 129 MacDougal Street in Greenwich Village, for obscenity and disorderly conduct. Six days ago, officers confiscated lewd material found in Miss Adams' possession, which she is believed to have distributed elsewhere in the city. She is also charged with engaging in improper behavior toward a female police officer. Eve Adams' Teahouse is well known as an establishment that caters to unorthodox types and political dissidents, and is not healthy for teenagers or comfortable for men. Miss Adams, a Jewish immigrant from Poland, is being held in custody until her case comes to trial.'

She wiped up the spilled coffee and read the article again, trying not to imagine Eve in prison—or worse, deported. Then she grabbed the telephone and called Sidney.

He answered on the first ring. "I just finished reading about it."

"It's all because of that horrid Bobby Edwards," Lizzie said, meaning the publisher of the *Greenwich Village Quill* who regularly reported on events held at the teahouse. "Why can't he just stick to singing his silly little ditties and keep his nose out of other people's bedrooms?"

"Nothing's ever as enticing as what goes on in someone else's bedroom, Bearcat. Especially if that someone is enjoying what you'd like to partake of but are too hidebound to actually try."

"What's going to happen to Eve?"

"I guess it depends on who she can get to take her case and how much money she can scare up."

Lizzie looked out her apartment window in the direction of Washington Square, although she couldn't see the tearoom. "I'm going to walk over and try to find out more."

"If you happen to spot any cops skulking about, turn around and walk away as fast as you can," Sidney warned her. "We can't afford to have you get tossed in the hoosegow. Remember, we've got a job tonight."

"Okay-ski."

"Oh, and by the way-ski. Why were you singing on KDAZ yesterday, and without me?"

"I got us some free publicity, didn't I?"

"We could've made more of the opportunity if you'd let me know," he said, a hint of pique tinging his words.

"I'll explain tonight," Lizzie promised.

* * *

A dozen or so women stood in a line on the sidewalk in front of Eve Adams' Teahouse. Some held signs stating their outrage; others wore expressions of dismay and anxiety. Nearby, a group of men taunted them, yelling insults, laughing, and making lewd gestures. Lizzie spotted a woman named Vera, whom she'd met a few times at Eve's, a heavy-set, gray-haired poet who'd been active in the suffragette movement, and made a beeline toward her.

As Lizzie passed the jeering men, one of them pointed her out and shouted, "That one's too pretty to be a lesbo."

She shouted back at him, "And you're ugly enough to put any woman off men."

One of his buddies guffawed and punched him on the arm. Another man whistled at Lizzie. She ignored them and joined the women on the sidewalk.

"Vera, do you know anything beyond what the newspapers reported?" she asked the poet.

"That cop, Margaret Leonard, claims Eve tried to fondle her bosom. I don't believe a word of it. Leonard's trying to make a name for herself." Vera shook her head sadly. "Eve never should've befriended that snake in the grass."

"What will happen to Eve if they find her guilty?"

"They'll probably send her to the workhouse on Welfare Island."

A big-bellied man with tobacco-stained teeth approached the two women. He reached for Lizzie's arm and said, "Dolly, you oughtn't to be wastin' your time with these perverts. What you need is a real man."

She slapped him hard with her handbag. "You couldn't buy nooky in a fifty-cent house if you offered to pay fifty bucks."

The man drew back, startled, and spit a stream of tobacco juice on the sidewalk. Scowling, he retreated into the group of men who hurled teasing insults at him.

Vera laughed. "I'm going to use that line in a poem. It'll be easy to come up with a rhyme."

* * *

On this pleasantly warm evening, Sidney drove north on Broadway with the breezer's top down, enjoying Manhattan's cornucopia of sights, sounds, and smells. Although Lizzie had hoped to spare Bert the embarrassing details connected with Jim Jenkins's death, so many people already knew about the record producer's indiscretions–even women in Auntie Edith's church—that the saxophonist would surely hear about it soon, if he hadn't already. Better to deal with it now, she decided, even if that meant tarnishing the image of the man Bert thought of as an uncle. So, on the way to Jock's, a nightclub at the edge of the Garment District, Lizzie related the story to her young colleague.

"I know this isn't the best time to tell you, Bert, and I hope it won't put you off your game tonight," she began. "I was at KDAZ yesterday. Maybe you heard me sing a few songs?"

"No, sorry, I missed it," Bert said.

"Anyway, while I was there, Sweet William Bly told me something about Jim Jenkins that I thought you should know. JJ had syphilis, which might be why he used mercury bichloride."

Okay, that's not exactly the way it went down, Lizzie admitted to herself, *but it's better than telling him I got the dirt from Detective Perry.*

"Yeah, I know. Mom and Daisy do too. We've known for a while."

"Really? What about his wife?"

"I don't know. I haven't spoken to her about it."

"Do you think it's connected with his, uh, death?" Lizzie almost said "murder," but caught herself just in time.

"Lizzie, can we talk about this another time?" Bert asked.

"Good idea," Sidney interjected. "You still haven't said why you were at KDAZ this afternoon, singing without us."

She answered carefully, trying to be honest without letting Sid and Bert know she'd been snooping around in Jenkins's affairs. "I was visiting a friend, and Victor asked me to sing. I couldn't say no, could I?"

Sidney stopped to let a woman walking her dog cross the street. "You don't have any friends in Brooklyn."

"I have lots of friends, in high places and low," she countered, figuring Sweet William could loosely be considered a friend. "Anyway, guess who was waiting for me when I left the studio?"

From the backseat, Bert answered, "Daisy. She told me you wouldn't let her play with you on the radio."

"She showed up, unannounced, while I was already on the air. I had no idea she was there."

"She said you also told her she can't play with The Troubadours."

Lizzie noticed an uncharacteristic hint of accusation in his voice. Bert rarely expressed displeasure at anything. Rather, he accepted life's ups and downs with the stoicism of someone who's seen hard times and is grateful for the small comforts that other people take for granted. She let out an exasperated sigh. She loathed being caught in the middle between her two colleagues, but she agreed with Sid that they'd be foolish to admit the girl into their group.

"Daisy's too young to play in the places we perform," Lizzie explained. "We can't take the risk."

"It would be bad enough if we got busted in a raid, but if we got a minor involved, the cops would savage us," Sidney added.

"She was really disappointed," Bert said.

Sidney turned into a narrow alleyway and parked in an unpaved lot behind a brick warehouse. A mixed bag of businesses occupied the building's first floor, among them Jock's nightclub. People who wanted to enter the speakeasy had to knock on a door that opened onto the alley, then whisper a password through a hole in the door in order to be admitted. Tonight's code was "I've come to see the dancing bear."

Sid got out of the Buick and motioned for Bert to help him pull up the car's ragtop and fasten it in place. "Look, Bert. I'm sorry your sister got her feelings hurt, but if she wants to be in the music biz, she'd better get used to disappointment. It comes with the territory." He reached into the backseat and grabbed one of Bert's instrument cases. "You're only as good as your last performance. No matter how much talent you've got, there's always somebody better."

Chapter Twenty-One

"A man cannot be too careful in his choice of enemies."

—Oscar Wilde

The ornate Victorian elevator bumped to a stop in the lobby of Lizzie's apartment building. The metal door creaked as she opened it and stepped out onto the black-and-white tile floor. From behind a scuffed oak desk, the building's janitor—who referred to himself as the superintendent—looked up from his newspaper and called out to Lizzie. The gray tiger tomcat who kept the building's rodents under control dozed on the desktop.

"Top o' the mornin', miss. Got a letter here for ya."

"Good morning," she said, taking the envelope he proffered.

Instead of an address and postage stamp, it bore only her name configured in mismatched letters cut from a magazine: **Miss** L. Crane. *How odd,* she thought as she tore open the envelope and withdrew a single sheet of folded paper. Like the address, the sender's message was conveyed in magazine letters: STOP **nosing** *around* in his Death.

"Who gave this to you?"

"Didn't see 'im, miss," the janitor said, stroking the cat. "I stepped out for a minute, an' when I come back it was lyin' here on the desk."

Lizzie tucked the letter in her purse and handed the man a coin. "If any more of these letters show up, try to get a good look at the guy who delivers them, will you?"

"Yes, miss."

At first, the letter piqued her curiosity—who would take the trouble to cut out all those words from a magazine when he could simply write down what he wanted to say? The more she thought about it, though, the more the idea worried her. Obviously, whoever sent the message meant to remain anonymous. But that person knew who Lizzie was and where she lived.

She walked east on Bleecker Street, then turned north on MacDougal toward Eve's Hangout. Today, no protesting women or jeering men gathered in front of the controversial teahouse. A "Closed" sign hung on its door. *If Eve went to prison, would her partner, Ruth Norlander, be forced to close the place?* Lizzie wondered. Both possibilities made her want to cry, and she forced them out of her mind for the time being.

She bought a cannoli from an Italian bakery and sat on a park bench in Washington Square to eat the sweet, ricotta-filled pastry. When a squirrel approached, begging to share her treat, she broke off a bit of flaky crust and tossed it to him. She pulled the letter from her purse, staring again at the pieced-together message as she tried to determine who might have delivered it. *Who knows I'm trying to figure out what happened to Jim Jenkins?*

Mentally, she began compiling a list of people she'd talked to recently about the dead man. Sweet William Bly yesterday, which meant by now half of New York's music scene probably knew she'd asked about JJ's secret lady friend. KDAZ's manager, Victor Fosse. The music store owner Frankie Woods, who told her Jenkins had enemies but refused to name names. Kitty Taylor, who'd known the deceased record producer for years and used to play music with him. Lizzie couldn't recall if she'd broached the subject with the restaurateur Rory Moynihan. Was there anyone else?

As she ticked off the names, she couldn't imagine any of them leaving the cryptic letter warning her to stop snooping into Jenkins's death. But she had no idea who they might have talked to. Maybe even the person who killed him.

If somebody killed him, Lizzie reminded herself. The police had yet to establish whether JJ's death was an accident or murder. She folded the letter and slipped it back into her purse, uncertain if she should take the warning seriously. She considered showing it to Detective Perry. However, the policeman would likely agree with the letter's author and insist that she quit nosing around in the case. Washing her hands of the whole business made sense, she had to admit. Except Jim Jenkins played an important role in Bert's life, and the man's death had clearly affected the Halley family. Lizzie's heart went out to her young friend who'd lost both his father and his surrogate uncle, and whose mother seemed as fragile and vulnerable as a bird with a broken wing.

She stood and brushed cannoli crumbs from her frock. Despite a thick cloud cover, the day was warm and pleasant. Tucking her purse under her arm, she decided to peruse the shops to see if she could find a smashing dress for Malcolm MacGregor's party Friday night. She couldn't imagine donning a sailor outfit, but what other attire did the yachting set wear?

As she passed under the park's arch, she had a prickly feeling that someone was watching her. Accustomed to men's stares, Lizzie looked around but saw no one ogling her. An elderly couple strolled by, arm in arm. A young mother watched two little girls playing hopscotch. A boy in short pants tossed a balsa wood airplane into the wind. None of them seemed the least bit interested in Lizzie Crane.

For the next hour, she poked about in store after store without finding anything that caught her fancy. Finally, she chose two pairs of silk stockings, then remembered her intention to buy a garter flask. When she asked a shopkeeper where she might acquire one, the woman reached into a cabinet underneath the lingerie counter and pulled out a circle of lace with a satin pocket sewn on it that held a small silver flask.

"Perfect," Lizzie said. "I'll take it."

Chapter Twenty-Two

"We can never know when they are upon us; we can never be sure they are at a safe distance."

—Aristotle

Lizzie dashed down the stairs from Penn Station's concourse to the tracks below and waited on the platform as Alan's train pulled in. Travelers emerged from the passenger cars into the afternoon sunlight that filtered through arched skylights overhead.

Alan stepped down from the first-class car, settling his fedora on his flame-red hair, and searched for her in the crowd. Ordinarily, Lizzie would have run along the platform and thrown herself into his arms. Today, however, she held back, watching him. Willing him to come to her. She admired his fluid stride, his impeccably tailored suit, the air of confidence he exuded that caused women and men alike to notice him as he made his way through the crowd. After a few moments, he sensed her eyes on him and met her gaze.

While he was still a car-length away, Lizzie removed her sweater, baring her arms. He smiled and took a dozen steps in her direction. As he drew closer, she undid the top button of her blouse, then the second one. When he was only a few feet away, he stopped, letting his eyes slide leisurely from her lips to her ankles, and back up again. Then he pulled her to him and kissed her longer than might be considered proper in a public place.

* * *

An hour later, Alan sat up and swung his long legs over the side of Lizzie's bed. He stood and crossed the tiny bedroom to the adjoining bath. As she lay there admiring his backside, he suddenly toppled forward, hitting his knee on the tile floor and slamming his cheek against the tub. Lizzie heard his cry of surprise, followed by several words he'd never uttered before in her presence. She jumped out of bed and rushed toward the bathroom.

"Stop," he ordered, holding up his hand. "Don't come in. Bend down and check the doorway."

Puzzled, Lizzie knelt and ran her fingers along the door jam. About six inches above the floor, she discovered a nail hammered into the wooden frame. A piece of filament attached to it was stretched tight across the opening and nailed into the other side of the doorway. It looked like a length of fishing line.

"What's this?"

Alan touched his injured cheek and found a cut about an inch long there. "It seems someone booby-trapped the doorway."

"But why?"

"Good question."

Cautiously, she stepped over the thin, almost invisible barrier. "You're hurt."

"Yes, damn it. Not seriously, though, I hope." He examined his kneecap, fingering it gently and prodding the area around it. "Help me stand, will you?"

Lizzie gripped the sink with her right hand for support, then crooked her left arm for him to grasp. He took it and slowly pulled himself up. Tentatively, he put his weight on his injured leg and winced.

"Should we go to the hospital?" Lizzie asked.

"No, that won't be necessary. I don't think anything's broken. It just hurts like hell." He leaned against the sink, studying his reflection in the mirror. Blood trickled from the cut on his cheek.

"Do you think you should get stitches?"

He dabbed at the cut with a Kleenex. "No, but I need a bandage."

Lizzie reached around him into the medicine cabinet, grabbed a box of Band-Aids, and pasted one on Alan's cheek.

"Do you have some scissors?"

She pulled a manicure set from a drawer in the sink cabinet and withdrew the fingernail clippers.

"Cut that blasted cord, so neither of us trips on it again," he told her. "But don't remove the nails. The police should see this."

She snipped the fishing line, tied it in a knot, and hooked it on one of the nails. Then she helped Alan hobble back to her bed. Gently, she lifted his banged leg onto the mattress. She slid a pillow under his knee and plumped a couple others behind him, so he could lean against the headboard comfortably.

Frowning, she asked, "Are you sure you don't need a doctor?"

"I'm sure."

"I'll get some ice to keep the swelling down."

Lizzie chipped two chunks from the block in her icebox and wrapped each one in a linen napkin. Next, she poured Lagavulin into two glasses, set them on a tray, and brought everything back to her bedroom.

"Hold one piece of ice on your cheek and the other one on your knee," she said.

"How am I supposed to drink my scotch?"

"I'll serve you."

"Why don't you see to my knee, and I'll see to my drink?"

"Deal," she agreed.

They sat together on her bed, sipping scotch and holding cold compresses on Alan's wounds, while worrisome questions swirled in Lizzie's mind. Who strung the fishing line across her bathroom doorway? Why would anyone do such a thing?

As the reality of the situation sank in, a sickening dread lodged in her stomach. *Someone broke into my apartment. Someone is trying to hurt me.* Fear gripped her first, followed by anger, and finally guilt that Alan had been injured in her stead.

"I need to report this to Detective Perry," she said. "I'm going to call Sid too and cancel tonight's performance."

"Don't do that. I know how much you want to play at this yacht party. Besides, if you cancel at the last minute, MacGregor might spread the word that you're unreliable and damage the reputation you've worked so hard to build."

Trying not to reveal how rattled she was, Lizzie said, "You're right."

"Do you have any idea who might have done this?"

"Not a clue."

"Does anyone else have a key to your apartment?"

"Only Sid and the building's superintendent."

Alan set down the ice he'd been holding against his cheek. Already, an ugly bruise had started spreading beneath his eye. "Why don't you wait to call your Detective Perry until first thing in the morning. There's probably not much he can do here tonight that he can't do just as well tomorrow. We'll both talk to him then."

Remembering the cryptic message somebody left for her earlier today, warning her to stop snooping into Jim Jenkins's death, Lizzie pulled the envelope from her purse and handed it to Alan. "Someone dropped this off for me this afternoon. The super said he didn't see the guy who left it."

He read the letter, a puzzled expression on his face. "Who might be threatening you?"

"Haven't the foggiest. But I can't help wondering if it's the same person who booby-trapped the bathroom door. I'll give the letter to Detective Perry when we see him tomorrow."

Alan took a sip of his drink, then asked, "Are you afraid to stay in your apartment now? We can go to a hotel if you prefer."

"Not as long as you're here with me."

He gestured at his injured knee. "Some protector I'd be. Look what happened to me."

"You prevented me from tripping on that fishing line and getting hurt," she reminded him.

Alan held the ice to his cheek again. "I suppose you could say that. What a shame it would be if you'd cut your pretty face. I can tell people I got this injury in a duel—it'll add a bit of mystique to my character, don't you think?"

She knew Alan worried even more than she did about her safety, but she appreciated that he hadn't tried to dissuade her from performing tonight–she didn't want to get on the wrong side of Malcolm MacGregor. Still, she couldn't quell the fear that set every fiber of her body on edge and made her tremble with trepidation. *Someone broke into my apartment and invaded my private space. Someone meant to hurt me.*

"I'm sorry, Lizzie, but it looks like I'm going to have to miss the party," he said. "I was looking forward to it too. But you won't want to show up with an escort who looks like he's just gone a few rounds in the ring with Jack Dempsey."

"I don't like leaving you here alone. Are you sure you're okay?"

"Obviously, I'm not okay. But I'm not seriously damaged, and I don't want to spoil your big event. So go, sing well, and try to put this out of your mind for the rest of the evening."

"What will you do while I'm gone?"

"Run up your telephone bill making long-distance calls to clients in California. It's only three o'clock there. I'll be hard at work while you play."

"All right," she said. "Why don't I fetch some supper for you before I leave, since you won't be eating whatever delicacies MacGregor offers up tonight on his yacht? There's an Italian restaurant around the corner that makes delicious lasagna. I'm friendly with the owners. Will that be okay?"

"Perfect. But first, how about another splash of that brown plaid?"

Lizzie topped off his drink, then examined the front door to her apartment on her way out. From what she could ascertain, no forced entry had occurred. No telltale marks scarred the door or its frame, and the lock didn't appear to be damaged. *Either the intruder knew how to pick a lock or had a key.*

When she returned twenty minutes later carrying a container brimming with meat, cheese, pasta, and spicy tomato sauce, Alan was sitting on the sofa wearing only a pair of blue silk boxer shorts, his foot propped up on the coffee table. He held her telephone receiver to his ear. Lizzie spooned lasagna onto a plate and set it on the dropleaf table beside the window. Then she opened a bottle of Chianti, carried it and a glass to the table, and headed for the bathroom.

Alan interrupted his conversation and covered the phone's mouthpiece with his hand. "Don't bathe," he told her. "I want you to wear my scent to the party, just in case any other fellas come sniffing around."

Lizzie laughed. "Marking your territory?"

"You bet."

She threw him a kiss, then went into the bedroom to change clothes. She opened her jewelry chest and took inventory of its contents. Nothing was missing. And the Edward Hopper painting—the most precious thing she owned—still hung above the living room sofa. Evidently, the intruder wasn't a thief, but that knowledge gave her little comfort. She could understand a burglar breaking in to steal her valuables–burglars were as common as rats in the Village. Why someone wanted to hurt her made no sense. *If some crazy guy is trying to scare me, he succeeded.*

Lizzie washed her face, applied fresh makeup, and brushed her coffee-colored hair. Knowing a stranger had entered her home made her skin crawl. What other nasty surprises might be in store for her? Cautiously, she opened her walnut wardrobe, half-expecting to see a snake curled at the bottom. She withdrew an aqua gown with a V-neck, a bodice studded with hundreds of tiny rhinestones in a chevron pattern, and a beaded fringed skirt that barely covered her knees. After slipping into it, she rolled up her stockings, then shook out her *peau de soie* pumps–just in case scorpions hid inside—before putting them on.

As she fastened an aquamarine choker around her neck, she heard a knock on the apartment door. She went to open it, then reconsidered and called out, "Who is it?"

"It's Sid. If you're expecting Rudolph Valentino, you'll be seriously disappointed. Open up."

Lizzie unlocked the door and let her friend in. Alan had managed to limp to the table, pour himself a glass of Chianti, and was just about to dig into the lasagna. Painfully, he stood and extended his hand to Sidney.

"What happened to you, old man?" Sidney asked.

"I fell in the bathroom."

Sid shook his head and tsk-tsked. "Alan, you should know better than to make whoopee in the shower. It's too dangerous. All that slippery soap—"

"Someone broke into my apartment," Lizzie interrupted. As succinctly as possible, she explained the situation. "I can't imagine who did this or how the guy got in. Only you and the janitor have keys to my flat."

"You're not fingering me for the job, are you?"

"Don't be a dumb Dora, of course not. Let's just shelve it for the time being, okay? I don't want this to put a crimp in our evening. We'll get it all sorted out in the morning."

Sidney frowned, but didn't push the issue. "Whatever you say, Bearcat."

Lizzie kissed Alan, reluctant to leave him. Then she grabbed a silk shawl and tucked her purse under her arm. "I'll probably be late. No need to wait up."

"Sorry you're not coming with us, Alan. It's going to be a doozy of a party," Sidney said in a forced casual tone, although Lizzie sensed his underlying concern that matched her own.

"Don't rub it in," Alan grumbled. "Have fun and be careful."

Chapter Twenty-Three

"How fine you look dressed in rage."

—*Lewis Carroll, Alice's Adventures in Wonderland*

Docked on the Hudson River, Malcolm MacGregor's yacht glowed like polished ivory. Portholes ringed the bottom deck, which Lizzie presumed held the sleeping cabins. Teak siding and casement windows enclosed most of the mid-level, except for the pointed bow and an open area outfitted with wicker furniture at the stern. The wheelhouse perched on top. Behind it stretched a long, uncovered deck where passengers could dance, drink, and gaze at the stars. To her mind, the yacht lacked the grace of the sailing ships she'd seen in Massachusetts last year, but it was certainly impressive.

A young man with a barrel chest, broad shoulders, and muscular arms that strained the shirt of his white sailor uniform stood on the dock, ready to greet arrivals or turn away gatecrashers. When The Troubadours approached, he touched his hand to his cap. Sidney showed him a business card and introduced the trio.

The man waved them toward the yacht. "Welcome aboard."

"Pretty ritzy," Lizzie said as they climbed the gangplank.

"What did you expect?" Sid asked.

"Nothing less."

Another young man dressed in sailor's garb met them at the boat's entrance gate. Again, Sidney introduced the musicians.

"Take those stairs," the man said and opened the gate. "I believe you'll find Mr. MacGregor topside."

The deck stretched some thirty feet long and twenty feet wide, surrounded by metal railings that Lizzie assumed were meant to keep tipsy passengers from falling overboard. Built-in banquettes ran along both sides of the deck. A handsome teak bar situated behind the wheelhouse displayed a distinguished array of bottles. At the stern sat an upright piano lacquered bright red.

Malcolm MacGregor lounged on a stool at the bar, chatting with a thin, swarthy bartender who might have been Italian or Spanish or Greek. Instead of evening attire, their host wore a captain's navy-blue uniform with a double row of brass buttons down the front and gold stripes on the sleeves. A jaunty white cap adorned with a military-looking shield perched on his head of thick, graying hair. *Did he really serve in the Navy, or is his get-up just for show?* Lizzie wondered. Beside him stood the pretty, fashionably thin blonde who'd accompanied him at the birthday bash he threw for Jim Jenkins three weeks ago, the night before the record producer died. Both of them held martinis.

MacGregor waved the musicians over. "Top o' the evening," he said, raising his glass in greeting. "Welcome to the *Highland Lassie.*"

"Thank you, Mr. MacGregor," Sidney said. "We're happy to have this opportunity to entertain you and your guests on this beautiful sailing vessel on this beautiful evening. You remember my colleagues, Elizabeth Crane and Bert Halley?"

MacGregor eyed Lizzie as if she were a piece of cake on a dessert tray. "How could I forget?"

"Ahoy, Captain," she said, wishing she'd worn something a bit less revealing.

Bert hung back a few steps behind the others, shifting his weight nervously from foot to foot. He smiled awkwardly, but didn't speak.

The blonde elbowed MacGregor, who took the hint and introduced her perfunctorily. "This is Nadine. Now, how about one of these dirties?" he asked, tapping his glass.

"I'm in," Sid answered.

"Me too," Lizzie agreed.

Bert simply nodded.

The bartender poured a generous amount of gin and a small splash of vermouth over ice in a silver shaker. He rattled it vigorously a few times, as if playing maracas, then filled three crystal glasses. After serving the musicians, he topped off his boss's and Nadine's drinks.

"Here's to a *braw eenin*," MacGregor said, raising his martini.

Uncertain what she was toasting, Lizzie followed suit. "Cheers."

For several minutes, they discussed the fine weather, the quality of the gin, and the tunes The Troubadours planned to play tonight. Finally, Lizzie asked something she'd been thinking about since Sidney accepted this venue.

"Will we be sailing out into the ocean tonight, Captain?"

MacGregor grinned, revealing large, slightly crooked teeth. "No, Miss Crane, we'll be enjoying the river on this pleasant evening. The ocean can be rambunctious at times. Not the best for dining or dancing. I'd rather not cause my guests any discomfort. Have you sailed the high seas?"

"Good heavens, no. I did enjoy sailing in a lovely sloop off the coast of Massachusetts last summer, though."

"I have a sloop as well that I moor at Martha's Vineyard. Perhaps you'll let me take you sailing there this summer?"

"What a nice idea," she said without enthusiasm, hoping he'd casually tossed off the suggestion and would forget about it after he'd finished another martini.

Two young couples, beautiful and lively and flush with the infinite possibilities that stretched before them by virtue of their birth, ambled onto the deck. The men hailed MacGregor, demanded drinks, and swapped playful insults with their host. The women posed prettily, as if cameramen for the *New York Times* society pages hovered nearby waiting to snap their photos.

Sidney used their appearance as an excuse to get away. He saluted MacGregor, then steered Lizzie and Bert toward the rear of the yacht.

"I can't believe he leaves the piano out in the weather this way," Sidney groused as they approached it. "It'll be as flat as a tire with ten nails in it."

But when he opened the key lid and played a series of scales, his frown shifted to an expression of unexpected satisfaction. Watching him, Lizzie let out a small sigh of relief. She tapped her fingers on the piano's shiny, lipstick-red surface.

"Can I assume we're copacetic?" she asked, guessing the instrument had been made in the Astoria factory where Kitty Taylor worked.

"It's fine. Maybe our host has it tuned before every performance."

Bert ran his fingertips along the piano's lid. "Why is it red?"

"Maybe because it looks patriotic with the white boat and the blue water," Lizzie suggested.

"An affectation," Sid said. "It looks like a candy apple."

A half-dozen more guests joined the party. One of the men sported a white sailor outfit and cap instead of an evening suit; his date wore a navy-blue middy dress with a pleated skirt and red necktie. No sooner had they collected their drinks from the bartender than another group of revelers burst on the scene.

"Time to earn our fee," Sid said and began playing "Everybody Loves My Baby."

Bert unsnapped his trumpet case, took up his horn, and quickly captured the attention of MacGregor and his friends. Lizzie adjusted the microphone and sang along. For the next half-hour, they played a series of jazz numbers and popular show tunes, while men and women wearing expensive suits, flashy dresses, and attitudes of privilege came aboard.

When the last invitees had been accounted for and the gangplank pulled up, the yacht eased away from the dock and out into the great river that separated New York from New Jersey. Although stiff winds could make the Hudson turbulent at times, tonight only the wakes of passing freighters and barges ruffled its blue-green surface. The sixty-foot *Highland Lassie* cruised along unaffected by such disturbances. Her occupants shimmied, foxtrotted, and danced the Charleston as easily as if they were in the ballroom of MacGregor's Upper East Side townhouse. If a guest spilled a drink, it was due to his own clumsiness, not the boat's.

When the full moon climbed high enough in the sky to change from orange to silver, Sidney announced, "Good evening, everyone. We're The Troubadours from right here in the Big Apple, and we're delighted to entertain all you wonderful people tonight at the invitation of our illustrious host, Mr. Malcolm MacGregor. We're going to take a short break, but we'll be back soon with more of your favorite music."

While they'd been playing, MacGregor's staff set up a buffet laden with culinary delights. Every sort of shellfish Lizzie could imagine—shrimp, scallops, crab, cherrystone clams, raw oysters, lobster—rested on ice. Slices of turkey, smoked ham, and rare roast beef lay in fan-shaped arrangements on platters made of the new stainless steel. A colorful array of vegetable salads nestled in heavy ceramic bowls. Two young men attired in crisp, white chef's garb stood ready to serve hungry guests.

"What's your pleasure this evening, miss?" one of the men asked her.

Lizzie pointed to several dishes, and he placed generous portions on a plate for her. She carried her supper to one of the banquettes and sat down to eat. All around her, handsome, well-dressed couples bantered, postured, and flirted with each other in the deliciously cool evening. Whenever another pleasure craft passed, they waved and called out greetings.

After she finished eating, Lizzie returned her plate to the man who'd served her at the buffet table, then made her way to the bar. While she waited for the bartender to mix a gin-and-tonic, she heard a man's voice behind her, so close she could almost feel his breath on her neck.

"It's a bonnie evening we're gifted with, eh, Miss Crane?"

She turned to see MacGregor ogling her and took a step back, away from him. "Yes, indeed. I hope you're enjoying our performance."

"Aye. I have Jim Jenkins to thank for bringing you to my attention." He grasped her elbow, grinning broadly. "Fetch your bevvy, and I'll give you a tour of the *Highland Lassie.*"

"I must admit I'm curious to see what the interior of a yacht looks like," she said. "I've never been on one before."

The bartender handed Lizzie a chilled glass, then her host led her to the wheelhouse, situated at the front of the topmost deck. The walls and floor were made of polished mahogany. Windows formed a 180-degree arc around the front half of the room. A huge nautical map hung on the back wall. Two men in their middle years dressed in summer white Navy uniforms sat in leather swivel chairs on either side of a wooden steering wheel. Before them stretched a console replete with gauges, dials, and an array of gadgets Lizzie couldn't begin to identify.

Both men stood and saluted when their boss and Lizzie entered. After introducing her, MacGregor good-naturedly slapped the shoulder of the man with the most ribbons pinned on his shirt and said, "Carry on, Captain."

"Yes, sir," he replied, then turned to Lizzie. "Stop back by later, miss, if you'd like to try your hand at sailing."

"That's a swell offer, but I can't imagine sailing a huge boat like this."

"Don't worry," the captain said. "We won't let you run into anything."

Lizzie laughed, then let MacGregor guide her downstairs to the yacht's middle deck. He opened a door into a sitting room furnished with leather sofas and chairs and paneled with gleaming mahogany, like the wheelhouse. An oriental carpet lay on the floor. Open windows along one wall provided stunning views of the river. Across the hall, she saw a game room with a well-stocked bar at the far end.

"The card tables are bolted to the floor to keep them from bouncing about in rough seas," he explained. "Wouldn't want nature to ruin a good game of poker."

A dining room furnished with a linen-draped table and eight campaign chairs, plus a galley kitchen that boasted the latest appliances, completed the second level. Lizzie complimented each room enthusiastically, impressed not only by the fine craftsmanship but also how everything had been cleverly designed to utilize the space efficiently.

"This way, Miss Crane."

MacGregor gripped her arm and guided her down another flight of stairs to the *Highland Lassie*'s lowest level. She could no longer hear the sounds of the party going on above, only the constant hum of the yacht's engine. Four bedrooms and bathrooms for guests, as well as sleeping quarters for the crew, occupied the bottom deck. As he opened the door to the first cabin, Lizzie ventured to ask a question that had perplexed her since the party at his Upper East Side townhouse.

"How did you and Jim Jenkins become friends? You don't seem to be, well…"

"Cut from the same tartan?" MacGregor laughed. "I'm thinking of buying Jupiter Records."

Surprised, Lizzie asked, "Is that why you threw the birthday bash for Jenkins?"

"I wanted to hear the musicians he already had under contract, as well as those he was considering. Jim knew music, and he had a sixth sense about who and what would be the next sensation. But our man was a right eejit when it came to business."

"If The Troubadours had made a record with Jenkins as planned and you bought Jupiter Records, we'd be working with you, right?"

"Aye, so you would."

Shifting back into his tour-guide persona, MacGregor showed her into one of the guest bedrooms. He pointed out a few of the room's features that he seemed especially proud of, including an elaborately carved teak chest from faraway Indonesia and a lamp with a tulip-shaped shade designed by the renowned glass artist René Lalique.

"Take a gander at the doorknobs. They're plated with gold from one of my South African mines," he bragged.

He waited a few moments while she admired them, then closed the door and opened another one. Inside, a half-dressed young couple who'd escaped the party upstairs to pursue private entertainment stared at MacGregor and Lizzie in wide-eyed embarrassment.

"Whoops, sorry, chief. Carry on." MacGregor chuckled and retreated.

Farther down the hall, he unlocked the door to yet another bedchamber, this one larger and more elegantly appointed than the others. He nudged Lizzie inside and closed the door. He removed his cap and tossed it on the bed, then plucked her drink from her fingers and set it on a bureau.

"Records are the wave of the future," he continued. "I expect to make a good deal of money in this business."

Lizzie remembered the two Mississippi musicians she'd met only days before Jenkins died, who claimed the record producer swindled them. She thought about the contract Jenkins offered The Troubadours, which gave Jupiter all rights to their royalties and music if they didn't live up to the terms of the agreement—or if one of them died. Now with Jenkins dead, would MacGregor get the record company on the cheap because of the scandal associated with it?

"You and your friends can still make a record with me, Miss Crane. Jim's untimely demise needn't change anything," he said, putting his hands on her shoulders.

She recoiled at his touch. Her muscles tensed; her skin prickled as if a spider were crawling along her body. Although she didn't want to offend her host, his familiarity and what it insinuated made her stomach churn. She eased away from his grasp, hoping she could dash out of the cabin and back upstairs, but he stood between her and the door.

"I really should get back to the party. My friends will be wondering what happened to me."

"How about a wee bit of fun first? It's my party," MacGregor reminded her. "I'll decide when it's time for you to return."

"Excuse me, Mr. MacGregor. I've enjoyed the tour of your boat, but our contract plainly stipulates you've hired me to perform music, period."

His eyes dropped to the V-neckline of her dress and lingered there for what seemed an interminable time. He stepped toward her again, reaching out to touch the necklace she wore. Lizzie forced herself to stand still while he examined the aquamarines in the choker, and his fingers strayed to caress her neck. Her mind raced, struggling to find a dignified way out of this indecorous situation.

"Nice stones," he said. "I can give you gems much more exquisite than these. I have investments in diamond mines, you know."

When she didn't answer, MacGregor said, "I'll make that record for you. I might even sweeten the deal with a little bonus." He bent and kissed the hollow at the base of her throat. "Your neck was designed to wear diamonds."

"This isn't the way I do business."

"Truly now? Surely you don't expect me to believe that. Everyone knows lady entertainers are whores. It's simply a question of price."

Laughing coldly, he ran his hand from her neck to her shoulder. He hooked his fingers around the strap of her evening dress and yanked it down, baring her left breast. Lizzie dug her fingernails into his hand, pried his grip loose, and pulled the beaded bodice back into place. Angrily, she pushed him away, scanning the bedroom for something she could use to defend herself.

"You realize I have the power to make or break you in the music world."

"I'm sure you do," she admitted. "But fame bought at the expense of one's self-esteem is no success at all."

MacGregor grabbed Lizzie again, pushing her toward the bed—just as the cabin's door opened and Nadine burst in. The woman's eyes narrowed. Her cheeks flushed magenta. Her pretty face contorted into a mask of fury. She plucked a bronze statue of the Greek goddess Aphrodite from a shelf and held it above her head as she stormed across the room toward MacGregor. When he turned to face his assailant, Lizzie twisted loose from the startled man's grip.

"Nadine, honey, it's not what it looks like," he pleaded, holding up his hands to protect himself.

"The hell it's not, you lying snake in the grass!" Nadine shouted, waving the bronze statue like a war club.

Lizzie dashed out of the bedroom and raced up the stairs to the top deck. She paused briefly to catch her breath, straighten her dress, and smooth her hair into place before rejoining her colleagues. Struggling to regain her composure, she made her way through the crowd of guests to the cherry-red piano at the yacht's stern.

"Where have you been, Bearcat?" Sidney chided her. Then, seeing the look of rage mixed with worry and the sadness of broken dreams on her face, he asked, "What's happened?"

She gazed up at the full moon, its all-seeing face shining above the city that never sleeps, and shook her head. "We need to rethink this business of making a record."

Chapter Twenty-Four

"It isn't for the moment you are struck that you need courage, but for that long uphill climb back to sanity and faith and security."

—Anne Morrow Lindbergh

Detective Lawrence Perry observed Alan's bruised face, the cut on his cheek, and the eye that had swollen nearly shut. "What's the other guy look like?"

Alan didn't find the remark funny. In his clipped, upper-class Boston accent, he said, "Thank you for coming over on this rainy Saturday morning."

"This is my younger brother, Officer Fred Perry. Greenwich Village is his territory, so I notified him after you telephoned. I've filled him in on the basics of the Jenkins matter."

"Please have a seat, gentlemen," Lizzie said. "Would you like coffee? I don't know how to make chai tea."

"Coffee sounds good," Officer Perry said.

She poured strong, dark coffee into two cops, freshened Alan's cup and her own, then sat next to her lover on the sofa. "As I said on the telephone, someone broke into my apartment yesterday and nailed a piece of fishing line across the doorway to my bathroom. Alan tripped on it and sustained the injuries you see. I believe whoever did this meant to harm me. Unfortunately, Alan was the victim instead."

"I'll take a look in a few minutes, but we'd like to ask you both a few questions first," Officer Perry said. "Do either of you have any known enemies? Hostile relationships with anyone? Former spouses, family members, business rivals, that sort of thing?"

Lizzie and Alan shook their heads.

"No, nothing like that," she answered.

"Miss Crane," Detective Perry said in his harsh, raspy voice that to Lizzie seemed at odds with his otherwise smooth manner. "As an entertainer, you no doubt attract the attentions of many fans and admirers. Could someone who felt spurned by you have attempted revenge?"

Immediately, she thought of Malcolm MacGregor. But the intruder had broken into her apartment before MacGregor tried to force himself on her. "I can't think of anyone who fits that description."

Detective Perry took a sip of his coffee, then shifted his attention to Alan. "Mr. Peabody, you invest money for people who expect to profit from your advice. Have you failed to fulfill any of your clients' expectations? Perhaps lost money for them?"

"No, the market's been strong lately. My clients are enjoying good returns on their investments."

"Law" Perry thumbed the prominent mole that clung to his jutting chin like a barnacle on a rock. "Miss Crane, you and I have spoken on a couple occasions about the death of Jim Jenkins, who owned Jupiter Records, a company with whom you planned to make a recording. Do you think there might be any connection between Mr. Jenkins's recent demise and this incident?"

"What makes you think that, Detective?" Alan asked.

Lizzie laid a hand on his arm, wishing they'd had more time to discuss the details surrounding this situation before meeting with the police. She didn't like springing what she'd discovered in the past week on Alan like this, but she'd had no opportunity since his arrival yesterday afternoon to lay out the whole scenario and prepare him for the cops' questions.

"Actually, I've considered the same thing," she admitted.

From her purse, Lizzie pulled the letter composed of words cut from magazines and handed it to the detective. He read it, looked up at her, then read it again.

"Where did you get this?" he asked.

"Someone left it for me at the apartment building's front desk. The superintendent didn't see who delivered it, though." *I should have shown this to him before. I should have taken the warning more seriously. If I'd gone to the police earlier, maybe none of this would have happened.*

"I'd like to keep this as evidence."

"I understand."

"May we have a look at your bathroom?" Officer Perry asked.

She nodded and stood up. "This way."

Pulling on a pair of gloves, the younger Perry knelt in the doorway between the bathroom and bedroom. He ran his fingers along the jamb until he came to the nail that held the piece of fishing line in place. Carefully, he unwound the filament and stretched it across the opening to the nail on the other side to recreate what Alan had described as a booby-trap.

"This is what tripped your friend?" he asked Lizzie.

"Yes."

Detective Perry bent down to examine what his brother had observed. "And you have no idea who did this or why?"

"No, sir."

"I'd like to have someone from the department come by and take photos," Officer Perry said. "Maybe a guy to dust your apartment for fingerprints, too. Please don't clean or disturb anything in the meantime."

Lizzie nodded. "Okay."

"While I'm here, I want to check all the other ingresses to your apartment," the detective said. "It doesn't appear that the intruder entered through the front door."

"Did you open the windows? Yesterday was nice and warm," Officer Perry pointed out.

She thought for a moment, trying to recall if she'd left the windows open to air out her flat when she went to meet Alan at the train station. "Yes, I believe I did. But we're on the third floor. If a fella wanted to break in, he'd need a tall ladder to gain access. Surely a neighbor or someone passing by would've seen him and called the cops."

"Maybe. Nonetheless, let's check your windows. Any other ways to get in and out?"

"The fire escape."

While the younger brother examined the windows in her apartment, the elder Perry opened the door that led from the kitchen to the fire escape. "Do you have an umbrella?"

Lizzie fetched one for him, and he stepped out onto a narrow metal landing attached to the side of the brick building. Two ceramic pots of salmon-colored geraniums crouched in one corner, soaking up the rain. A window box overflowing with purple petunias hung on the railing. The stairs that would allow her to climb down to the street in an emergency were secured in their usual position. An identical staircase led to the building's top floor.

"It's about twenty feet to the ground," the detective said, leaning over the railing. "From there, you'd need a ladder as well as something to pull down the stairs in order to access your apartment."

"Like a shepherd's crook, you mean?"

"More likely a hoe or a rake—not many shepherds tending their flocks in Greenwich Village these days. Unless someone climbed down from the floor above." He squatted to get a closer look at the stairs. "When was the last time you used these?"

"Never." In the four years she'd lived here, she'd never even tried them to see if they actually worked. For all she knew, the metal steps might be rusted and useless in case of a fire.

"Hello, what have we here?" Law Perry plucked a scrap of pale blue cloth from the stairway's hinge. He held it out for her to see. "Recognize this?"

Lizzie examined the wet bit of fabric: lightweight cotton, cheaply woven, faded from wear. "No, sorry. Do you think it's relevant?"

He shrugged. "You never know."

She backed away from the door so he could view the entryway more closely. With his gloved index finger—a finger Lizzie knew lacked the first digit—he traced the line where the door met the jamb, wiping away rainwater that had beaded up there. He closed the door, paused, then opened it again.

"Look here," he said.

Lizzie leaned closer, her eyes following the path his finger indicated. A bit of paint on the door jamb near the lock had been scraped off, leaving raw wood behind.

"The door doesn't close very tightly, and the exposed wood is clean, indicating this scrape is new. The person who broke into your apartment may have jimmied the lock. He could've slid a knife blade in here and opened it easily." The detective collapsed the umbrella and leaned it against the outside wall beside the doorway. "You really should replace this with a deadbolt lock."

He stripped off his gloves, shook rainwater from his cap, and stepped inside her tiny kitchen, leaving wet footprints on the linoleum. His suit smelled of damp wool.

Lizzie closed the door behind him. "What now?"

"Honestly, I don't know. I haven't enough evidence to even put together a theory about what's going on here. The ball's in your court, Miss Crane. You *must* report to me everything curious that happens, no matter how insignificant it may seem. I can't stress the importance of this strongly enough. We don't know what your intruder has in mind, but it's not good. Clearly, you're in danger. I think Mr. Peabody would agree." He nodded in the direction of her living room, where Alan still sat on the sofa, his injured leg propped up on the coffee table.

"I understand. I have your card. I promise to contact you if anything out of the ordinary occurs in the future."

"Or if you have any information that might help us in this case. Let me remind you that we may be dealing with more than a break-in. This incident may be linked to Jim Jenkins's death—and his death may not have been an accident."

When Lizzie and Detective Perry returned to the living room, Alan started to stand, but the policeman held up his hand to stop him. "Don't get up. Fred, what's your assessment of the windows?"

"They look okay, screens intact. I doubt our man got in that way."

"All right, then. We're finished here, for the moment at least," Law Perry said. "Miss Crane, if you think of anything that might aid the police in this matter, don't hesitate to contact me. In the meantime, take care of yourself."

"Thank you, gentlemen, for coming over today," Alan said. "I hope if we meet again, it will be under better circumstances."

"So do I."

After she saw the policemen out and locked the door behind them, Lizzie sat on the sofa beside Alan.

"I'm so sorry," she said. "I should've told Perry about the letter as soon as I got it. Honestly, I didn't take it seriously at the time. Now, in light of all this, I realize I made a mistake."

He took her hand and held it between both of his. "In less than a year, you've been attacked four times and almost killed on at least three occasions. None of that would've happened if you'd minded your own business. Need I remind you that you're a jazz singer, not a detective?" He turned to gaze out the rain-streaked window. "I couldn't bear to lose you, Lizzie. I can't protect you—usually I'm two hundred miles away, and I have no idea what you're doing, who you're seeing, whether you're safe. Do you have any idea how much I worry about you?"

"I'm sorry, Alan," she apologized again. "I never meant to worry you. You have enough to worry about with your mother's illness."

"Yes, and I can't shield her either. A man is supposed to protect and care for the woman he loves, yet I'm helpless to do that."

For the first time, in the ten months she'd known him, Lizzie sensed a hint of vulnerability in his confident demeanor. Accustomed to taking charge, making decisions, and having his wishes carried out by the people around him, Alan Peabody, she realized, had trouble accepting that some things were beyond his power to control.

It was also the first time he'd intimated that he loved her. She didn't doubt his attraction to her, but love was something else. *Do I dare believe this?*

He stroked her hair, then kissed the top of her head. "So, what did the cops determine from their investigation of your apartment?"

"Detective Perry thinks whoever broke in pried open the door from the fire escape. He found a bit of fabric caught in the hinge of the fire escape stairs—maybe it got torn from the intruder's clothing. His brother will probably send somebody over to take photos and check for fingerprints."

"I think you should come back to Boston with me until this mess is resolved."

"Lovely as that sounds and much as I enjoy being with you, my work is here. I can't just abandon my friends, cancel our engagements, and leave everyone in the lurch for weeks or longer."

"Could you move in with Sid for the time being?"

She laughed, trying to envision *that* scenario. "Having a woman in residence would seriously cramp his lifestyle."

"How about your girlfriends—could you stay with one of them?"

"I don't have any girlfriends, other than Melody, and she's in Europe on her honeymoon."

Often, Lizzie wished for friendships with other women. But the girls she grew up with in the Bronx had married, borne children, and settled into ordinary family routines, while she pursued the unconventional life of a jazz singer. Even her peers in the music world didn't invite closeness, partly because of the inherent competitiveness of the business, but also because Lizzie's beauty aroused jealousy. Women with whom she might have sought camaraderie steered clear of her—and kept their men away from her too.

"What about Bert? Maybe he could stay here with you temporarily, so you wouldn't be all alone."

"In this six-hundred-square-foot apartment? Camping out in my dinky living room, sleeping on my sofa, and underfoot all the time?" Lizzie shook her head. "I don't think so. Besides, he's got his mother and sister to look after."

"I thought Bert and his family weren't close. Has that changed?

"Since Jenkins's death, yes. From what I can gather, Jim Jenkins sort of took care of the family after Bert's father died."

Alan frowned, which further contorted his bruised, cut, and swollen face into a grotesque mask. "Bert left home after his father died, didn't he?"

"The way he tells it, his mother and the man she took up with after Tommy Halley's death forced Bert out to fend for himself. Now, he seems to be trying to re-establish himself as the head of the household."

"Who was that man? Is he still in the picture?"

Lizzie searched her memory and realized she didn't know the answer to either of those questions. Bert had never volunteered the information, and she'd never pressed him to reveal those parts of the story. She got up and poured herself another cup of coffee.

"Want more?" she asked.

"No thanks."

Alan shifted his position and bent his knee slightly, testing the swollen joint. Lizzie studied his face, trying to ascertain his level of discomfort, but his expression gave nothing away.

"I don't know," she admitted. "Now that you mention it, I can't believe I didn't pursue it further. I wanted to respect Bert's privacy. I guess I just assumed the man was gone now."

"If the guy's still around and, as you say, Bert's trying to reassert himself as head of the household, your friend may be inviting trouble."

"You're right. I didn't think of that," Lizzie said as another idea pushed its way into her awareness. An idea that led down a route she hadn't considered before. *What if that man had a hand in JJ's death?*

Chapter Twenty-Five

"Run from what's comfortable. Forget safety. Live where you fear to live."

—Jalāl al-Dīn Rumi

Alan telephoned a locksmith who complained about coming out on a rainy Saturday morning to replace the locks in Lizzie's apartment until Alan offered to pay extra for immediate service. By noon, the man had secured the front door and the door that led to the fire escape with new deadbolts. In addition, he installed heavy metal latches that looked as if they'd be impossible to pry open.

"If'n this was my place," the locksmith said, "I'd get bars put on them windows too. I could do the job for you next week. In the meantime, you can jam these here double-hungs with wooden dowels so's they won't open."

"But then I wouldn't have any fresh air," Lizzie said. "Plus, I'd feel like I was living in a prison."

The locksmith packed up his tools and wiped his hands on his denim overalls. "Suit yourself, lady."

After paying the man, Alan limped to an Art Deco cabinet that housed a radio and turned the dial to KDAZ. Instantly, a song by a band from Chicago that Lizzie didn't recognize filled her living room. She couldn't help wondering if either the musicians or their producer had paid the station's manager, Victor Fosse, to play their music.

"Why don't you have a Victrola?" Alan asked.

"They're rather expensive," Lizzie answered. "Besides, I'm hardly ever here, and the radio works just fine."

"I'd like to buy one for you, so you can stay abreast of the competition—and listen to your own record when it comes out."

Lizzie's thoughts swept back to last night aboard the *Highland Lassie* and Malcolm MacGregor's revelation that he planned to buy Jupiter Records. If The Troubadours agreed to make a recording with Jupiter, they'd be making it with him. Then she'd be obligated to MacGregor with all the smarmy details that implied. She still hadn't mentioned the man's unwanted overtures toward her to either Alan or Sidney and hoped she'd never need to do so. The incident had left her feeling both ashamed and weak—not the way she wanted either her lover or her business partner to view her.

"I didn't mean to insinuate anything of the sort, Alan," she said, looking at the Edward Hopper painting he'd given her only a few months ago. Much as she appreciated his generosity, she didn't want him to feel she cared about him only for his money. "Please don't think I led you to make that offer."

"I don't, but I'd like to listen to the latest recordings when I'm here visiting. Now, as I recall, you know a fella who owns a music shop."

Before she could reply, the telephone rang. Lizzie grabbed the receiver and heard Sidney's voice on the other end of the line.

"Get decent. I'm on my way over to see how Alan's doing."

"You don't think I can take care of him myself?"

"I regret to remind you, Bearcat, that you're the reason he's in this condition in the first place." He paused for a moment to let that sink in.

"Don't make me feel guiltier than I already do."

"Okay, sorry. Anything you need me to bring over? How about lunch— have you eaten?"

"Lunch would be swell." She thought a moment, then added, "And a cane. Remember the scene we did from *Gatsby* last month at the Cherry Hill Theatre's improv, where you played Jay Gatsby? Do you still have the cane you used with a daisy on the handle?"

"I'm sure it's around here someplace. You know I never throw anything away."

"Dig it out, will you? If Alan had a cane, he could get around better. He's not used to sitting still for so long, and he's getting restless." She glanced at him, sprawled on the sofa where he'd spent far too much time since his arrival yesterday afternoon. He gave her a thumbs-up.

"See you in an hour," Sidney said and hung up.

A look of enthusiasm brightened Alan's injured face. "Is Sid bringing me a sword cane? That could come in handy if I need to defend us against more intruders."

"Sorry to disappoint you, but it's just an ordinary cane. No secret sword concealed inside. Still, it might help you walk more easily."

Alan consulted his Patek Philippe watch. "It's quarter past twelve. What would you like to do on this rainy afternoon until Sid gets here?"

"We could play backgammon or dominoes." She threw him a teasing look.

"I have another game in mind." He smiled at her, then tapped his injured knee. "Of course, due to my injury, you'll have to be on top. I hope that agrees with you."

Lizzie laughed. "It's one of my sixty-four favorite positions."

* * *

As promised, Sidney arrived an hour later with prosciutto and provolone sandwiches, potato salad, and dill pickles. He handed an ebony walking stick with a brass head to Alan.

"Thanks, Sid, this is super." Alan twirled the cane a few times for dramatic effect, then limped back and forth with it across the apartment a few times. "Lizzie, does this make me look dapper? Or maybe a bit of a rogue?"

She raised one of the table's leaves into position. "Both."

While the coffee finished brewing, Sidney prowled around her apartment examining the locksmith's work.

"Don't touch the doorjamb in the bathroom or the fishing line nailed to it," she told him. "Detective Perry might send somebody over from the police department to photograph it and take fingerprints."

CHAPTER TWENTY-FIVE

"I still can't imagine why anyone would do this," Sidney said.

"I can't either. It's all very confusing."

"Why string fishing line across your bathroom doorway? If some bad man really wanted to put you out of commission, wouldn't he grab you, drag you into an alley, and give you a .22-calibre headache?"

"We think it's a warning," Alan told him. "Obviously, if the guy wanted to kill Lizzie, he would've found a way to do it. That doesn't appear to be the case."

"I hope you're right."

"Me too," Lizzie agreed, as she set lunch on the table and poured coffee. "Okay, gentlemen, time to eat."

Alan slid into his chair, careful not to bump his sore knee. "Do you even know any fishermen, Lizzie?"

"Henry, our former saxophonist, the one who was murdered last summer, came from a family of fishermen from Gloucester, Massachusetts. Bert gave fishing a try when we were at Halcyon Castle in October, but that was just a lark. A distraction from all the weird goings-on there."

"Anyone could buy fishing line at a hardware store, or even from the Sears catalogue," Sidney pointed out.

"Well, I feel quite secure with the new locks on my doors," Lizzie said, trying to sound confident.

Sid's right, she thought. Someone could easily nab her while she walked in the park or waited for the subway. She had to admit she wasn't particularly cautious about her comings and goings. She'd never been a Nervous Nellie, afraid that strangers lurked in the shadows, ready to rape or strangle her. More likely, the intruder who booby-trapped her bathroom was someone she knew, or at least someone who knew her.

"Did you show Sid the letter?" Alan asked.

Lizzie shook her head, wishing he hadn't brought it up.

Sidney laid down his fork and raised an eyebrow. "What letter?"

"Somebody left an anonymous note downstairs at the front desk telling me to stop looking into Jim Jenkins's death."

"When?"

Alan's voice took on a sharp edge as he answered, "Last Saturday."

"Why didn't you tell me?" Sidney stared at Lizzie, then Alan, and then back at Lizzie again.

"Good question," Alan said. "She just told me this morning."

"I didn't take it seriously at the time. And I didn't want you both to make a big deal of it. Really, it seemed kind of cartoon-ish—a note composed entirely of letters cut from magazines, like something a child might do."

"Or a person who didn't want to leave any trace that could identify him," Alan added. "I think the same person who broke into Lizzie's apartment left the note as a threat."

"Show me the letter, Bearcat."

"I gave it to Detective Perry. He came by this morning to talk to us and check the place out. He's on the case."

Sidney rapped her lightly on the head with his knuckles. "At least there's an inkling of sense in that pretty head of yours. Does 'Law' think the intruder left the letter?"

"He didn't say. He just took it as possible evidence." Lizzie finished her coffee and got up to get more. "Anybody else want a refill?"

"I do," they said in unison.

As she poured coffee into their cups, Alan said, "I still haven't heard much about the yacht party last night. This break-in has overshadowed what should've been quite a stellar event."

Sidney's countenance brightened as the conversation shifted to a more upbeat topic. "Wish you could've come, old man," he said. "We played splendidly, if I do say so myself. I think MacGregor and his guests had a smashing good time, wouldn't you agree, Bearcat?"

"Ab-so-lute-ly," Lizzie answered.

But her host's boorish behavior had tarnished her pleasure at having given a standout performance for an audience of rich and influential people on a beautiful evening on a luxury yacht. She hadn't told Alan or Sidney about MacGregor's improper advances toward her, and she didn't intend to. Nor did she intend to make a recording with Jupiter Records if it meant The Troubadours would be under MacGregor's thumb. *An alliance with Jupiter has been doomed from the start,* she realized. *If Sid doesn't find another company we can work with, I'm scratching the whole plan off my list.*

Letting go of the dream brought tears to her eyes, and she retreated to the kitchen so the men wouldn't notice. All these years, she'd chased fame and fortune. She longed to share her music–the music she loved, the music that brought her joy and made her heart sing—with listeners near and far. *We came so close.*

"What do you say we all go out and listen to some music tonight?" Sidney asked. "Do you feel up to it, Alan?"

"I could probably hobble to the elevator with your cane, but I look like I was in a train wreck. I'd rather not run into anybody I know."

"I have an eyepatch and a fake beard left over from a show we did a couple years ago. If you tie a bandana around your head and wear one of Lizzie's gold earrings, we can pass you off as a pirate."

Alan threw him a dubious look, then laughed. "Okay, I'll take you up on the eyepatch. It might add to my air of mystery."

"Where are we going?" Lizzie asked as she collected their dishes and carried them into the kitchen.

"No place fancy," Alan insisted. "Certainly not the Blue Lagoon—I don't want to have to explain my condition to our pal Rory Moynihan."

"How about Jock's?" Sidney suggested. "It's out of the mainstream, both location- and music-wise. We've played there a few times."

"Their lighting's poor, so no one will notice you," Lizzie said. "Besides, Sid's hot for the club's owner."

"We can eat at that Chinese place on Sullivan Street. I'll pick you up at eight, and we'll make an early night of it. What do you say-ski?"

"Alan?" she asked.

He nodded. "I think I can handle it."

"Then okay-ski."

Chapter Twenty-Six

"I don't know that I should care for a man who made life easy; I should want someone who made it interesting."

—*Edith Wharton, The Fruit of the Tree*

By Sunday afternoon, the pain and swelling in Alan's knee had diminished significantly, though he still used the ebony walking stick for support and, Lizzie suspected, for dramatic effect—he knew it would look smart with a tuxedo and top hat. He leaned over and lifted it from its resting place against her bedside table, where he'd positioned it an hour ago, and laid it across his lap. Not for the first time, he examined the brass head, as if he still hoped it might unscrew to reveal a rapier inside.

"Do you think Sid will mind if I take his cane back to Boston with me temporarily?" he asked. "Just until I'm fully back on my feet again."

"I can't imagine why he would. He probably forgot he even had it until I reminded him."

Lizzie traced the daisy design on the cane's brass head with her fingertip, but instead of F. Scott Fitzgerald's character Daisy Buchanan, Bert's younger sister came to mind. Lizzie and Bert had spoken only sparingly about MacGregor's party, and she wondered if he was still annoyed because she and Sid wouldn't let Daisy play with The Troubadours.

We're scheduled to perform at the Queen of Diamonds Saturday night, and we need to practice before then, Lizzie thought. We've got to be on top of our game. I can't let tension between us interfere. For months, she'd pestered Sidney to get them a booking at the exclusive club—her favorite nightspot in the entire city—and she meant to dazzle not only the nightclub's patrons, but also any reviewers who might attend the show. *Maybe I should take a trip to Brooklyn and check on the Halley family. See how Bert's doing.*

"I wish I didn't have to leave you," Alan said, taking her hand.

"So do I. It's lovely having you here, even under these unfortunate circumstances."

"I worry about you staying here alone."

"But you just paid a bundle to have all these nice new locks installed," she reminded him.

"We both know they won't keep you safe. If somebody really wants to hurt you, he'll find a way." He put an arm around her and pulled her to him. "I still think you should come back to Boston with me. I can protect you better there."

She laid her head on his shoulder, remembering her visit two months ago to his Beacon Hill townhouse, when his butler chauffeured her around the city, and his staff catered to her every whim. Where his cook prepared exquisite meals for them, and they shared bottles of vintage wine from his well-stocked cellar. Since then, she'd often imagined what her life might be like if she lived with Alan. Each time that Cinderella dream unfolded in her mind's eye, however, she felt a tightening in her stomach. Claustrophobia gripped her as if she were trapped in a small room with no windows. As she breathed in the familiar scent of the man she loved, feeling his warm skin against her cheek and listening to the rhythmic beat of his heart, Lizzie wondered, *Could I be happy living like a canary in a gilded cage?*

The question, she realized, was a hypothetical one. Alan hadn't asked her to marry him. He'd only suggested she come for a brief stay until the threat posed by her unknown antagonist passed. For the umpteenth time, she reminded herself that men of his status didn't marry showgirls who'd grown up in the Bronx and never even graduated from high school. The thought made her feel both sad and free.

* * *

Lizzie rode with Alan in the taxicab to Penn Station to catch the two-forty train that would get him into Boston by eight o'clock. His butler, Norman, would pick him up at South Station in Alan's silver Bentley and whisk him home, where the entire household would fuss over him as if he were a wounded king returning victorious from battle. She couldn't help being amused as she imagined the fanfare that would accompany his homecoming, even though she still felt guilty for having been the cause of his injuries.

She promised to telephone him every evening to let him know she was alive and well. She also agreed to check in with Sidney at least once a day, so her friend would also know her whereabouts and could alert Detective Perry if anything seemed amiss.

"You're not taking this matter seriously enough, Bearcat," Sidney said in the big-brother tone of voice he used when he disagreed with her. "Maybe you should hire a bodyguard."

"And have some gun-toting, muscle-bound hulk hanging around my apartment, following me wherever we perform, dogging me when I shop or go out to eat?" She shook her head. "No can do-ski."

Sidney shrugged in resignation. "It's up to you-ski."

"Now let's talk about our show at the Queen of Diamonds."

Chapter Twenty-Seven

"A problem is a chance for you to do your best."

—Duke Ellington, Music is My Mistress

Monday morning, Lizzie awoke alone in her bed, with no plans for the next five days. For several minutes, she lay on her back watching sunlight filter through the window blinds, casting stripy shadows on the wooden floor, while she tried to think of something constructive to do with all her time. Finally, she threw off the covers and made her way to the kitchen. She ground Colombian beans, poured water into the coffee percolator, and set it to brew while she washed and dressed.

She ate breakfast, looking out at the parade of pedestrians and motor vehicles hurrying along the street below. At least the locksmith had configured the locks so she could still raise the bottom half of the double-hung windows six inches to let in the sounds and smells of the city on what promised to be a lovely day.

Ever since that awful morning when she found Jim Jenkins's lifeless body lying in a pool of vomit, she'd wondered what would happen to Jupiter Records in the wake of its owner's death. And ever since the yacht party Friday night, she kept imagining Malcolm MacGregor buying Jupiter. But what if someone else purchased the company? Or if Edith Jenkins decided to keep it and run it herself? In either case, The Troubadours could negotiate a deal with the new owner. Her dream of making a record needn't die with JJ.

Lizzie poured herself a second cup of coffee and set it down on her bedroom vanity. She hadn't visited Jupiter Records since Jenkins's death almost a month ago—she didn't even know if the place was still open for business. Now seemed like a good time to find out. She applied a bit of rouge and powder to her cheeks, then painted a red cupid's bow on her lips. From her walnut wardrobe, she withdrew a pretty blue-and-white flowered daytime dress, then put it back in favor of a more business-looking two-piece ensemble of beige linen. She set a straw hat with a blue ribbon on her bobbed hair, tucked her purse under her arm, and keyed the new lock on the front door of her apartment. Then she took the train to Queens.

When Lizzie entered the reception area of Jupiter Records, she saw a slim, dark-haired man in his mid-twenties sitting on the corner of Irene Warner's desk. He turned to assess her, but didn't stand. Irene began shuffling papers around the desk in an attempt to look busy.

"Hello, may I help you?" the secretary asked.

"I'm Elizabeth Crane, of The Troubadours. You probably don't remember me. The only time we met was when we discovered Mr. Jenkins's body the morning he died."

"Oh, yes, of course, Miss Crane." Irene blushed, either because Lizzie'd caught her chatting up a suitor on company time or because she hadn't remembered a client, especially one who should've stuck in her mind considering the circumstances.

Lizzie decided to dispense with small talk and get right to the point. "I'm curious about Jupiter's future, now that Mr. Jenkins is gone. Will the company continue on without him? I've heard rumors it might be sold."

"I wouldn't know about that. You'd have to ask Mrs. Jenkins."

"It's just, well, I've got a contract pending with Jupiter Records, and now that things have taken this unfortunate turn, I don't know whether to look for another record producer or negotiate with whoever will take over here."

The telephone rang, and Irene answered it, holding up an index finger to signal "one minute." Lizzie smiled and offered her hand to the secretary's young man, who still perched on Irene's desk like a piece of office equipment. He limply shook her hand and mumbled his name, without looking her in the eye.

No sooner had Irene placed the phone's receiver back in its cradle than it rang again. Again, the young woman grabbed it and said, "Good morning, Jupiter Records. May I help you?" After a brief exchange, the secretary hung up, only to be summoned by yet another telephone call.

"Looks like you're pretty busy. Isn't anybody else here to help out?" Lizzie asked, trying to appear sympathetic.

Irene shook her head and let out a long, plaintive sigh.

"It must be hard for you handling everything by yourself, especially now," Lizzie said.

"Harder than you can imagine."

The phone rang again, and Irene rolled her eyes before picking up the receiver, then glanced apologetically at the dark-haired young man. While the secretary patiently discussed a matter about sound quality with the caller, Lizzie addressed him.

"Looks like Miss Warner could use a break. It's almost one o'clock. Why don't you two go out for lunch someplace? I'll hold down the fort while you're gone."

The man's face brightened and, for the first time, Lizzie noticed he was nice-looking in a studious sort of way. *Maybe he's not rude, only shy.*

"Gee, you'd do that?" he asked.

"Sure. Miss Warner and I both want the best for Jupiter Records."

Irene hung up the telephone and scribbled some notes on a pad of paper. Before the phone could ring again, Lizzie nodded at the young man and said, "Irene, your friend and I have decided it's lunchtime. I'll watch things here while you go grab something to eat."

"I don't know…" the secretary said dubiously.

"Look, I can answer the phone, write down messages, and call-back numbers. You'll only be gone an hour or so. Nothing earth-shattering is going to happen in that amount of time."

"She's right," the young man said, reaching for Irene's hand. "Let's get out of here."

Through the front window, Lizzie watched the couple stroll down the sidewalk arm-in-arm. Then she opened the top drawer of an oak file cabinet and began rummaging through a battery of file folders. She had to give Irene points for orderliness. The second drawer yielded Jupiter's contracts with musicians, arranged alphabetically and color-coded according to the year the contract went into effect. Lizzie quickly figured out that a red star drawn on a folder meant the contract was still pending. A black X indicated the artist had died.

Near the back of the drawer, Lizzie found a folder labeled "The Troubadours" and noted the red star on it. She opened it and skimmed the contract inside, which appeared to be the same as the copy Sidney had shown her. The signature lines at the end remained blank. Next, she located a folder marked "Delta Jazz Boys" and read it. Their contract described conditions similar to those outlined in the one Jim Jenkins had drawn up for The Troubadours, including the clause granting all rights and royalties to Jupiter Records if a musician died. Jenkins and the two Mississippi musicians, Lizzie, met at the Blue Lagoon, Charles Tippett and Hank Fowles, had signed it.

Lizzie grabbed a notepad and pen from Irene's desk, then thumbed through the folders and pulled out one with a black X on the cover. She opened it and scanned the contract to make sure it included the death clause. The folder also contained a copy of the musician's death certificate as well as an obituary clipped from a newspaper. Lizzie wrote down the name and address of the deceased artist, the date of his death, and the names of his relatives. After returning the folder to its place, she continued searching the files for black Xs and turned up nine. She had no way of determining if nine in a drawer that held about fifty folders constituted an unusually high percentage of deaths, considering the intemperate lifestyles musicians led and the possibility that some of them might have been in their later years.

As she jotted down information for a forty-two-year-old man who died three months ago in Brevard, North Carolina, the door to Jupiter Records swung open. An attractive, well-dressed woman in her middle years entered. Lizzie recognized her immediately. Edith Jenkins. The surprised look on the woman's face suggested she couldn't place Lizzie, however.

"Where's Irene?" Mrs. Jenkins asked.

Lizzie shoved the file back in the drawer and slammed it shut. "At lunch. I'm filling in for her temporarily, fielding phone calls and the like."

As if on cue, the telephone rang, and Lizzie answered it. "Good afternoon, Jupiter Records. May I help you?" She listened to the caller for a few moments, then wrote down a name and telephone number on a notepad. "I'll ask someone to get back to you later today, sir."

"You look familiar," Mrs. Jenkins said, stepping closer to Lizzie. "Ah, now I remember. You're Bert's friend."

"Yes, you and I met at your husband's funeral." Lizzie started to convey condolences, but Jenkins's widow cut her off with a wave of her hand.

"Why are you here?"

"Like I said, I'm filling in while Irene's at lunch."

Mrs. Jenkins's scowl told Lizzie the woman wasn't buying it. "What were you looking for in the file cabinet?"

"Our contract with Jupiter. Bert and I and our other partner, Sidney Somerset, planned to make a record with your husband's company—didn't he tell you? But Mr. Jenkins passed away before we could finalize it."

"Jim may have mentioned it, but I don't recall. Before his death, I never got involved with his business matters. Now, unfortunately, I'm forced to."

Lizzie saw her chance to press Bert's Auntie Edith for more information. "Do you intend to continue operating Jupiter Records? Or are you thinking of selling the company? I imagine a lot of people would be interested in buying it—records, they're the wave of the future, aren't they?"

"I haven't decided yet," the woman said in an icy tone of voice. Bert's description of her "as cool as a cucumber" flashed in Lizzie's mind.

The telephone rang again, and Lizzie answered it. After listening to a creditor complain that Jupiter Records was three months late paying its bill, she said, "The person you need to talk with is at lunch now, but if you'd like to leave your number, I'll ask her to return your call when she gets back."

After Lizzie hung up, Mrs. Jenkins took off her hat and set it along with her purse on a chair beside the reception desk. "Miss Crane, you can go now. I'll take over until Irene comes back from lunch. If you have any questions regarding your contract, please get in touch with my attorney." She wrote a name and phone number on a piece of paper and handed it to Lizzie.

Lizzie took the note and tucked it in her purse beside the list of dead musicians. "Good day, Mrs. Jenkins."

Lizzie stepped out into the warm, cloudy afternoon and started walking in the direction opposite the one Irene and her beau had taken, hoping to find a place to eat lunch. She couldn't imagine Edith Jenkins running Jupiter Records by herself. Most likely, JJ's widow would sell the company to the highest bidder, perhaps to Malcolm MacGregor, and wash her hands of the whole mess.

Savory smells emanating from a café with yellow awnings and a turquoise door drew her in. A waitress about Lizzie's age with a strawberry-blond bob and a face full of freckles greeted her. She motioned with a menu for Lizzie to follow her to a white cast-iron table with S-curved legs that would look pretty in a garden. Baskets of ferns hung from the ceiling. Tiny vases of carnations sat on the tables.

"Will a friend be joining you?" the waitress asked.

"Not today," Lizzie answered. "Would you please bring me a cup of black coffee, while I peruse the menu?"

"Sure thing. Let me know if you have questions. Oh, by the way, the chicken pot pie is especially good today."

"Why today?"

The waitress leaned closer to Lizzie and whispered in a conspiratorial tone of voice, "I think the chef's girlfriend gave him a little sugar last night—that always spills over into his cooking."

Lizzie laughed and handed the menu back to the waitress. "How can I resist? I've got to try the chicken pot pie."

While she waited for her lunch, Lizzie opened the list of deceased musicians and scanned it, searching for similarities that might provide clues. Unfortunately, the limited information she'd gathered from the files didn't reveal the circumstances that took those artists to their graves. Had Jenkins been collecting their royalties? Perhaps sold the rights to their songs before he died, too? The possibility that Jenkins might have played a role in hastening their deaths made her skin crawl, as if a snake had slithered over her feet.

Her thoughts shifted back to what Kitty Taylor surmised at Melody's wedding reception: "My money's on the wife. Especially if he not only cheated on her but gave her the pox too." *What if Edith Jenkins had a financial reason as well as an emotional one for wanting her husband out of the way?*

Chapter Twenty-Eight

"I want to be with those who know secret things."

—*Rainer Maria Rilke*

After finishing the chicken pot pie, which lived up to its billing, Lizzie decided to visit the Steinway factory and try to find Kitty. Considering the glamour that surrounded the Western world's most prized pianos, the plain brick building where these treasures were crafted was a bit of a letdown. *Shouldn't elves build them in a Bavarian castle?*

At the front desk, Lizzie told the receptionist, "I'm here to see Kitty Taylor," and handed the woman her business card.

The receptionist read it and asked, "Do you play piano, Miss Crane?"

"No, I'm a singer. But my business partner in The Troubadours is one of the finest pianists in New York—and he owns a 1910 Steinway Grand O."

"The gentleman has good taste." The receptionist smiled and stood up. "Come with me, I'll show you to Miss Taylor's office."

Kitty, two men, and two other women shared the large, brightly lit room, crowded with drafting tables, worktables, desks, and file cabinets. A gray-haired woman sat at what looked like a typewriter with extra keys, attached to an array of other gadgets Lizzie couldn't identify. A reed-thin, older man with spectacles stood at an easel, painting a watercolor picture of a pretty young woman in an evening gown standing beside a grand piano played by a man in a tuxedo. *That looks like Sid and me,* Lizzie realized, wondering if

"

they'd actually served as inspiration for the artist or if they were merely a cliché. Another man pasted artwork and type onto thick sheets of paper. Kitty, wearing a low-waisted green frock that made her unfashionably large hips seem even broader, bent over a drafting table, giving directions to a woman who sketched as rapidly as Kitty spoke.

"Miss Taylor," the receptionist said. "You have a visitor."

Kitty straightened up, and the surprised look on her face quickly changed to a big smile. "Lizzie, how nice to see you. What brings you to Steinway and Sons?"

"I was in the neighborhood and took a chance you might be in."

Kitty glanced at a wall clock. "I'll be tied up here for maybe another hour, but if you can hang around, we'll go someplace for coffee. You might want to take a tour of the factory while you're here. As a musician, I think you'll find it pretty amazing."

"I'd like that."

"Great." Kitty nodded at the receptionist. "Mrs. Ulrich will arrange for you to see the inner workings of the factory, and I'll meet you later in the front lobby."

"You're on."

Mrs. Ulrich introduced Lizzie to a portly man with plump, flushed cheeks and asked him to show her around.

"You're in luck, miss," the man said, grinning to expose a gold incisor. "This is my last tour of the day, and you've got me all to yourself."

"Thank you, I appreciate your time."

For the next hour, her guide explained the time-honored art of crafting pianos. He recounted the story of the boy Heinrich Engelhard Steinweg, who lost most of his family during Napoleon's campaign in Germany. The enterprising young Steinweg became a carpenter and organ player who built guitars, zithers, and finally pianos—the first as a wedding present for his wife—in his kitchen. He immigrated to New York in 1850 to escape political unrest, anglicized his name to Henry Steinway, and established the Astoria piano factory three years later.

"It's the only Steinway factory in the world. We ship pianos to the four corners of the earth," the guide told her proudly.

Four strong men carrying a twenty-foot-long slab of rock maple crossed in front of Lizzie and the tour guide. "That will form the body of a concert grand," the guide told her, pointing as the men made their way through the factory to a press that would mold the wooden rim into its characteristic curved shape.

The guide showed her the patented press, the 95-degree room where the wood was cured to exactly the right moisture content, and the delicate operation of installing the instrument's steel strings. She watched skilled workers cut felt hammers, fit ivory keys into place, and test them with tiny weights to be sure the action of each key was identical.

"Everything is done by hand," the guide said, admiration evident in his voice.

At the end of the tour, Lizzie listened to a man who looked a bit like Sidney, though not as handsome, play a finished piano to make certain it met expectations and was fit to bear the Steinway name. *Sid would love this,* she thought. *I must bring him here.*

The guide escorted her back to the building's lobby, where Kitty Taylor awaited her. She thanked him and shook his hand.

"My pleasure, miss," he said with a slight bow of his head. "I'm glad you enjoyed it."

"Kitty, the tour was fascinating. Thanks for arranging it for me."

"I thought you'd like it." Kitty positioned a wide-brimmed straw hat trimmed with a green sash and a yellow silk rose on her bleached blond hair. "Unless you have someplace in mind where you'd like to go, I have an idea."

"I'm completely at your disposal."

"Good, then I think you'll find this interesting."

Outside, Kitty hailed a taxi and gave the driver the address of a pub in a neighborhood of small shops and working-class housing. A carved wooden sign hanging over the door said "The High Note."

Kitty paid the cabbie and stepped out onto the sidewalk. "This is where Tommy Halley and I used to play. Given your relationship with his son Bert and the questions you've been asking, I thought you might want to see the place."

The pub's interior looked pretty much like any other beer joint except for the dozens of photographs of musicians displayed on its walls. An upright piano sat at one end of the room. Above it, a brass trumpet hung on a peg. On this Monday afternoon, the pub's only customers were four elderly men drinking coffee and playing cards.

Behind a long wooden bar, a tall man with a bushy mustache polished glasses with a white linen cloth. When he saw the two women enter, he called out, "Hey, Kitty girl. Long time no see."

"Hi, Mick. This is my friend Lizzie Crane. She sings in a band with Tommy Halley's son Bert."

"Is that a fact?" He pantomimed tipping an invisible hat. "Please to meet you, Miss Crane. Welcome to The High Note."

Kitty leaned both elbows on the bar's worn surface. With two fingers on her right hand, she tapped her left wrist three times. Mick nodded and retreated into a room behind the bar. A few minutes later, he returned and set a glass of sparkling golden liquid in front of each woman, along with a bowl of peanuts.

"Thanks, Mick." Kitty slid onto a barstool and motioned for Lizzie to do the same. "Have a seat."

Lizzie took a sip of what she assumed to be ginger ale and was pleased to discover Mick had spiked it with a healthy dose of gin. *That must be what Kitty ordered with her secret finger signal.*

The mustached man picked up his cloth and resumed polishing glasses. "So, how'd you meet Bert?" he asked Lizzie.

"He was playing for change in Central Park. We needed a saxophonist, and I hired him on the spot." She pulled a calling card from her purse and handed it to him. "He's very talented."

"Yep, Bert's a good kid," Mick agreed.

"Takes after his old man," Kitty said. She tasted her drink, then smiled at Mick. "I sure do miss those good ol' days when we played here."

"You know I'd be glad to have you back anytime, Kitty. It wouldn't be the same, but still..."

"Thanks, Mick. I'll consider it."

"I understand Tommy Halley played here the night of his death," Lizzie said, hoping to draw Mick out and learn more about what happened. Although she'd tried to talk to Bert about it several times, he remained reticent, revealing only the most basic facts.

"He did, him and his buddy Jim…what's his surname?"

"Jenkins," Lizzie answered. "Owned a record company. He died recently."

"Sad, both of them gone now," Mick said. "Kitty wasn't here the night Tommy died, thank God for small favors." He crossed himself. "But Bert was. He played sometimes with his dad and Jim."

Lizzie hoped her surprise didn't show on her face. *Bert played here that night with his father and Jenkins?* Her mind flashed back to the night of Melody's wedding reception. Bert sitting on the back porch of the restaurant, crying in the rain. He told her then that JJ was with Tommy Halley when the taxicab hit and killed him. What Bert left out of the story was that he, too, was there.

Chapter Twenty-Nine

"To know your Enemy, you must become your Enemy."

—Sun Tzu

The subway car rumbled and screeched and groaned its way through the dark, narrow tunnels into Greenwich Village. Hot, fetid air blew in the half-opened windows. Occasionally, the overhead lights flickered, went out briefly, then snapped on again, bathing the passengers in a harsh, yellow glare. Again and again, the car braked at a station and sat rumbling while men and women got on and off, before roaring to life once more and speeding to its next stop.

During the entire ride home from her meeting with Kitty Taylor, Lizzie kept imagining the horror her friend Bert must have felt, witnessing his father's death. One minute, the men were playing music to a room full of cheerful patrons at The High Note. Next, Tommy Halley lay fatally broken and bleeding on the street. To lose someone you loved like that, suddenly and at such a young age, seemed unbearably cruel. *No wonder Bert doesn't want to talk about it.* Her heart ached for her shy, awkward friend, and she felt proud of him for holding up as well as he had under the circumstances.

The sky over the Village had turned deep purple by the time Lizzie reached her apartment building. The super sat on the front steps, smoking a cigarette and catching the cool evening breeze. The gray tiger tomcat crouched at his side, eyeing a bird in a nearby bush.

The man waved to her and called out, "They's another of them funny notes come for you today."

"With letters cut from magazines, you mean?"

"That's right. C'mon in, I'll fetch it for you."

Lizzie followed him into the lobby, where he pulled an envelope addressed to her from under the front desk. Like the previous note, this one was a pastiche of individual words cut out of magazines and pasted together to form phrases. Lizzie shivered involuntarily as she took it from him. The colorful and seemingly playful composition gave her the creeps, the way she felt when she saw clowns: darkness hidden behind a jovial mask.

"Who gave this to you?" she asked.

The super shrugged. "Didn't see 'im. He just left it lyin' here on the desk, same as before. Say, does this mean the coppers gonna show up again?"

Lizzie handed him a coin. "Please let me know if you see anyone or anything unusual."

With a trembling hand, she slid her key into her apartment's new lock and opened the door. She tossed her hat and purse on a chair, then tore open the envelope. She pulled out a folded sheet of paper, opened it, and stared at her adversary's message: STOP. **Now**. Or *else*.

Even though it was after eight o'clock, she telephoned Detective Perry. While she waited for him to pick up, Lizzie wondered if the policeman had a life outside the force. Did he have a wife? Play softball with his sons or bowl with his pals on Saturday afternoon? Escape now and again for a weekend in the Catskills?

"I got another of those weird letters," she said when he answered.

After a long pause, Perry asked, "Are you alone?"

"Yes."

"How do you feel? Are you afraid?"

"A little," she admitted, thinking his questions sounded more like those of a concerned friend than a cop investigating a crime.

"Do you notice any signs that your apartment has been broken into again? Any more booby-traps?"

"I haven't had time to check yet. I called you as soon as I got this annoying threat."

"Please examine everything and get back to me," Perry said. "Don't disturb anything that might be evidence."

"Okay, thanks. I will."

"Be careful."

Lizzie mixed herself a gin-and-tonic and took a few sips before starting her survey of the apartment. "I don't even know what I'm looking for," she muttered to herself. First, she inspected the locks on the front door and the one that led to the fire escape, but noticed no signs of damage. Likewise, the windows appeared secure. Cautiously, she opened closet doors, kitchen cabinets, and dresser drawers, half-expecting a monster to jump out and grab her. She peeked under the bed and sofa but saw nothing except dust balls. No demons hid behind the shower curtain or under the living room rug. All her kitchen knives nestled safely in their rack.

Instead of relief, she felt frustrated and confused. Danger could lurk anywhere–poison in her orange juice, a black widow spider in her bed, crushed razorblades in her toothpaste. If her adversary was the same person who killed Jim Jenkins, he might even have diluted a mercury bichloride tablet in water and poured it into her bottle of gin. She started to dump her drink down the drain, but stopped and took a few deep breaths to calm the anxiety that burned in her chest.

I can't safeguard myself against every possible peril, she realized. If someone really wanted her out of the way, he could find a million ways to accomplish it—inside her home or, more likely, outside. Her enemy knew who she was, but Lizzie had no clue to his identity. Unless she was willing to give up her freedom and remain a captive cowering in a locked fortress, she remained vulnerable.

She tossed back a swig of her drink, straightened her shoulders, and dialed Detective Perry's number again.

"What have you discovered?" he asked.

"Nothing. Everything appears copacetic. But any number of dangers may still exist—I just haven't uncovered them yet."

"Would you feel more comfortable if I came by and checked your apartment myself? I need to get this new letter from you anyway, as possible evidence to support the previous threat and the intrusion into your apartment Friday night."

Lizzie heard in his voice what he didn't say: *In case there's another break-in, or something worse.* She considered it for a moment, then asked, "Doesn't the police department have more pressing demands on your time?"

"You're in luck, Miss Crane. Things are unexpectedly quiet at the moment. I can be there in, say, half an hour?"

"Thank you. I appreciate your concern for my well-being."

Next, she called Alan, as she'd promised to do every night. The sound of his voice, even over a telephone line from a distance of two hundred miles, made her feel less alone and sent a tingling warmth rippling through her body. She glanced at the piece of paper in her hands and thought, *Maybe I should've gone back to Boston with him.*

They chatted for a while. He talked in professionally guarded terms about landing a new and prestigious client. She congratulated him, then discussed her tour of the Steinway factory and her drink with Kitty Taylor, but stopped short of telling him what she'd learned about Bert's presence at his father's death. She didn't want Alan to know she was still looking into Jim Jenkins's demise and felt guilty about what might not exactly be lying, but certainly fringed on deceit. Nor did she tell him about the second cryptic note she'd received. Alan couldn't do a thing about it, and until she arrived at some sort of plan, it didn't make sense to worry him further.

After he wished her a good night, Lizzie telephoned Sidney. "You've simply got to take a tour of the Steinway factory. It's incredible," she told him, and described what she'd seen and learned there. She considered telling her friend about the second note, but decided he wouldn't be any more help than Alan and would simply get in a lather.

Before hanging up, Sidney reminded her, "See you here Wednesday at 2:00 for practice."

"Got it on my calendar. I'll tell Bert. G'night-ski."

"Sleep tight-ski."

As promised, Law Perry knocked on her door half an hour later. When

Lizzie threw back the heavy new latch and opened it to admit him, the policeman frowned.

"You should get a peephole installed in this door so you can see who's outside before you open it." He tapped a spot at eye level where he thought the peephole should go.

"Good idea," Lizzie agreed, stepping back to let him in. "I'll see if the fella who installed these nice locks can provide yet another device to safeguard this princess in her tower."

Perry's eyes swept her tiny living room, as if searching it for intruders or booby-traps or anything else amiss. "You seem to resent the protection the police are trying to offer you, Miss Crane."

"I resent being forced to live in fear. Unless I hire a bodyguard to follow me everywhere I go and a taster to sample my food before I eat, it seems I'm going to have to get used to the fact that someone doesn't like me and wants me out of the way. I'll have to learn to watch my back, question the motives of everyone I meet—"

"You have another option, Miss Crane. You can stop poking your nose into the death of Jim Jenkins and leave this matter to the police."

"That's why I telephoned you." Lizzie handed him the letter. "Whoever left this warning is someone who knows me. Someone who's close enough to know that I'm still curious about what really happened to Jenkins."

"And just what do you think really happened to Jenkins?"

"Haven't the foggiest. I'd need a scorecard to keep track of the suspects and possibilities." Lizzie sighed dramatically to demonstrate her frustration. She longed to pour herself another gin-and-tonic, but not with Perry here. Instead, she said, "I'm going to make tea. Would you care for some?"

"Yes, thank you."

"I know you're itching to search my apartment, so now would be a good time to do it."

After setting the kettle on the stove to boil, she filled a tea ball with Earl Grey and warmed the teapot. She placed cups, saucers, spoons, a sugar bowl, and a small pitcher of milk on a tray, while the big cop with the prominent mole on his jutting chin prowled around her apartment, searching for anything that might justify his reason for being there. *Perry doesn't seem to be any closer than I am to solving the murder of Jim Jenkins—if, indeed, JJ was murdered.* She poured water into the teapot and carried the tray to her living room. For a moment, she considered adding a plate of cookies from the Italian bakery around the corner, but ruled it out. Proper tea was a civility; cookies suggested friendship.

"What have you found, Detective?" she asked.

"Nothing, I'm pleased to say." Perry sat on the sofa and helped himself to a cup of tea with two sugars and a splash of milk.

"So, I'm in the clear?"

"I wouldn't say that. Whoever authored these threats obviously wants to keep you from figuring out what happened to Jenkins. My guess is he's involved in Jenkins's death, or he knows something he doesn't want revealed. If you continue this quest, he's going to try to stop you."

Lizzie stirred sugar in her tea, gazing into the cup as if she hoped to scry an answer in the fragrant brew. "Who do you think fits that description?"

"As you said yourself, Miss Crane, the list of candidates is a long one."

"But you must be getting close by now. With all the intelligence and muscle and money the New York Police Department has at its disposal?"

Perry chuckled. "Even so…"

Until now, Lizzie hadn't shared with the cop what she knew about Bert's relationship with Jenkins. She was still reluctant to do so. The idea that Detective Perry might descend on her shy, young friend and ply him with questions about his painful past made her want to protect Bert. Yet she had to admit that keeping information from the police not only hampered their ability to do their job, it put her in jeopardy. If Alan and Sidney knew she hadn't cooperated fully with Perry, they'd be furious. *Maybe it's time to stop protecting Bert and start protecting myself.*

Chapter Thirty

"Under a government which imprisons any unjustly, the true place for a just man is also a prison."

—Henry David Thoreau

Lizzie tucked her newly minted passport—which she hoped would one day grant her access to Paris, London, Rome, and the world's other great cities—into her purse, along with a letter written on official stationery from Detective Lawrence Perry that suggested she had backing from the New York Police Department. She glanced at her image in her vanity mirror one last time, noting her lack of makeup and her nondescript afternoon frock with its long sleeves and high neck. Even though she'd tried to downplay her looks as much as possible, she knew she'd still attract attention when she least wanted it. Positioning a floppy straw hat on her bobbed hair, she locked her apartment door, pocketed her key, and took the creaky old elevator to the ground floor.

On this warm, overcast morning, she walked to East 26th Street, where a boat ferried passengers to one of New York's most dismal and disturbing places: Welfare Island. Located in the East River between Manhattan and Queens, the cigar-shaped stretch of land, almost two miles long and only 750 feet across at its widest point, once provided pastureland for colonial Dutch settlers' hogs. Now it held a prison and hospital that confined the city's most destitute and despised human beings.

Lizzie's stomach churned in apprehension of what she might find in this terrifying place. Eighteen days ago, a judge condemned her friend Eve Adams to the notorious workhouse on what people once called "Damnation Island" after the raid on her Greenwich Village teahouse, for the crime of writing a book about love between women.

The penitentiary, four stories tall and made of gray granite, stood like a fortress on the flat strip of land. Lizzie shivered as she entered the oppressive building, despite the close, damp heat. She waited in line behind five other visitors for her turn to speak to a husky guard in a faded uniform who was missing a few front teeth. He studied her passport, then eyed her for longer than necessary to make sure she matched the photograph. Lizzie felt as though vermin crawled on her skin. After handing her passport back, the man read Detective Perry's letter.

"What's your business here today, Miss Crane?"

"I've come to see a prisoner, Miss Eva Zloczower, sir. She's also called Eve Adams."

The guard flipped through the pages of a ledger, then ran a finger down a long list of names until he found Zloczower. "Your purse, please. Gotta check for weapons or drugs."

Lizzie gave it to him, and he rummaged through its contents, finding nothing of concern. He read Perry's letter again before handing it and her purse back to her. Pointing at a backless wooden bench, he said, "Wait over there."

He conferred briefly with a heavy-set matron, who strode away down a shadowy hallway, then he addressed the next person in line. Twenty minutes later, the matron returned and motioned for Lizzie to follow her deeper into the prison, which stank of human waste, rotten food, and misery. Tiers of cells–hundreds of them stacked four stories high–ran through the center of the structure. From those cells came the anguished cries of the inmates.

The matron unlocked the barred door of a tiny cell and opened it to let Lizzie enter. "Fifteen minutes," she said, then locked the door behind her.

Inside on a narrow bed sat Eve Adams. Garbed in a baggy, blue-checked dress, a dirty kerchief tied over her dark hair, Eve appeared to have aged ten years in the past eighteen days. Mauve half-moons hung under her eyes; her skin was yellowish, lined, and dry. Instead of her usual erect posture, her shoulders now hunched, and she seemed about to implode.

"It is good to see you, Lizzie. Thank you for coming."

Eve smiled, stood, and held out her hands. Lizzie grasped them, noticing the brown stains and calluses on her friend's skin.

As if reading her mind, Eve said, "I no longer serve tea. Now I spend my days rolling cigars for a company that contracts with the prison for cheap labor." She released Lizzie's hands and shrugged. "It is better than some jobs in this workhouse. Others make coffins for those of us who die here."

Lizzie tried to keep the shock and horror she felt at Eve's circumstances from showing on her face. "Surely they can't keep you here for long," she said, not knowing if that was true.

She started to sit on the bed, but Eve stopped her. "Don't sit, it has lice. I'm sorry, I cannot offer you even a scrap of hospitality or comfort. And I hope you don't need to relieve yourself, because that is the only toilet here." She pointed to a wooden bucket in one corner of the cramped cell.

Struggling to hold back tears, Lizzie asked, "What does your lawyer say?"

"That he's working on it. My uncle offered to pay $1,000 bail, but the City of New York refused to release me." Eve sighed in resignation. "Well, I am in only for six months. That I can endure. Now, tell me news of my friends and life in the Village."

"You probably know the teahouse is closed for the time being."

Eve nodded. "Yes, Ruth told me. This is hard on her, you know. Perhaps you could visit her? Water my petunias, too? Ruth sometimes forgets."

"Okay."

"Where are you performing now? How's Sidney? And what about that man you were seeing, the one from Boston?"

Lizzie glanced around the fetid cell, hearing the moans and shrieks of desperate prisoners, smelling the overwhelming stench of decay and degradation. *How can I chat casually about my everyday life when hers is in tatters?*

"We all miss you, Eve." Lizzie reached under her skirt and withdrew a small roll of ten-dollar bills from the pocket of her garter flask. She slipped it to Eve.

"What's this?"

"Bribe money. Maybe you can buy a few favors or creature comforts. Hide it in secret places."

Eve shook her head slowly. "We have no secrets here. They look *everywhere*." But she tucked the cash under her kerchief anyway until she could find a safer spot. "Thank you."

"What can I bring you the next time I come?"

"Books. Nothing provocative, though." Eve forced a grim smile, acknowledging the reason for her imprisonment.

The matron returned and unlocked the cell door. "Time's up."

Lizzie moved to hug her friend, but Eve held out her hand instead and shook Lizzie's formally. "I hope to see you again. Please tell my friends that I miss them."

"I will."

On the boat ride back to Manhattan, Lizzie clung to the railing, trying not to throw up. Tears streamed down her cheeks. She inhaled deeply in an effort to clear away the dreadful stench of the prison, but she couldn't shake the images of debasement she'd seen inside those granite walls. *I've got to talk to Detective Perry about this. Maybe he can pull some strings and get Eve out of that wretched place.*

Chapter Thirty-One

"If you want to keep a secret, you must also hide it from yourself."

—George Orwell

Detective Perry promised Lizzie he'd look into Eve Adams's situation and see what he could do to help, but he didn't sound very hopeful. "If she were a common prostitute or a vagrant or a drunk, like many of the inmates at Welfare Island, it would be easy enough to spring her. But your friend is a unique case. She's notorious. All the newspapers covered her arrest, and the reporting hasn't been favorable, as you probably know. Frankly, it appears some people want to make an example of her and her friends."

"But why?" Lizzie asked. "Eve isn't a danger to anyone."

"I guess that depends on what you mean by 'a danger' and to whom. Sorry if I sound condescending, but you're a musician. You live in Greenwich Village. You may not realize how folks outside your circle feel about women like Eve Adams and her *avant-garde* pals with all their unconventional ideas—and I'm not talking only about sex. Eve and her ilk threaten ordinary people by questioning the status quo that gives them a sense of security."

Lizzie contemplated the policeman's words while she walked through the Village to Sidney's apartment for their afternoon practice. Struggling to shuck off the morose mood that hung around her like a miasma, she reasoned, *I can't do anything to help Eve, not today at least. Right now, I need to keep my mind on my music.*

Ever since The Troubadours began playing together, she'd wanted to perform at the prestigious Queen of Diamonds. Finally, Sidney's efforts to arrange a booking had paid off. Saturday night, they'd get their chance. It was a dream come true, especially on this momentous holiday weekend, when the nightclub expected a huge crowd of revelers to celebrate the nation's 150th birthday. But as she crossed under the arch at Washington Square, Lizzie's thoughts turned back to Eve Adams. *What happened to our founding fathers' dream of life, liberty, and the pursuit of happiness?*

* * *

Sidney opened the door to his penthouse apartment and invited her in. Sunshine streamed through the Palladian windows, spilling golden light into the comfortable living room. Bert, she saw, had preceded her, and he'd brought his sister Daisy with him. The siblings sat—rather stiffly, Lizzie thought—in a pair of Beidermeier chairs near the marble fireplace, unlit on this balmy summer day.

As Lizzie greeted them both, she recalled her last unpleasant meeting with Daisy outside KDAZ radio's studio two weeks ago and Bert's comments about how disappointed his sister was that The Troubadours wouldn't let her perform with them. Nevertheless, Daisy's scuffed guitar case lay on the floor beside her chair. *Is this some sort of attempt on Bert's part to get us to change our minds?* Lizzie wondered. *Or is Daisy just here to listen to her brother play jazz?*

Usually, Lizzie would have led their practice. As the group's creative director, she decided everything from the songs they played to the clothes they wore on stage. Today, sensing her discombobulation, Sidney took charge.

Last night she'd called him in tears after her trip to Welfare Island and described the wretched conditions at the prison. "Detective Perry thinks Eve is being scapegoated."

"It's out of your hands," Sidney told her. "You can't fix every problem you encounter. Sometimes you can even make things worse by getting involved."

Lizzie felt pretty sure he wasn't talking about Eve's situation, but rather her attempt to figure out what happened to Jim Jenkins, and why.

Sid motioned for Bert to pick up his clarinet, then took his seat at the piano and placed his long, slender fingers on the keyboard. The two of them launched into "Rhapsody in Blue"–one of Lizzie's favorites, even though the Gershwins' instrumental didn't allow her an opportunity to sing–and she realized her friends were giving her time to relax and ease into the music that soothed her soul.

The trio ran through the first hour of their repertoire, then Sidney suggested they break for tea, and he put a kettle on the stove to heat. He set out cups and saucers and arranged Italian cookies flavored with amaretto and sprinkled with confectioner's sugar on a plate. Bert ate three cookies before Sid poured the tea.

Trying to be friendly, Sidney asked Daisy, "What are you doing these days?"

"I'm working in a hospital part-time. For the summer at least."

"Do you like it?"

Daisy shrugged. "It's a job. Mostly, I empty bed pans, change sheets, and help the nurses however I can. I'm learning from them how to care for Mom."

"Is your mother ill?" Lizzie asked, remembering how pale and fragile Gladys Halley had seemed. She shot a questioning glance at Bert, but he turned away and busied himself with clearing the mouthpiece of his saxophone.

"I'd rather not talk about it, if you don't mind." Daisy looked down at her lap and rubbed the frayed cuff of her light blue blouse, where she'd mended a tear.

Appraising the girl's faded skirt and worn shoes, Lizzie thought, *I should take her to the church charity shops to get some better clothes.* Unless Tommy Halley had some savings or a minimal pension from his teaching job, the family must be getting by on what Bert gave them, and the pittance Daisy earned at the hospital.

Sidney shifted the conversation back to music. While he and Lizzie tossed around options, she made a list of the songs they agreed to play and in what order, although it was all subject to change depending on the audience's mood. In recognition of the holiday, they added several patriotic numbers, including the "Star-Spangled Banner," "Grand Old Flag," and "My Country, 'Tis of Thee" to their usual repertoire of jazz, blues, and show tunes.

"Bert, any suggestions?" Lizzie asked.

"How about 'Yankee Doodle Dandy'?" he suggested and reached for another cookie.

"Good idea. Okay, let's rehearse for another hour. I realize we know all this stuff inside and out, but this event is really important. We want to sparkle like fireworks."

For the rest of their practice session, Daisy sat quietly, listening, tapping her feet, and nodding her head in time to the music. Once, she got up and walked around the living room, observing Sidney's artwork and his collection of records. *She probably hopes I'll invite her to play with us,* Lizzie surmised. But although she wanted to support Daisy's musical aspirations, she refused to stoke the girl's desire to join The Troubadours.

When they finished, and Lizzie felt certain the trio was ready for the big night, Bert packed up his instruments. He lifted his saxophone and trumpet cases. Daisy grabbed her guitar case and the battered leather one that held her brother's clarinet.

"I'll fetch you Saturday evening at eight," Sidney told him.

"Wear your tux and a big smile. I'll see if I can find a couple red-white-and-blue bow ties for you fellas," Lizzie said, ruffling Bert's brown hair affectionately, as if he were her own kid brother. "Hey, it's our country's birthday. This is a celebration. It's going to be fun."

After the Halleys left, Sidney pulled out a bottle of I. W. Harper, plunked ice cubes in two glasses, and poured golden liquor into both of them. He handed a glass to Lizzie and raised his own. "Cheers."

"Thanks for getting us this show at the Queen of Diamonds, Sid—and at such an auspicious time. This is so exciting!"

Sidney dipped his head ever so slightly, feigning modesty. "All in a day's work."

"Do you think some celebrities will come?"

"Undoubtedly. I wouldn't be surprised if our mayor, Jimmy Walker, showed up. He's a music lover, and I hear the Queen is one of his favorite nightspots."

"The press will be there too, right? If we get enough media attention, we can attract another record producer."

"And raise our rates," Sidney pointed out. "I'll see if I can set up a few interviews. KDAZ will give us a shout—Vic Fosse's sure to be in attendance. Maybe we can swing by the station to do an on-air promo tomorrow or Friday. But I'd like to get some ink coverage too."

Lizzie sipped her drink and let her imagination run free. "It's really happening, isn't it?"

"What do you mean?"

"We're going to be famous."

Sidney lit a cigarette and took a few puffs before answering. "I hope you're right, but the road to success is strewn with obstacles and pitfalls, sometimes landmines. Remember the old saying, 'Don't count your chickens before they're hatched.'"

"I know, I know. But just for the moment, I want to believe in my dreams."

"So do I, Bearcat. So do I."

They drank in companionable silence for a few minutes, each lost in thoughts about Saturday's engagement and what might come of it. Sidney finished his cigarette, then lit another. He topped off their drinks. Finally, he broached a topic he'd been reluctant to bring up earlier.

"Bert seems distracted, don't you think?"

Lizzie nodded. "He's always quiet, but today he was more aloof than usual. Still, he played well."

"True," Sid agreed. "Why do you suppose he brought his kid sister along?"

"My guess is they still hope we'll let her play with us." She took a sip of her bourbon before asking, "Do you think their mother is really sick?"

"Physically or mentally?"

"Either. Maybe both."

"You want my opinion? The lady's got some flat keys on her piano. I just hope that won't interfere with Bert's ability to perform." Sidney flicked cigarette ash into a glass ashtray. "Damn it, Bearcat. We need him. What are we going to do if his trolley skips the track?"

"For what it's worth, Bert told me when we were at Melody's wedding that the only thing holding him together is music. Plus, Bert's the family breadwinner now. He needs us as much as we need him."

She considered what she'd learned from Kitty Taylor–that Bert had been present, along with Jim Jenkins—the night Tommy Halley died. Now seemed like the right time to finally share that information with Sid.

"I think everything's connected with his father's death."

"How so?"

"It's a bit of a story," Lizzie said. "Pour me another glass of that Kentucky comfort, and I'll fill you in on what I know."

* * *

"Holy moly," Sidney said after Lizzie revealed what Kitty Taylor told her about the night Tommy Halley died. "Bert actually saw his father get run down by a taxi?"

Lizzie nodded. "According to Kitty, both men were blotto. As they staggered down the sidewalk, JJ tripped, lost his balance, and fell against Tommy, knocking him into the street. Right in front of the speeding cab."

"Jeepers creepers, that's horrible."

"Yes, it is. I can't imagine how awful it must have been for Bert, seeing his father die like that." After another sip of bourbon, she added, "Jenkins must have felt dreadfully guilty about his part in his friend's death, even if it was an accident."

"*If* it was an accident?" Sidney repeated. "Are you suggesting otherwise?"

"No, of course not."

But as she spoke, fragments of conversations flitted through Lizzie's mind. Bert crying on the porch during Melody's reception dinner, when he linked JJ's death and his father's as being "all of a piece." How Jenkins hung around after Tommy Halley died, trying to "fill a gap that couldn't be filled." Gladys

Halley took up with another man after her husband passed and threw Bert out of his childhood home to fend for himself. Then there were the rumors about Jim Jenkins's secret paramour. Like pieces of a jigsaw puzzle, the individual bits began to fit together and form a disturbing picture.

Chapter Thirty-Two

"When the world goes wrong, and I've got the blues

He's the guy who makes me put on both my dancin' shoes."

—King Oliver, "Dr. Jazz"

The Queen of Diamonds' owner, who went only by the name Xavier, had a flair for the dramatic. The walls of the upscale supper club were painted the glossy black of patent leather with art deco friezes in gold and silver. The floors were made of white Carrara marble dotted with diamonds of red jasper. The master glassmaker René Lalique had designed the glittering chandeliers. One hundred tables draped in crisp white linen and adorned with vases of red roses furnished the spacious room that walked a fine line between chic and gaudy.

Patrons already occupied most of those tables when The Troubadours arrived at eight o'clock. Lizzie opened the door of her dressing room a crack and peeked out, watching holiday revelers stroll into the club. She didn't see New York City's mayor, Jimmy Walker, among them, but KDAZ's Victor Fosse sat at a table near the stage, accompanied by a stylish young couple and an attractive woman in her forties dressed in a sequined gown. *Could this be Vic's wife who doesn't like jazz?* Lizzie wondered. *Or is the radio station's manager stepping out?* She spotted several of the city's top music reviewers, too, whose write-ups could sizzle or scald. She crossed her fingers, closed her eyes, and made a wish: *Please let them praise us to the highest heavens.*

Just as she started to close the door and prepare herself mentally for the show, Sidney and Bert pushed their way in. Sid held a bottle of bubbly in one hand and three champagne flutes in the other.

"How about a drink to celebrate our nation's birthday?" he said as he popped the cork. "A gift from Xavier."

"I'm game-ski." Lizzie took one of the glasses from him.

Sidney filled hers, then Bert's. "To fortune and fame-ski," he toasted.

"Hear, hear," Bert said and clinked his glass against theirs.

As she raised the flute to her lips, Lizzie's hand trembled with pre-performance jitters. After several sips of what turned out to be exceptionally good champagne, she felt it start to work its magic, easing her into a place of happy anticipation. She clipped two red rosebuds from the vase of flowers Xavier had placed in her dressing room and pinned one on each of her friends' lapels. Then, with fingers wet from the icy champagne glass, she smoothed Bert's cowlick into place.

"You both look smashing," she said.

Sidney eyed her strapless red evening gown with its dramatic train that cascaded from her right hip to the floor like a waterfall of rubies. "So do you."

"I certainly should," Lizzie said, wishing Alan could be here to watch their performance. "It's Coco Chanel, and it cost a fortune."

"If all goes well, we can name our price from now on," Sid assured her.

Two drinks later, Sidney glanced at his watch. "Time to make my appearance. Bert, join me in fifteen minutes. We'll warm up the audience for you, Bearcat."

"Thanks. I just hope my royal entrance goes off without a hitch."

Left alone with Bert, Lizzie's mind slipped back to the conversation she'd had with Sidney about their fellow musician and the night his father was killed. She'd always viewed Bert as shy, awkward, and naïve. Now she eyed him through a different lens. As she adjusted a rhinestone tiara on her head, her stomach knotted–not from stage fright, but from the close proximity of the young man in her dressing room. A man she'd considered a friend, until now.

A knock on the door snapped her back to the present. She opened it to admit two tall, muscular bouncers carrying an ornate wooden chair painted gold and studded with fake gems.

"I guess I'll go join Sid onstage," Bert said and gave her a thumbs-up. "Knock 'em dead."

The bouncers set down the glitzy chair, and the blond one motioned for Lizzie to sit. "Okay, Queen Elizabeth. Let's give it a trial run here, to make sure we've got the balance right. Wouldn't want you to take a tumble."

After Lizzie took a seat on her "throne" and arranged her red silk gown around her, the men lifted her to their shoulders. She laughed, feeling simultaneously silly and glamorous, and thrilled in her role as queen for the night. They turned in a circle three times, the men adjusting their grip on the chair until they seemed satisfied they had everything under control.

"Ready, ma'am?" the dark-haired man asked.

"Ready."

Moving with a slow, stately gait, the men carried "the Queen of Diamonds" seated on her throne onstage, while Bert and Sidney played "Chaconne" from Purcell's seventeenth-century opera *The Fairy Queen*. As the audience broke into applause, Lizzie waved to her adoring subjects. The bouncers set her down center stage, then helped her alight amid the cheers that rang through the club. The chandeliers dimmed, leaving only a candelabra on the piano burning.

After a moment, a spotlight came on and followed Lizzie as she strode to the microphone, head held high like the dignified regent she pretended to be. With Bert's clarinet and Sidney's flashy piano backing her, she launched into King Oliver's lively song "Dr. Jazz." For just a moment, Lizzie wished Daisy Halley could have played clarinet with them tonight, so her brother could have wowed the audience with his trumpet and added some extra pizazz.

For the next hour, The Troubadours performed a mélange of hot and cool jazz, blues, and Broadway hits that had the audience clapping and tapping their feet. Lizzie's spirits soared with the music. By the time Sidney announced the trio's break, she'd managed to put aside worries about her apartment break-in, the threatening notes, Jim Jenkins's death, and Eve Adams's imprisonment. Dr. Jazz had done his job.

She exited the stage and headed for Victor Fosse's table to thank him for coming and for giving them airtime on his radio station yesterday to promote tonight's performance. Before she got there, however, a man with a bronze tan and thick graying hair, wearing an elegant tux and an air of entitlement, stepped in front of her. Malcolm MacGregor.

"Inspiring set, Miss Crane."

"Thank you," she answered coolly.

She waited for him to offer an apology for the way he behaved the night The Troubadours played at his yacht party, but none came. Instead, he moved uncomfortably close to her, and she fought an impulse to push him away or run.

"In case you haven't heard," he said, "I've purchased Jupiter Records."

"Congratulations."

"Let's get together next week and discuss a record contract. We'll pick up where Jenkins left off." He waved his hand to indicate the nightclub's full house. "You've got quite a following, Miss Crane. I'm ready to offer you an agreement I think you'll find most enticing."

"My business partner, Sidney Somerset, handles those things."

MacGregor fingered her rhinestone tiara, then stroked her hair in an overly familiar manner. "A lady like you shouldn't be wearing paste."

Repulsed, she took a step back. "This isn't a good time to talk, Mr. MacGregor. I'm in the middle of a show. I hope you enjoy the rest of it. Now, you must excuse me."

* * *

Bert's clarinet trilled and soared as he began their second set with George Gershwin's dramatic fusion of classical and jazz "Rhapsody in Blue." After a minute, Sidney joined in with a flourish on the piano as Lizzie took the stage. The spotlight followed her, while the rest of the club's illumination dimmed. When she reached center stage, Xavier, dressed in a beautifully cut tuxedo, approached her. His bald head and gold hoop earring glowed. His graceful steps brought him to within an arm's length of his "queen," and he dropped to one knee before her. Lizzie held out her left hand. Her respectful "subject" took it, bowed his head, and kissed her ring.

Lizzie waved her right hand, and a cascade of glittering gold confetti rained down on them from the ceiling. Xavier stood, grasped her hand, and they danced. Although they'd only practiced this scene once, her host was an excellent dancer, and they flowed together as if they'd been partners for years. For the next ten minutes, he swept his queen around the stage as the musicians changed tempo, volume, and intensity numerous times. Finally, Sidney's piano brought the drama to its conclusion. Xavier bowed to Lizzie and backed slowly away.

The lights snapped off. When they came on again, Lizzie stood alone at the microphone. The audience erupted into a cacophony of applause, cheers, and even a few whistles. She blew a kiss to Xavier, who'd resumed his role as proprietor of the nightclub, and he waved back. Then The Troubadours shifted pace to Ida Cox's sultry "Wild Women Don't Get the Blues," followed by songs made popular by Louis Armstrong, Bix Beiderbecke, Ben Bernie, Ma Rainey, and Bessie Smith.

As she worked her way through a series of songs she loved, Lizzie felt the worries of the past few weeks slowly dissolve. She surrendered to the music's healing balm, thinking *music really does soothe the savage beast in all of us.*

* * *

When The Troubadours came back from their break to play their third and final set, Lizzie noticed Xavier's staff had hung a colorful banner above the stage that said "Happy 150th Birthday, America." As waiters slid gracefully between tables, serving customers glasses of ginger ale and tonic water that would surreptitiously be laced with spirits, the musicians played "My Country 'Tis of Thee," which was first performed publicly in Boston on this holiday nearly a hundred years ago. They followed it with "I'm a

Yankee Doodle Dandy" from the Broadway musical *Little Johnny Jones.* When they launched into Irving Berlin's "God Bless America," a man wearing the uniform of his European War service stood up beside his table, leaning on a cane, and sang along with such passion it overshadowed his lack of talent.

Just before midnight, two young men rolled out a giant cake frosted with red, white, and blue icing and blazing with 150 candles. Dozens of sparklers, arranged in an arc around the back of the stage, shot off sizzling, white-hot flames. One of the waiters brought a slice of cake to Lizzie, then served Sidney and Bert. But as a mouthful of the rich devil's food melted on her tongue, she remembered eating cake at Jim Jenkins's birthday party—the last birthday the record producer would ever celebrate.

* * *

After two encores, The Troubadours bade their audience goodnight and retreated to Sidney and Bert's dressing room. Four reporters seeking interviews awaited them. Sid waved them in. The six men and Lizzie crowded into the tight space, where the newsmen pulled out their notepads and began firing questions at the musicians.

"I hear you're making a disc with Jupiter Records," one of them said.

Sidney lit a cigarette and took a deep drag before answering. "Jim Jenkins's untimely death tabled that agreement."

"But now that Malcolm MacGregor owns the company, will you go ahead?"

"We'll take it under consideration," Lizzie said and shot Sid a quick look that meant *I'll explain later.*

"What's the inside scoop on Jenkins's death?" asked another reporter.

"I don't know. You'll have to discuss that with the police," Sidney replied dismissively. "Can we talk about our music?"

"Right-o," agreed the senior member of the group, a veteran journalist whose reviews, Lizzie knew, were read by thousands of music lovers.

She moved a little closer to the man whose opinion could make or break careers and focused her smoky gaze on him. "What did you think of my royal entrance?"

"Fantastic," he said. "And your dance scene was sublime."

Lizzie laid her hand on his and playfully nudged his pencil. "Would you please put that in print?"

The writer laughed and scribbled on his notepad. "Your wish is my command, Your Highness."

"May I kiss your hand, O Queen?" a younger newsman asked in a teasing voice.

Lizzie extended it to him. "Of course. If you like, you can show obeisance too."

Grinning, the senior writer elbowed him. The young man knelt and kissed Lizzie's hand, amid guffaws and cheers from his colleagues. One of them snapped a photograph she hoped would appear in tomorrow's newspaper.

After she'd answered a few more questions, a journalist whose name was unfamiliar to her turned to Bert. "You're a newcomer on the jazz scene," he said. "How'd we miss you before now?"

"Been playing music all my life. Guess you just weren't listening."

Sidney interrupted, trying to smooth over a remark that might have seemed impertinent. "Bert joined us only about nine months ago. As you heard tonight, he plays sax, trumpet, cornet, and clarinet—pretty much any wind instrument that gets near his mouth. He's a terrific addition to our group."

"I speak best through my horns," Bert explained. "Maybe you should talk to them instead of me."

The journalist laughed. He picked up Bert's sax and spoke into its bell. "So, who's your biggest inspiration? I hear some of Satchmo in your riffs."

"My dad," Bert answered. "He was a musician too."

"Halley…Halley," the reporter repeated slowly, thoughtfully, struggling to drag a long-forgotten name from his memory vault. "I used to hang out at a pub called The High Note. A guy named Tommy Halley played there. Any relation?"

"My father."

"Hell of a musician," he said. "I heard he died a couple years ago."

Bert nodded.

"I'm sorry for your loss. A loss to the music world, too." The reporter shrugged his shoulders, as if trying to shake off thoughts of those lively nights at the pub and the sudden, unexpected death that brought them to an end.

For half an hour more, The Troubadours fielded questions. The photographer snapped dozens of pictures. Finally, the newsmen seemed to have all they needed to write their columns and shook hands with the musicians. Sid grabbed Bert's trumpet case. Bert picked up the two that held his sax and clarinet. They bid adieu to Xavier, and Lizzie kissed him on both cheeks.

"Great show," the restaurateur said.

"It was fun," Lizzie said. "Thanks for inviting us to perform for your guests."

"Sure, you don't want to stay for the rest of the party? We'll be celebrating 'til dawn, unless the cops shut us down."

Lizzie lifted Sidney's arm and studied his watch. "It's past two o'clock. I'd love to, Xavier, but this girl needs her beauty sleep."

"I hope you'll consider having us back," Sidney suggested.

"Consider it done," Xavier agreed. "I'll have my secretary telephone you Monday and set up something soon."

Still flying high with the excitement of a successful performance, Lizzie looked out over the neon-splashed city as Sidney drove to Brooklyn to drop Bert off at the boarding house where he resided now. Even though New York had been her home all her life, it still seemed magical to her, full of promise and mystery and beauty. And despite the city's drawbacks, she couldn't imagine living anywhere else.

Chapter Thirty-Three

"Revenge may be wicked, but it's natural."

—William Makepeace Thackeray

Lizzie finished reading the newspaper reviews of The Troubadours' performance at The Queen of Diamonds, then telephoned Alan and read them to him.

"Congratulations," he said. "I wish I could've been there."

"So do I. How was your family gathering on Cape Cod?"

"No one drowned or blew off any fingers lighting fireworks."

"That bad, huh?"

"All in all, it went okay. But next year, what would you think about taking a trip someplace where people don't celebrate the Fourth of July?"

"I'm game. I've never been out of this country, so the whole world is up for grabs."

"Good. And while you're considering where to go next year, give some thought to what you'd like to do when you're here this weekend."

"I will," she said. "I should probably let you get back to your work now."

"Probably, although I fear thoughts of you might prove to be a distraction. Let me know which train you decide to take, so I can have Norman pick you up at South Station."

They said their goodbyes, then Lizzie hung up and dialed Sidney's number.

The time had come to fill her friend in on her concerns about Bert. And

Malcolm MacGregor.

"Can you meet me for lunch at The Place at one o'clock?" Lizzie asked him.

"Are you buying?"

"Yes. Just come, okay? We need to talk."

"Sounds serious."

"It is."

At one sharp, Lizzie entered the café with its crimson walls on which dozens of paintings hung, giving it the ambiance of an art gallery that also served food. Sidney was already seated at a table near the back of the room. He stood as she approached and pulled out a chair for her.

"Did you hear from Xavier?" she asked.

"His secretary called this morning. We agreed to a Saturday, September 25th, performance unless you have a problem with that."

"Whatever you arrange is fine with me. I have no plans after this weekend."

A waiter approached their table and handed them menus. "Would you like something to drink while you decide on lunch?"

"Chai tea," Lizzie said.

"What's that?" Sid asked.

"I'm not sure. Something Detective Perry developed a fondness for when he lived in India. I thought I'd give it a try."

"Perry lived in India?"

"So he says."

"Coffee for me, please," Sid told the waiter, then asked Lizzie, "Well, Mistress of Mystery, are you going to tell me why you invited me to lunch today, other than the fact that I'm charming company?"

"Malcolm MacGregor purchased Jupiter Records. He approached me Saturday night and suggested we get together to negotiate a contract."

"Ah," Sidney said and lit a cigarette. "I noticed him chatting you up and thought there might be something more to it than mere flirtation. What did you tell him?"

"That you handle our business affairs." She paused, uncertain how to proceed. She shifted her gaze to a painting of a pastoral scene hanging above

Sidney's head. *What a bucolic and peaceful life that picture portrays,* she thought, wishing her own life could be so simple. Then she took a deep breath and let it out slowly. "Sid, I don't want to do business with MacGregor. I don't care how much money he offers or what promises he makes. If I never see him again, it will be too soon."

The waiter brought their drinks and asked, "Are you ready to order?"

Without even looking at the menu, Lizzie chose familiar comfort food. "Ham and Swiss on rye, with potato salad on the side, please."

Sidney ordered beef tongue on pumpernickel. After the waiter had topped off his coffee, he asked, "Why not? We dazzled the crowd at his yacht party. And after our performance at the Queen, we can command a hefty price. We're in the catbird seat."

As unemotionally as possible, Lizzie described how MacGregor had attempted to assault her. "He made it clear that if we wanted to deal with him, I'd better give up the goods."

"Why didn't you tell me this when it happened?"

"What could you have done? We were in the middle of a performance, out in the Hudson River on MacGregor's boat, surrounded by his influential friends. I didn't want to anger him—he's got clout, and he can hurt us if he wants to."

Sidney took a last drag on his cigarette, then stubbed it out. "You're right, Bearcat. But I wish you'd given Bert and me a chance to get in a few licks."

"Before his bouncers tossed you overboard?" Lizzie shook her head, trying to imagine foppish Sidney with his pianist's delicate hands throwing a punch. The idea was laughable, yet the fact that her friend would try to defend her made her feel loved and valued. "I just hope his girlfriend hit him where it hurts."

"We won't do business with him ever again," Sidney promised, making an X in the air with his finger.

"Here's another point. Do you think there's any connection between MacGregor's acquisition of Jupiter Records and Jenkins's death?"

"What do you mean?"

"Let's say Jenkins didn't want to sell his company and MacGregor decided to put the pressure on."

"Are you suggesting that Mac killed Jenkins so he could take over Jupiter?" Sidney asked. "That seems a bit far-fetched."

"According to Frankie Woods, my friend who owns the Tin Pan Alley record store, Jenkins was bumped off because he 'stepped on some toes.' I got the impression those toes belonged to somebody important."

"You're playing sleuth again, aren't you?"

The waiter served their lunch, interrupting their conversation. "May I bring you anything else?" he asked after setting their plates on the table.

"Not at the moment, thanks," Sidney said.

"The night we played on his yacht," Lizzie continued, "MacGregor told me records are the wave of the future, and he expected to profit handsomely from them. I can't help wondering how far a guy like him would go to get what he wants. Maybe he threw that birthday party for Jenkins as a way to drum up publicity for the company he planned to take over. Maybe he hoped to acquire some new talent as well." She bit into her sandwich and chewed contemplatively, recalling her run-in with Edith Jenkins at Jupiter Records' office a week ago. "Then there's the possibility he and JJ's wife were in on the scheme together."

"What makes you think that?"

"Rumor has it Jenkins had a mistress. Maybe she's the one who gave him the pox. If that's true—and my new friend Kitty Taylor, who knew Tommy Halley, claims it is—Bert's 'Auntie Edith' may have realized both she and Mac wanted to get rid of JJ and teamed up."

"I think you've been reading too many Agatha Christie novels," Sidney said dismissively. But he ate in silence for a couple minutes, contemplating the ideas Lizzie laid out, trying to decide if they had the ring of truth.

Lizzie patiently watched her friend finish half his sandwich and then start on the second half, giving him time to consider those ideas before going further. She sincerely hoped Malcolm MacGregor was the villain. That would fit nicely into the unsavory picture she already had of him. And if Edith Jenkins murdered her unfaithful husband—alone or in collaboration with MacGregor—well, that would be better than the third option.

The waiter stopped by to refill their cups and asked if they were enjoying their lunch. "Everything's copacetic," Lizzie said.

Sidney, with his mouth full, simply nodded. When he finally stopped chewing, Sid stared at her with narrowed eyes and asked, "Why do I have the feeling you've got another card to play?"

"The Jack of Spades." *The card of mystery, deceit, and dark forces at work.*

"Spill."

Lizzie raised her cup of chai tea to her lips, took a sip, hoping it might settle her nerves, then set the cup back in its saucer. "I think Bert killed Jenkins."

"What? That's insane." Sid stared at her in absolute astonishment.

"Hear me out."

He pushed his plate aside, then lit a cigarette. "This better be good."

"Alas, it's pretty awful. Since we talked last week, I've thought a lot about Bert and his relationship with Jim Jenkins. And Jenkins's relationship with Tommy Halley. We know Jenkins stumbled into Bert's dad after they'd both been drinking at The High Note. JJ knocked Tommy into the street, where he was hit and killed by a taxicab."

"Yeah, so?"

"What if it wasn't an accident?"

Sid shook his head. "Why would Jenkins want to kill his friend?"

Lizzie recalled Bert's tearful words, spoken at Melody's wedding, about the deaths of his father and Jenkins. *It's all of a piece.*

"After Tommy died, Bert said Jenkins tried to 'fill a gap that couldn't be filled' with the Halley family. JJ started hanging around their house more, ostensibly providing comfort and care to the widow Gladys Halley." She paused for a moment, letting her words sink in. "Then Bert's mom took up with another man and threw Bert out of the house to fend for himself."

"And you think the man she took up with was Jenkins?"

"I do."

"Why?"

"It seems to be common knowledge that JJ was fooling around. People in the music world knew it. I even heard a couple women in Jenkins' church talking about it at his funeral. But nobody knew who the mystery woman was. If it was another musician or some floozy, Sweet William Bly or Frankie Woods surely would know who–there aren't a lot of secrets in this business. But they didn't, and neither did Kitty Taylor. The affair was very hush-hush."

Sidney took a long drag on his cigarette, then exhaled out a lungful of smoke. "Go on."

"We also know Jenkins had syphilis. What if he gave it to Gladys Halley?"

Sid frowned, his countenance darkening. He puffed harder on his cigarette, blowing out smoke like a dragon. He cast his confused gaze about the art-strewn café as he slowly pieced together Lizzie's suppositions.

"Bert's sister Daisy said she's been working at a hospital where she's learning to care for her mother," Lizzie reminded him. "That could mean Gladys Halley is ill. It could also mean Daisy has access to mercury bichloride. Although, of course, if Jenkins was using the drug to treat his condition, any one of the Halleys could probably have found it in his bathroom medicine cabinet and appropriated it."

"That's quite an assumption, don't you think, Bearcat?"

"Maybe," Lizzie agreed. "While I'm at it, here's another assumption that may or may not be relevant."

Sidney crushed his cigarette butt in the ashtray. "I'm almost afraid to hear it."

"Remember when we were at Halcyon Castle last October? Bert took up fishing to occupy his spare time."

"So?"

"Someone booby-trapped my apartment with fishing line, causing Alan to fall and get hurt. That was intended for me."

"You think Bert strung up that trap?"

"There's no logical explanation for why someone would break into my apartment and try to harm me. None of my jewelry or other valuables were stolen, so the culprit wasn't a thief. It doesn't make sense, unless you tie it in with the rest of the pieces of this sordid drama."

Sidney shook his head slowly. "I'm not buying it. It's too absurd. Bert's our colleague and our friend. He wouldn't hurt you, Lizzie."

"Unless he feared I'd expose his crime. What about those threatening notes composed of letters cut from magazines, warning me to stop snooping into Jenkins's death? Those were left by someone who knows me, who knows where I live. Someone who didn't want me to recognize his handwriting or know his identity."

Their waiter came by again and asked if they wanted dessert, but both declined.

"Just bring our check, please," Sidney said. He drummed his long, delicate fingers on the tabletop. "What are we going to do, Bearcat?"

Lizzie shook her head. "I wish I knew."

Chapter Thirty-Four

"Truth is always present; it only needs to lift the iron lids of the mind's eye to read its oracles."

—Ralph Waldo Emerson

Lizzie spent most of Tuesday morning standing by her living room window, staring out at the rain. On the street below, people with umbrellas scurried here and there, trying not to step in puddles or get splashed by passing motorcars. Occasionally, she went to the kitchen to make coffee or get something to eat. Several times she tried doing a crossword puzzle or picked up a book to read, but she couldn't concentrate. Even listening to her favorite jazz tunes on the radio didn't calm her restless mind. Her thoughts always returned to Bert and what she planned to say to him.

She considered just letting the whole matter slide. Feign ignorance. Wash her hands of it and move on. Those awful ideas were only suspicions, after all. She had no proof. But if Bert really had murdered a man—even a man who'd done irreparable harm to Bert's family—could she condone such an act? Could she continue working with someone she knew had intentionally taken a human life? And if Bert admitted it, what then? Should she tell Detective Perry?

I should've listened to Sid and stayed out of it.

* * *

After a fitful night, Lizzie awoke Wednesday morning and realized she'd have no peace until she at least talked to Bert. Perhaps she'd completely misinterpreted things. Maybe he could offer an explanation that made sense. She telephoned the boarding house where Bert lived; the landlady said he'd gone to his mother's house to help with some chores. Next, she called Gladys Halley's number, but nobody answered.

She brewed a pot of strong coffee, toasted two slices of rye bread, and scrambled an egg. Then she sat at the dropleaf table by the window and gazed down at the ongoing street scene below while she ate her breakfast. At least the rain had stopped. She considered asking Sidney to come with her, but nixed the idea. Bert might be more willing to open up if she met with him alone.

Lizzie took the subway to Brooklyn and got off two blocks from KDAZ. Still uncertain how to approach Bert, she walked to the radio station, hoping Sweet William Bly might offer some insight. When she entered the lobby, she found him pouring a cup of coffee from the station's percolator.

"Just the man I'm looking for," she said.

"Hey, lady. What good fortune brings you here to visit Sweet William?"

"I doubt you'll consider it good fortune when you've heard me out. Do you have a few minutes to talk?"

He grinned broadly, flashing a mouthful of sparkling white teeth. "Always got time for the hottest white female jazz singer in the Big Apple. Congratulations on your performance at the Queen Saturday night. Sorry, I missed it."

Although The Queen of Diamonds, like other nightclubs, including the Cotton Club, hosted Negro performers, Lizzie knew their audiences were white. She followed William into the studio where Reggie, the technician, slid records onto a turntable inside his soundproof booth. She waved to him, and he waved back.

"Can we talk privately?" she asked.

"Sure thing. Vic's out and about. Just me and Reggie holding down the fort. What's on your mind?"

They sat at a table scarred by numerous cigarette burns. William sipped his coffee slowly, waiting for her to get comfortable enough to open up. Finally, Lizzie revealed her suspicions, one at a time, like a dealer laying down cards until they formed a pattern.

"Woo-ey," William said. "Looks like you got one helluva mess on your plate."

Lizzie nodded. "I hope you can give me a bit of advice."

"You think Sweet William's some kinda oracle?"

"Just tell me honestly what you'd do if you were in my place."

"I wouldn't have stuck my nose in it at all. If I was you, I'd bury everything I knew in a deep, dark place and put a big ol' Keep Out sign on top." He ran a finger along his lips as if zipping them shut.

"I don't know if I can do that, William."

He shrugged. "Hey, you asked me, and I said my piece. What you do is your own business. But you never told me none of this."

Lizzie reached out and laid her hand on his. "Thanks for your thoughts."

"Where you headed now?"

"To find Bert."

* * *

Lizzie walked to the simple, two-story brick house where Bert had grown up and where his mother and sister still lived. Someone, Bert most likely, had cut the grass in the front yard since her last visit and replaced the broken pickets in the fence. For a couple minutes, she stood staring at the house and almost turned around. Then, strengthening her resolve, she decided, *I've come this far, I may as well see what he has to say.* She pushed through the wooden gate, walked to the front door, and knocked.

Daisy Halley opened it.

Lizzie smiled, trying to appear friendly. "Hi, Daisy. I came to see Bert. His landlady said he's here doing some handyman stuff."

Daisy's mouth hardened, and she narrowed her eyes. "He's gone to the hardware store to get some supplies."

She's still mad at me, Lizzie thought. "May I come in and wait for him?"

The girl appeared to consider the request, shifting her weight from one foot to the other. Just when Lizzie thought Daisy would slam the door, the girl stepped back and reluctantly invited the singer in. Despite the warm and pleasant day, the living room curtains were drawn, the windows closed. The green davenport, worn armchairs, and an upright piano sat in shadows. A guitar leaned against one of the chairs.

"I apologize if I'm disturbing you," Lizzie said, gesturing at the guitar. "You don't have to work at the hospital today?"

"Nope, I worked over the weekend. Got today off."

"How's your mother?"

Daisy shrugged. "Okay, I guess. She's resting upstairs."

"Please give her my regards," Lizzie said politely. "Say, may I use your bathroom?"

"Down the hall." Daisy pointed. "On the left."

The bathroom was none too clean and barely big enough to accommodate an old clawfoot tub, a commode, and a pedestal sink. Lizzie locked the door and opened a medicine cabinet mounted on the wall above the sink, its mirror foggy with age. Inside, she saw the usual personal care items: toothpaste, a jar of Mum deodorant, talcum powder, various lotions, ointments, and cosmetics. She rummaged around looking for a jar of salve or a bottle of mercury bichloride tablets that could be dissolved in water, but saw nothing bearing that name. Disappointed, she shut the cabinet's door, used the toilet, and flushed.

When she returned to the stuffy living room, Daisy was gone. Lizzie sat on the horsehair davenport, its scratchy fabric prickling the backs of her thighs through her thin cotton dress. She picked up an out-of-date copy of *The Ladies' Home Journal* from the maple coffee table, hoping she wouldn't have to wait long for Bert to return. Idly, she flipped through the pages, glancing at ads for perfume, stockings, and household products. She read a few sentences from an advice column that recommended ladies should spritz their bed linens with lavender water to calm their husbands' "manly nature" and laughed. *The last thing I want to do is calm Alan's manly nature. When he's in my bed, I want him to be lusty and passionate and full of joy.*

She turned the page and stopped. A few words had been cut out of an article about preparing a garden for spring planting. As Lizzie continued scanning pages, she noticed more holes in fashion columns, advertisements, and recipes. She ran her fingertips over the clipped sentences, wishing she could remember the exact words pasted on the threatening notes an unidentified person had delivered to her apartment building. Did those snippets come from this very magazine?

The sound of footsteps brought Lizzie out of her ruminations, and she looked up to see Daisy staring at her. When the girl recognized the magazine Lizzie held open on her lap, her expression shifted from curiosity to fear, and then to anger.

"What are you doing?" Daisy demanded.

The fury in the girl's eyes sent chills running up and down Lizzie's spine. She shut the magazine and set it aside. "Just looking at this magazine while I wait for Bert."

"It's none of your business," Daisy said, her voice low and harsh, almost a growl. "Why couldn't you just stay out of it?"

"Stay out of what?" Lizzie asked, feigning innocence.

"My family's affairs." She turned to look at a collection of framed photographs sitting on the piano. Photos of the Halleys at Christmastime when the children were little. Of Tommy playing a trumpet and Bert playing a saxophone. Of Jim and Edith Jenkins with Bert fishing on a motorboat. "Did you come here today to tell Bert you knew?"

Again, Lizzie pretended ignorance. "Knew what?"

"That Jim Jenkins killed my dad."

"No, Bert told me. But wasn't it an accident?"

"Nope, he did it on purpose." Daisy snorted and stamped her foot. She reminded Lizzie of an angry young colt. "Did my brother also tell you Uncle Jim had the pox?"

"The police did. Jenkins died from mercury bichloride poisoning. The drug that killed him is used as a treatment for syphilis."

"And the bastard gave it to my mom."

So there it is. Confirmation. Jenkins's mystery mistress was none other than Gladys Halley. His dead friend's wife.

Keeping her voice low, calm, and steady, as if she were, indeed, talking to an angry, frightened animal, Lizzie asked, "Is that why Bert killed JJ?"

Daisy raised her eyebrows in a look of surprise and confusion. "Bert didn't kill him. I thought you knew."

Lizzie turned away from the girl's hard, accusing glare, reassessing her ideas and doubts about Bert. Relief flowed through her. She hoped she could believe Daisy and that Bert, her colleague and friend, wasn't guilty.

Her gaze fell on the guitar. As she stared at the instrument's strings—strings similar to fishing line, and equally strong—a memory of the filament stretched across the doorway to her bathroom flashed in Lizzie's mind. Another almost forgotten detail followed that thought: a piece of blue cloth caught in the fire escape after someone broke into her apartment, and the mended tear in the cuff of Daisy's blue blouse. And now, here was the magazine with its excised words.

Daisy hadn't attended Jim Jenkins's birthday party, but she'd accompanied her brother to Jupiter Records' studio the day before. According to Detective Perry, "mercury bichloride can kill in a matter of hours or days, depending on the strength of the dose and the person's constitution." Did Bert's sister slip the drug into Jenkins's coffee that morning?

"You killed him," Lizzie said softly.

"He deserved it. Scum like him shouldn't be free to keep preying on other people."

When Lizzie tallied up all the crimes, real or alleged, ascribed to Jim Jenkins, she agreed that people like him shouldn't be allowed to continue harming others. But she couldn't condone murder as the solution.

"He killed my father. My mother will die too because of him. Uncle Jim destroyed my family." Daisy laughed a bitter, painful laugh that held no mirth. "I don't regret what I did. I only wish I'd done it sooner."

"I understand why you did it. But his death can't bring your father back or prevent your mother from suffering."

Daisy's eyes blazed with rage. She planted her feet and tensed her body, ready to fight if challenged.

"I wish you and your mother well," Lizzie said, grabbing her purse.

Daisy snatched a pair of scissors from the coffee table, perhaps the scissors she'd used to cut out threatening words from a ladies' magazine, hoping to stop Lizzie from prying deeper into the Halleys' sad past.

"You're gonna rat me out to that copper, aren't you?" the girl said, brandishing the scissors like a weapon.

"You've got your own demons to deal with, Daisy. You don't need me to make things worse. Take care of your mother. She needs you."

Daisy raised the scissors above her head and charged at her adversary. Lizzie shoved the coffee table at the girl, banging it into her knees and knocking her off balance. As Daisy yelped and toppled over, she dropped the scissors. Lizzie kicked them under the davenport and ran for the door. Behind her, she heard Daisy's plaintive wail, a sound so anguished it broke Lizzie's heart. But she kept running, away from this place of lies, betrayal, and pain. Away from a girl's desperation, a mother's shame, and a brother's helplessness.

Chapter Thirty-Five

"Three things cannot long be hidden: the sun, the moon, and the truth."

—*Confucius*

Lizzie rode the subway back to the Village, but instead of going home, she walked to Sidney's apartment building near Washington Square. When she reached his penthouse, Sid opened the door, his face radiant with joy.

"Bearcat, where have you been? I've been telephoning you for hours."

"Well, I'm here now," she said, pushing past him into the light-filled living room. "What's up?"

"Stellar wants to make a recording with us."

"Stellar Records? Really?"

"They want to meet with me a week from Monday to discuss a deal."

Juxtaposed against Daisy's disturbing confession, Sidney's good news caught Lizzie off guard. Instead of jumping up and down and clapping her hands, she simply stood there, uncertain how to respond.

"Let's have a toast," he suggested. "What's your preference?"

"How about a martini?"

Sidney retreated to the kitchen to prepare their drinks, while Lizzie roamed about the apartment, torn between excitement at making a record with one of the nation's most venerable companies and dismay at what she'd learned about Jim Jenkins's death. Although she didn't want to dampen Sid's soaring spirits, she needed to tell him what happened at the Halley house this afternoon.

While she sipped her martini, Lizzie listened to Sidney spin out his plans. For months—long before Jenkins's death—she'd urged him to strike a deal between a major recording studio and The Troubadours. "A record will give people all over the country a chance to hear us," she'd insisted. Now, when the opportunity lay on the table before her, Lizzie wondered whether the goal they'd chased for so long still mattered in light of all that had transpired.

Sidney lit a cigarette and studied her, perplexed by her lack of exuberance. "What's wrong, Bearcat? I thought you'd be thrilled that we're finally going to make a record."

"I went to see Bert today, to ask him about Jenkins."

"What did he say?"

"He was out, but his sister Daisy was there." She took another sip of her martini, then set the glass on the cocktail table. "Daisy killed Jenkins."

"Jeepers creepers. How'd you figure that out?"

"She admitted it. She's also the one who booby-trapped my bathroom. She stretched a guitar string across the doorway. And she sent those threatening notes, too."

After Lizzie told him the rest of the story, Sidney asked, "Does Bert know?"

"I haven't talked with him, but I'm guessing he does."

Sid stubbed out his cigarette, then ran a hand through his thinning hair. He leaned back in his chair and crossed his right ankle over his left knee. "What are you going to do?"

"I don't know. I suppose I should tell Detective Perry, but I can't bring myself to do it. Daisy's only seventeen."

New York sentenced convicted murderers—even minors—to life in prison. Memories of Eve Adams, locked in the workhouse on Welfare Island, flooded Lizzie's mind. Deplorable as those conditions were, the situation at Bedford Hills, the state's maximum security facility for women, would surely be worse.

"She killed a man," Sidney said.

"JJ wasn't exactly innocent, though, was he? And he was going to die of syphilis anyway. Maybe getting bumped off like that was better than years of suffering."

"Given the circumstances, a jury might let Daisy off with a lighter sentence."

Lizzie shrugged. "Maybe."

"She broke into your apartment, intent on doing harm—and succeeded in injuring Alan, although she meant to hurt you. Then she attacked you today with scissors. She might have killed you, too, Lizzie. What's to say she won't try again? The girl's dangerous."

"Daisy just wanted me to stay out of her family's affairs."

Sid lit another cigarette and took a few puffs. "If you'd listened to me in the beginning and kept out of it, none of this would've happened."

"You're right. Don't rub it in."

"Withholding evidence is a crime, you know," he reminded her.

Lizzie picked up her martini glass and finished the drink. "How do you suppose this will affect our relationship with Bert?"

"Hard to tell. We should talk to him, don't you think?"

"Not until I decide whether I'm going to tell Detective Perry."

* * *

After eating a lonely dinner of warmed-up take-out chop suey, Lizzie telephoned Alan. She'd barely begun to explain the complicated scenario before she broke down in tears. Patiently, he waited for her to cry herself out as she described Jim Jenkins's crimes, Daisy Halley's murderous rage, Eve Adams's imprisonment, and Malcolm MacGregor's assault.

When her weeping subsided, he said, "Lizzie, please get on the train to Boston tomorrow. Put all this aside for the time being and let me take care of you. We'll go to Cape Cod and bask on the beach if you like, or hike in New Hampshire's White Mountains. New England's at her best now and eager to welcome you. Or, we can just hide out here until you feel ready to face the world again."

Lizzie wiped her tears with a handkerchief. "I'd like that, Alan. Thank you."

"There's a train leaving Penn Station at nine-ten tomorrow morning. That should get you into South Station by three. I'll have Norman collect you."

"Okay, that sounds swell."

"Try to get some sleep. We'll figure out something when you get here."

* * *

Lizzie brought a trunk full of clothes to Boston, not knowing if she'd be wearing a bathing costume or an evening gown, a tea-time dress or hiking gear while she was there. Norman, Alan's efficient butler, directed two servants to carry her luggage to a lovely guest room decorated with a mahogany Hepplewhite four-poster bed, a Persian rug, and damask drapes–proper sleeping arrangements for unmarried couples, which the entire household knew she and Alan would ignore.

She took a bath, applied fresh face paint, and put on a sapphire blue silk dress with a petal skirt and a low-cut neckline that showed an immodest amount of cleavage. Then she grabbed a copy of Lucy Maud Montgomery's novel *The Blue Castle* and went downstairs to the front parlor with its striped silk wall coverings and Chippendale furniture to wait for her lover. On one wall hung the Van Gogh landscape, the notorious art collector and reputed thief, Isaac Roman, helped Alan acquire after the European War. For several minutes, Lizzie quietly observed the painting, captivated by its brilliant colors and bold brushstrokes that made the field of flowers seem to dance.

"May I bring you a libation, Miss Crane?"

Startled, she turned to see the butler Norman standing just inside the doorway in his immaculate black suit and starched white shirt. She hadn't heard him approach; his ability to move about as quietly as a cat was a bit unnerving.

"A martini would be lovely."

"Certainly," he said with a slight nod. "Mr. Peabody just telephoned to say he'll be home in half an hour."

"Thank you, Norman."

Before coming to Boston, Lizzie told Sidney she'd be away for a week but would return in time for their meeting with the top brass at Stellar Records. She'd tried to telephone Bert several times but failed to connect with him at his boarding house or his family's home.

Questions rose in her mind so quickly they tumbled over one another. Had Daisy told Bert she'd confessed to murdering Jenkins and tried to kill Lizzie, too? Did the shy young man fear Lizzie had gone to the police? That Detective Law Perry would descend on him and his family, peppering them with questions about their painful relationship with Jim Jenkins, and arrest Daisy? Bert, too, might be hauled in for aiding and abetting his sister. *I wish I could talk to him,* Lizzie lamented.

Seeking distraction, she opened Montgomery's novel, but her thoughts kept wandering. Unable to concentrate, she read whole pages over and over again without retaining anything. When Norman brought her martini on a silver serving tray, she gave up and laid the book aside. She stood and looked out the window at Louisburg Square's manicured private park and cobblestone streets. Below the hill lay Boston Common and the Public Garden, where people walked after work, children roller-skated or flew kites, families picnicked, and couples strolled arm-in-arm.

Lizzie had nearly finished her drink when she spotted Alan on the sidewalk. On this salubrious summer afternoon, he wore a white linen suit and a straw boater hat—attire fashion critics might deem too casual for a successful businessman in the financial world to wear to the office. But Lizzie thought he looked youthful, vibrant, and incredibly handsome. Her heart beat faster as she watched him mount the half-flight of steps to the townhouse, and heard Norman open the door to greet his employer.

She set her glass down on a piecrust table, forcing herself to remain composed as Alan entered the parlor. For several moments, they stood motionless, caressing each other with their eyes. Then he opened his arms, and she ran to him. He enfolded her in a comforting embrace, stroking her hair and kissing her gently. Succoring her wounds with his touch.

Alan took her hand and guided her to sit on the leather Chesterfield sofa.

Brushing the backs of his fingers along her cheek, he said, "It's good to see you, Lizzie. I'm glad you came."

"Me too. Thanks for inviting me. I really needed to get away."

"You know you're always welcome here," he said, still holding her hand. "My home is your home."

He didn't ask her about the troubles from which she'd fled, nor did she broach the subject. They simply sat in companionable silence, Alan rubbing the back of her hand with his thumb. Lizzie let herself unwind into the caring support he offered her. After they'd had time to relax together, Norman eased into the parlor and asked if he might bring them anything.

"Two martinis, please," Alan said. "And whatever hors d'oeuvres may be on hand."

"Certainly, sir."

Lizzie touched the scar on Alan's cheek, the result of the fall he'd taken when he tripped on the guitar string Daisy had stretched across Lizzie's bathroom doorway in an attempt to deter her. "I'm sorry," she said.

"Don't be. It wasn't your fault."

"Yes, it was. If I hadn't poked my nose into the whole Jim Jenkins affair, Daisy Halley wouldn't have broken into my apartment."

Alan nodded. "I hope you'll remember that if you ever get an inclination to play sleuth again."

"I will," she agreed. "Just for tonight, can we talk about things other than murder and mayhem? In the morning, I'll ask for your advice and be grateful for whatever you can offer. But right now, I just want to enjoy your company."

"Okay," he agreed, and kissed her.

When Norman returned with fresh martinis and a plate of spanakopita, Lizzie picked up one of the flaky hot pastries. "What's this?"

"Filo dough filled with feta cheese and spinach," Alan said. "My sister has a new cook from Greece who's introducing us to delicacies from her country. I hope you like it."

"How is your sister?"

"She's well."

"And your mother?"

"Holding on, but not for long, I fear."

For the past six months, Alan's mother had struggled with a heart condition that soon would "call her home," as she put it. Yet Mrs. Peabody remained in good spirits, refusing to succumb to self-pity or to demand special attention simply because she was a few steps closer to the inevitable than other folks. She'd always treated Lizzie kindly, despite the vast differences in their life stations, and Lizzie wished she'd known the woman when she was younger and still healthy.

"If she feels up to it, might I pay her a visit while I'm here?"

Alan nodded. "She'd like that."

* * *

After a supper of crab meat-stuffed sole, au gratin potatoes, and summer squash, Alan led Lizzie up to his retreat on the rooftop of the four-story townhouse. From here, they could view the city below in all its beauty. The Charles River and Boston Common lay at their feet, the city lights sparkling like jewels scattered along Back Bay and across the river in Cambridge. Above, a crescent moon hung in a star-spangled sky. For the first time in weeks, Lizzie felt at peace.

While they sipped after-dinner cognacs, Alan held her hand and told her about Ogunquit, Maine, a town nearly three hundred years old that he wanted to show her. "Its name means 'beautiful village by the sea,'" he explained. "It's one of this country's oldest shipbuilding towns. It also has three miles of the prettiest white sand beach you've ever seen. I took the liberty of renting us a waterfront cottage for the weekend. I can leave work early on Friday, and we can be there by suppertime. What do you think?"

"It sounds lovely."

"I must warn you, though. Even in summer, the ocean there is pretty cold, and the riptide can be fierce."

Recalling her misadventure last October, when she fell into the frigid sea in Massachusetts and nearly drowned, Lizzie said, "I can't swim, so I'll only

226

wade ankle-deep."

"A wise decision."

They talked a while longer until Alan suggested it was time for bed. "I'm sorry, I have to go to the office tomorrow. Will you be all right on your own?"

"Of course. I want to do some sightseeing anyway."

Lizzie went to the pretty guest room to wash and change into a silk nightgown. Then she walked down the hall to Alan's bedchamber. When she entered, he was sitting up in bed, the covers turned back, awaiting her.

She slid in beside him and whispered, "Make me forget everything but you."

Chapter Thirty-Six

"Time will bring to light whatever is hidden."

—Horace

A weekend of long walks on the beach, delicious seafood suppers, and intimate nighttime pleasures stitched the frayed fabric of Lizzie's soul together again. The salty air cleared her mind. Alan's support restored her confidence, and she felt ready to face what lay ahead. As they motored south along the coastal route, she rolled down the Bentley's window, letting the cool ocean breeze ruffle her dark hair.

"I'm not going to turn Daisy in to the police," she said.

"I never thought you would," Alan replied.

"Despite what she's done, she's just a girl. I can't condemn her to a penitentiary for the rest of her life." She paused a moment before asking, "Could you?"

"Probably not."

"If Detective Perry is worth his salt, he'll figure it out." Even to her own ears, it sounded like self-justification, but she knew she couldn't live with herself if she helped send Daisy to prison. "I still need to talk to Bert, though. This could ruin our relationship and devastate The Troubadours."

* * *

On Wednesday, Lizzie took the train from Boston back to New York. In her handbag, she carried the portable phonograph Alan had given her in honor of The Troubadours' forthcoming record. The device, known as a Mikiphone, could be hand-cranked to play a ten-inch, 78 rpm disc with reasonably good sound quality. Yet it was small enough to hold in the palm of her hand, and its Bakelite resonator and tone arm folded neatly into a circular nickel-plated case that fit in her purse.

"She shall have music wherever she goes," Alan quoted from the old English nursery rhyme.

"It's delightful," Lizzie said, charmed by the clever gadget. "Thank you, Alan. I'll have ever so much fun playing this."

When her train pulled into Penn Station, however, Lizzie's mood grew darker. She had no idea how she'd confront Bert, how much he knew about his sister's crimes, or if he was involved in the scheme as well. She took a cab to her apartment building and tipped the janitor to carry her luggage up to the third floor.

As she unpacked, she decided to give her colleague the good news about the record deal first, then hit him with the bad. *I better do it as soon as possible, before I lose my nerve.*

She telephoned Sidney to let him know she'd arrived home safely. Then she dialed Bert's boarding house and told him she wanted to visit tomorrow afternoon. "I've got some news."

* * *

Lizzie was surprised to see Gladys Halley sitting with Bert on the boarding house's back porch. She'd hoped to talk to her friend in private, not discuss the whole sordid business in the company of his frail, victimized mother. But she couldn't think of a way to dismiss the woman. *Well, maybe it's best if she learns the truth about her daughter,* Lizzie decided. *Gladys is at the heart of all this anyway.*

Bert pulled up a wicker chair for Lizzie, then sat down beside her, jiggling his long legs restlessly as if he'd rather be walking about. "You remember my mother, don't you?"

"Yes, I do. Good afternoon, Mrs. Halley."

Gladys Halley nodded, but didn't return the greeting.

Bert cracked his knuckles and asked, "So, what's the big news?"

"Stellar wants to make a record with us. Sid and I are meeting with them next week to discuss a contract."

Bert whistled through his gapped front teeth. "That's terrific!"

"Congratulations, son," Gladys said, patting his knee.

"I hope you can handle being famous," Lizzie said. "And maybe rich."

"I'll try to get used to it." He grinned, the left side of his mouth turning down while the right side turned up. "Do you think girls will swoon and fall at my feet?"

"I wouldn't be surprised if they did." Lizzie paused, uncertain how to take the next step. Her mouth felt dry. Her stomach knotted. *There's no way to soft-pedal this,* she realized, and plunged ahead. "I've got some bad news too. It's about Daisy."

"I know, she's still mad because you and Sid won't let her play with us," Bert said.

"She's more than mad at me. She tried to stab me with scissors last week."

A look of shock crossed Bert's face. Gladys Halley raised her eyebrows in curiosity.

"Three weeks ago, Daisy broke into my apartment and stretched a guitar string across my bathroom doorway," Lizzie continued. "She meant to hurt me, but Alan tripped on it instead and sustained some painful injuries."

"What makes you think Daisy did that?" Gladys asked.

"Your daughter told me herself. She wanted to make me stop looking into Jim Jenkins's death. She's also been harassing me with threatening letters–I've given them to the police. But the worst of it is, Daisy murdered Jenkins." Lizzie paused to let the awful revelation sink in. "She poisoned him with mercury bichloride."

"That can't be true," Bert said, shaking his head. No longer able to stay seated, he stood and began pacing the length of the porch.

Gladys twisted her hands in her lap. The last bit of color drained from her pale face. She watched Bert stride to the end of the porch, then turn and walk back to where the two women sat.

"Jenkins pushed your husband in front of that taxi," Lizzie said, leaning closer to Gladys.

"It was an accident," Bert insisted. "They were both drunk. Dad tripped and fell."

"Jenkins killed your father because he wanted him out of the way," Lizzie continued. "He and your mother were having an affair, weren't they?"

"But that was after Dad died."

Gladys's shoulders slumped in resignation. She stared down at her hands, slowly turning her head from side to side. After a few moments, she looked up at her son. "No, Bert. It started before Tommy's death."

Bert slammed his right fist into his left palm, as if he wanted to punch someone. "No, no, no. I can't believe this!"

"And he gave you syphilis, didn't he, Mrs. Halley?" Lizzie asked.

"Yes." Gladys took a deep breath, then let it out slowly. She rocked back and forth in her chair, hugging herself, struggling to come to grips with the truth. "I'm sorry for the trouble my daughter caused you, but Daisy was just trying to protect me. She didn't kill Jim. I did."

Bert stopped walking about and stood perfectly still, staring down at his mother in horror. "Mom?" he said in a little-boy voice. He reached out to lay his hand on her shoulder, then drew back, as if he could no longer bear to touch her.

"I slipped Jim the drug before he went to that big birthday party," Gladys admitted.

"How could you do it, Mom?" Bert asked, his voice shaking. His face contorted in a mask of pain, and he looked like he was about to cry.

"He destroyed my family." Gladys turned to Lizzie, her sad eyes pleading for understanding. "Did you tell the police that Daisy killed Jim?"

"No, I wanted to talk to Bert first."

Gladys rubbed the palms of her hands along her skirt, from her hips to her knees, again and again. Smoothing it with careful deliberation, as if doing so might smooth out the wrinkles in her life. "I'm going to turn myself in."

"Mom, you can't!" Bert exclaimed.

"Hush, son. I can't let Daisy take the fall for this." She held out her hand to him, and he took it. "It will be a weight off my shoulders. I'm tired of living a lie."

* * *

After a restless night, Lizzie rose and dressed, then went to a nearby deli for a bagel and coffee. For the next few hours, she walked the streets of Manhattan until her legs ached, but her mind still buzzed with regrets and what-ifs. She sat on a bench in Washington Square Park, watching children toss balls for dogs, *plein air* artists painting, and old men playing chess.

Even though she felt relief at having solved the mystery of Jim Jenkins's death—and that she hadn't made a terrible mistake by turning Daisy in to the police—she couldn't shake the sadness that filled her when she thought about Bert and his sister and the losses they'd suffered. Gladys Halley had been taken into custody and was awaiting trial for murder. She faced execution, most likely, although a jury might take pity on her and sentence her to life in prison. A life that promised to be grim indeed.

Bert had decided to move back into his family home and care for Daisy. Fortunately, he wanted to stay on with The Troubadours and make their record.

"I wish I didn't know what really happened, but I don't hold a grudge against you, Lizzie," he insisted.

Lizzie, too, wished she didn't know the truth. If only she'd stayed out of the matter and minded her own business. Let the police handle things, as Alan and Sidney advised her to do. She wished she'd never met Jim Jenkins or Bert's family. And she wished people would stop dying around her.

I can't change the past, she told herself as she got up from the bench and headed home. *Now I have to concentrate on my music. It's the only thing that can save me.*

Chapter Thirty-Seven

"If you love what you are doing, you will be successful."

—Albert Schweitzer

In September, Stellar Records released The Troubadours' first recording. Frankie Woods ordered one hundred copies to sell in his Tin Pan Alley music store. To promote it, he threw a party and asked the trio to perform.

Alan took the train down from Boston. Melody and her new husband, Douglas, drove in from Connecticut. KDAZ's Victor Fosse came with his wife, who didn't like jazz. So did Sweet William Bly. Kitty Taylor played a piano duet with Sidney and bought a copy of the record, which she insisted they all autograph. Rory Moynihan, the Blue Lagoon's owner, and Xavier, from The Queen of Diamonds, stopped by to congratulate the musicians and bought records to sell to their patrons. Malcolm MacGregor didn't show, nor did Edith Jenkins, but it seemed to Lizzie that nearly everyone else in New York's music world wandered in at some time during the night. Even the great Louis Armstrong made an appearance and joined the group for a tune.

At two o'clock, the celebration finally wound down. For the finale, The Troubadours played a song Sidney composed with words Lizzie wrote. The two of them sang the chorus together.

"When the blues come calling
And you hurt night and day
And the whole world's doing you wrong,
When your tears keep falling
But you can't run away
Then you might as well sing along."

After saying dozens of goodnights and thank-yous, Lizzie hugged Sid, then Bert. Alan pulled her into his arms and kissed her.

"We did it," Lizzie said, giddy with excitement. "We really did it!"

Sidney lit a cigarette and leaned against the piano. "You know what they say. Nothing completely bad happens to a musician; you can always get a song out of it."

A Note from the Author

This is a work of fiction, although it contains real places, people, and events that did happen. For example, Eve Adams, aka Eva Zloczower, really did own the Greenwich Village teahouse known as Eve's Hangout, and what I've included of her story is true; of course, my characters didn't know her, but they surely would have. Except in the case of historic fact, if any of my characters resembles an actual person, living or dead, it's purely coincidental.

I have endeavored to convey events, people, products, technology, music, literature, social norms, fashion, locations, and other details accurately, in keeping with the period. Some of the places in this story are real, including the Steinway factory, the Cherry Lane Theatre, Tin Pan Alley, and the former Welfare Island workhouse. The speakeasies and nightclubs, restaurants, shops, KDAZ Radio station, and Jupiter and Stellar Records are products of my imagination.

Acknowledgments

Many thanks to Level Best Books' Dames of Detection for making this book a reality: my wonderful editor Verena Rose, the talented Shawn Reilly Simmons for her terrific cover design, and Deb Well for more things than I realize.

Thanks also to the members of my writing group, who provided much-needed guidance, insight, and encouragement: Anne Barnhart, Sally Benson, Ron Cody, Betsy Fields, Daryl Herring, Pat Honc, Karen Jones, Dave Kaczynski, Karen McCready, David McCormick, Wanda McLaughlin, David Remschel, Mary Shaw, and Robert Swoboda. I'm especially grateful to fellow LBB author Gregory Stout for sharing his expertise about trains and for catching my mistakes. You all make me look a lot better than I would without your help.

Finally, I wish to acknowledge my mystery writer friends Kate Flora and Susan Oleksiw, who cofounded Level Best Books with me way back in 2003 to provide a venue for New England crime writers' stories. Over the years, LBB's subsequent owners have greatly expanded the company and taken it to new heights, winning all the important awards in the mystery/thriller field, and delighting readers not only in New England but worldwide. I'm grateful to still be part of the family.

About the Author

Skye Alexander is the author of more than fifty fiction and nonfiction books, including four previous novels in the Lizzie Crane mystery series: *Never Try to Catch a Falling Knife, What the Walls Know, The Goddess of Shipwrecked Sailors,* and *Running in the Shadows.* Her stories have been published in anthologies internationally, and her work has been translated into fifteen languages. With fellow mystery writers Kate Flora and Susan Oleksiw, she cofounded Level Best Books in 2003. After living in Massachusetts for thirty-one years, she now makes her home in Texas.

AUTHOR WEBSITE:
  skyealexander.com

Also by Skye Alexander

The Lizzie Crane Mysteries
Never Try to Catch a Falling Knife
What the Walls Know
The Goddess of Shipwrecked Sailors
Running in the Shadows

www.ingramcontent.com/pod-product-compliance
Lightning Source LLC
Chambersburg PA
CBHW020755310726
48969CB00002B/553